When Winston Niles Rumfoord flies his space craft into a chrono-synclastic infundibulum he is converted into pure energy and only materializes when his waveforms intercept Earth or some other planet. As a result, he only gets home to Newport, Rhode Island, once every fifty-nine days and then only for an hour. But at least, as a consolation, he now knows everything that ever has been and everything that ever will be. He knows, for instance, that his wife is going up to Mars to mate with Malachi Constant, the richest man in the world and the person destined to discover the secret of the universe. (Rumfoord's wife finds this piece of fortune-telling in extremely poor taste.) He also knows that on Titan there is an alien from the planet Tralfamadore who has been waiting 200,000 years for a spare part for this grounded spaceship. There is, however, one crucial thing that Winston Niles Rumfoord doesn't know...

Wacky, sentimental, bitterly funny, *The Sirens of Titan* teases at the most sensitive of human preoccupations – who's in charge of creation and what are they doing about it.

Kurt Vonnegut, who lives in New York, is a bestselling novelist on both sides of the Atlantic. His books include *Cat's Cradle*, *Slaughterhouse Five* and *Jailbird*. *The Sirens of Titan* was his second novel.

GOLLANCZ CLASSIC SF

GOLLANCZ CLASSIC SF

KURT VONNEGUT

THE SIRENS OF TITAN

LONDON
VICTOR GOLLANCZ LTD
1986

First published in Great Britain 1962
by Victor Gollancz Ltd,
14 Henrietta Street, London WC2E 8QJ

First published in Gollancz Paperbacks 1986

British Library Cataloguing in Publication Data
Vonnegut, Kurt, R.
  The sirens of Titan.
  I. Title
  813'.54[F]   PS3572.05
  ISBN 0-575-03819-5

Printed in Finland by Werner Söderström Oy

"Every passing hour brings the Solar System forty-three thousand miles closer to Globular Cluster M13 in Hercules—and still there are some misfits who insist that there is no such thing as progress."

—RANSOM K. FERM

DEDICATION

For Alex Vonnegut, Special Agent,
with love

CHAPTER ONE

BETWEEN TIMID AND TIMBUKTU

"I guess somebody up here likes me."
—MALACHI CONSTANT

EVERYONE now knows how to find the meaning of life within himself.

But mankind wasn't always so lucky. Less than a century ago men and women did not have easy access to the puzzle boxes within them.

They could not name even one of the fifty-three portals to the soul.

Gimcrack religions were big business.

Mankind, ignorant of the truths that lie within every human being, looked outward—pushed ever outward. What mankind hoped to learn in its outward push was who was actually in charge of all creation, and what all creation was all about.

Mankind flung its advance agents ever outward, ever outward. Eventually it flung them out into space, into the colourless, tasteless, weightless sea of outwardness without end.

It flung them like stones.

These unhappy agents found what had already been found in abundance on Earth—a nightmare of meaninglessness without end. The bounties of space, of infinite outwardness, were three: empty heroics, low comedy, and pointless death.

Outwardness lost, at last, its imagined attractions.

Only inwardness remained to be explored.

Only the human soul remained *terra incognita*.

This was the beginning of goodness and wisdom.

What were people like in olden times, with their souls as yet unexplored?

The following is a true story from the Nightmare Ages, falling roughly, give or take a few years, between the Second World War and the Third Great Depression.

There was a crowd.

The crowd had gathered because there was to be a materialization. A man and his dog were going to materialize, were going to appear out of thin air—wispily at first, becoming, finally, as substantial as any man and dog alive.

The crowd wasn't going to get to see the materialization. The materialization was strictly a private affair on private property, and the crowd was emphatically not invited to feast its eyes.

The materialization was going to take place, like a modern, civilized hanging, within high, blank, guarded walls. And the crowd outside the walls was very much like a crowd outside the walls at a hanging.

The crowd knew it wasn't going to see anything, yet its members found pleasure in being near, in staring at the blank walls and imagining what was happening inside. The mysteries of the materialization, like the mysteries of a hanging, were enhanced by the wall; were made pornographic by the magic lantern slides of morbid imaginations —magic lantern slides projected by the crowd on the blank stone walls.

The town was Newport, Rhode Island, U.S.A., Earth, Solar System, Milky Way. The walls were those of the Rumfoord estate.

Ten minutes before the materialization was to take place, agents of the police spread the rumour that the materialization had happened prematurely, had happened outside the walls, and that the man and his dog could be seen plain as day two blocks away. The crowd galloped away to see the miracle at the intersection.

The crowd was crazy about miracles.

At the tail end of the crowd was a woman who weighed three hundred pounds. She had a goiter, a caramel apple, and a grey little six-year-old girl. She had the little girl by the hand and was jerking her this way and that, like a ball on the end of a rubber band. "Wanda June," she said, "if you don't start acting right, I'm never going to take you to a materialization again."

The materializations had been happening for nine years, once every fifty-nine days. The most learned and trustworthy men in the world had begged heartbrokenly for the privilege of seeing a materialization. No matter how the

8

great men worded their requests, they were turned down cold. The refusal was always the same, handwritten by Mrs. Rumfoord's social secretary.

Mrs. Winston Niles Rumfoord asks me to inform you that she is unable to extend the invitation you request. She is sure you will understand her feeling in the matter: that the phenomenon you wish to observe is a tragic family affair, hardly a fit subject for the scrutiny of outsiders, no matter how nobly motivated their curiosities.

Mrs. Rumfoord and her staff answered none of the tens of thousands of questions that were put to them about the materializations. Mrs. Rumfoord felt that she owed the world very little indeed in the way of information. She discharged that incalculably small obligation by issuing a report twenty-four hours after each materialization. Her report never exceeded one hundred words. It was posted by her butler in a glass case bolted to the wall next to the one entrance to the estate.

The one entrance to the estate was an Alice-in-Wonderland door in the west wall. The door was only four-and-a-half feet high. It was made of iron and held shut by a great Yale lock.

The wide gates of the estate were bricked in.

The reports that appeared in the glass case by the iron door were uniformly bleak and peevish. They contained information that only served to sadden anyone with a shred of curiosity. They told the exact time at which Mrs. Rumfoord's husband Winston and his dog Kazak materialized, and the exact time at which they dematerialized. The states of health of the man and his dog were invariably appraised as *good*. The reports implied that Mrs. Rumfoord's husband could see the past and the future clearly, but they neglected to give examples of sights in either direction.

Now the crowd had been decoyed away from the estate to permit the untroubled arrival of a rented limousine at the small iron door in the west wall. A slender man in the clothes of an Edwardian dandy got out of the limousine and showed a paper to the policeman guarding the door. He was disguised by dark glasses and a false beard.

The policeman nodded, and the man unlocked the door

himself with a key from his pocket. He ducked inside, and slammed the door behind himself with a clang.

The limousine drew away.

Beware of the dog! said a sign over the small iron door. The fires of the summer sunset flickered among the razors and needles of broken glass set in concrete on the top of the wall.

The man who had let himself in was the first person ever invited by Mrs. Rumfoord to a materialization. He was not a great scientist. He was not even well-educated. He had been thrown out of the University of Virginia in the middle of his freshman year. He was Malachi Constant of Hollywood, California, the richest American—and a notorious rakehell.

Beware of the dog! the sign outside the small iron door had said. But inside the wall there was only a dog's skeleton. It wore a cruelly spiked collar that was chained to the wall. It was the skeleton of a very large dog—a mastiff. Its long teeth meshed. Its skull and jaws formed a cunningly articulated, harmless working model of a flesh-ripping machine. The jaws closed so—clack. Here had been the bright eyes, there the keen ears, there the suspicious nostrils, there the carnivore's brain. Ropes of muscle had hooked here and here, had brought the teeth together in flesh so—clack.

The skeleton was symbolic—a prop, a conversation piece installed by a woman who spoke to almost no one. No dog had died at its post there by the wall. Mrs. Rumfoord had bought the bones from a veterinarian, had had them bleached and varnished and wired together. The skeleton was one of Mrs. Rumfoord's many bitter and obscure comments on the nasty tricks time and her husband had played on her.

Mrs. Winston Niles Rumfoord had seventeen million dollars. Mrs. Winston Niles Rumfoord had the highest social position attainable in the United States of America. Mrs. Winston Niles Rumfoord was healthy and handsome, and talented, too.

Her talent was as a poetess. She had published anonymously a slim volume of poems called *Between Timid and Timbuktu*. It had been reasonably well received.

The title derived from the fact that all the words between *timid* and *Timbuktu* in very small dictionaries relate to *time*.

But, well-endowed as Mrs. Rumfoord was, she still did troubled things like chaining a dog's skeleton to the wall, like having the gates of the estate bricked up, like letting the famous formal gardens turn into New England jungle.

The moral: Money, position, health, handsomeness, and talent aren't everything.

Malachi Constant, the richest American, locked the Alice-in-Wonderland door behind him. He hung his dark glasses and false beard on the ivy of the wall. He passed the dog's skeleton briskly, looking at his solar-powered watch as he did so. In seven minutes, a live mastiff named Kazak would materialize and roam the grounds.

"Kazak bites," Mrs. Rumfoord had said in her invitation, "so please be punctual."

Constant smiled at that—the warning to be punctual. To be punctual meant to exist as a point, meant that as well as to arrive somewhere on time. Constant existed as a point—could not imagine what it would be like to exist in any other way.

That was one of the things he was going to find out—what it was like to exist in any other way. Mrs. Rumfoord's husband existed in another way.

Winston Niles Rumfoord had run his private space ship right into the heart of an uncharted chrono-synclastic infundibulum two days out of Mars. Only his dog had been along. Now Winston Niles Rumfoord and his dog Kazak existed as wave phenomena—apparently pulsing in a distorted spiral with its origin in the Sun and its terminal in Betelgeuse.

The earth was about to intercept that spiral.

Almost any brief explanation of chrono-synclastic infundibula is certain to be offensive to specialists in the field. Be that as it may, the best brief explanation is probably that of Dr. Cyril Hall, which appears in the fourteenth edition of *A Child's Cyclopedia of Wonders and Things to Do*. The article is here reproduced in full, with gracious permission from the publishers:

CHRONO-SYNCLASTIC INFUNDIBULA—*Just imagine that your Daddy is the smartest man who ever lived on Earth, and he knows everything there is to find out, and he is exactly right about everything, and he can prove he is right about every-*

thing. Now imagine another little child on some nice world a million light years away, and that little child's Daddy is the smartest man who ever lived on that nice world so far away. And he is just as smart and just as right as your Daddy is. Both Daddies are smart, and both Daddies are right.

Only if they ever met each other they would get into a terrible argument, because they wouldn't agree on anything. Now, you can say that your Daddy is right and the other little child's Daddy is wrong, but the Universe is an awfully big place. There is room enough for an awful lot of people to be right about things and still not agree.

The reason both Daddies can be right and still get into terrible fights is because there are so many different ways of being right. There are places in the Universe, though, where each Daddy could finally catch on to what the other Daddy was talking about. These places are where all the different kinds of truths fit together as nicely as the parts in your Daddy's solar watch. We call these places chrono-synclastic infundibula.

The Solar System seems to be full of chrono-synclastic infundibula. There is one great big one we are sure of that likes to stay between Earth and Mars. We know about that one because an Earth man and his Earth dog ran right into it.

You might think it would be nice to go to a chrono-synclastic infundibulum and see all the different ways to be absolutely right, but it is a very dangerous thing to do. The poor man and his poor dog are scattered far and wide, not just through space, but through time, too.

Chrono (kroh-no) means time. Synclastic (sin-classtick) means curved towards the same side in all directions, like the skin of an orange. Infundibulum (in-fun-dib-u-lum) is what the ancient Romans like Julius Caesar and Nero called a funnel. If you don't know what a funnel is, get Mommy to show you one.

The key to the Alice-in-Wonderland door had come with the invitation. Malachi Constant slipped the key into his fur-lined trouser pocket and followed the one path that opened before him. He walked in deep shadow, but the flat rays of the sunset filled the treetops with a Maxfield Parrish light.

Constant made small motions with his invitation as he

proceeded, expecting to be challenged at every turn. The invitation's ink was violet. Mrs. Rumfoord was only thirty-four, but she wrote like an old woman—in a kinky, barbed hand. She plainly detested Constant, whom she had never met. The spirit of the invitation was reluctant, to say the least, as though written on a soiled handkerchief.

"During my husband's last materialization," she had said in the invitation, "he insisted that you be present for the next. I was unable to dissuade him from this, despite the many obvious drawbacks. He insists that he knows you well, having met you on Titan, which, I am given to understand, is a moon of the planet Saturn."

There was hardly a sentence in the invitation that did not contain the verb *insist*. Mrs. Rumfoord's husband had insisted on her doing something very much against her own judgment, and she in turn was insisting that Malachi Constant behave, as best he could, like the gentleman he was not.

Malachi Constant had never been to Titan. He had never, so far as he knew, been outside the gaseous envelope of his native planet, the Earth. Apparently he was about to learn otherwise.

The turns in the path were many, and the visibility was short. Constant was following a damp green path the width of a lawn mower—what was in fact the swath of a lawn mower. Rising on both sides of the path were the green walls of the jungle the gardens had become.

The mower's swath skirted a dry fountain. The man who ran the mower had become creative at this point, had made the path fork. Constant could choose the side of the fountain on which he preferred to pass. Constant stopped at the fork, looked up. The fountain itself was marvellously creative. It was a cone described by many stone bowls of decreasing diameters. The bowls were collars on a cylindrical shaft forty feet high.

Impulsively, Constant chose neither one fork nor the other, but climbed the fountain itself. He climbed from bowl to bowl, intending when he got to the top to see whence he had come and whither he was bound.

Standing now in the topmost, in the smallest of the baroque fountain's bowls, standing with his feet in the ruins of birds' nests, Malachi Constant looked out over the estate, and over a large part of Newport and Narragansett Bay. He held up his watch to sunlight, letting it drink in the where-withal that was to solar watches what money was to Earth men.

The freshening sea breeze ruffled Constant's blue-black hair. He was a well-made man—a light heavyweight, dark-skinned, with poet's lips, with soft brown eyes in the shaded caves of a Cro-Magnon brow-ridge. He was thirty-one.

He was worth three billion dollars, much of it inherited.

His name meant *faithful messenger*.

He was a speculator, mostly in corporate securities.

In the depressions that always followed his taking of alcohol, narcotics, and women, Constant pined for just one thing—a single message that was sufficiently dignified and important to merit his carrying it humbly between two points.

The motto under the coat of arms that Constant had designed for himself said simply, *The Messenger Awaits*.

What Constant had in mind, presumably, was a first-class message from God to someone equally distinguished.

Constant looked at his solar watch again. He had two minutes in which to climb down and reach the house—two minutes before Kazak would materialize and look for strangers to bite. Constant laughed to himself, thinking how delighted Mrs. Rumfoord would be were the vulgar, parvenu Mr. Constant of Hollywood to spend his entire visit treed on the fountain by a thoroughbred dog. Mrs. Rumfoord might even have the fountain turned on.

It was possible that she was watching Constant. The mansion was a minute's walk from the fountain—set off from the jungle by a mowed swath three times the width of the path.

The Rumfoord mansion was marble, an extended reproduction of the banqueting hall of Whitehall Palace in London. The mansion, like most of the really grand ones in Newport, was a collateral relative of post offices and Federal court buildings throughout the land.

The Rumfoord mansion was an hilariously impressive expression of the concept: People of substance. It was surely one of the greatest essays on density since the Great Pyramid of Khufu. In a way it was a better essay on permanence than the Great Pyramid, since the Great Pyramid tapered to nothingness as it approached heaven. Nothing about the

Rumfoord mansion diminished as it approached heaven. Turned upside down, it would have looked exactly the same.

The density and permanence of the mansion were, of course, at ironic variance with the fact that the quondam master of the house, except for one hour in every fifty-nine days, was no more substantial than a moonbeam.

Constant climbed down from the fountain, stepping on to the rims of bowls of ever-increasing sizes. When he got to the bottom, he was filled with a strong wish to see the fountain go. He thought of the crowd outside, thought of how they, too, would enjoy seeing the fountain go. They would be enthralled—watching the teeny-weeny bowl at the tippy-tippy top brimming over into the next little bowl . . . and the next little bowl's brimming over into the next little bowl . . . and the next little bowl's brimming over into the next bowl . . . and on and on and on, a rhapsody of brimming, each bowl singing its own merry water song. And yawning under all those bowls was the upturned mouth of the biggest bowl of them all . . . a regular Beelzebub of a bowl, bone dry and insatiable . . . waiting, waiting, waiting for that first sweet drop.

Constant was rapt, imagining that the fountain was running. The fountain was very much like an hallucination—and hallucinations, usually drug-induced, were almost all that could surprise and entertain Constant any more.

Time passed quickly. Constant did not move.

Somewhere on the estate a mastiff bayed. The baying sounded like the blows of a maul on a great bronze gong.

Constant awoke from his contemplation of the fountain. The baying could only be that of Kazak, the hound of space. Kazak had materialized. Kazak smelled the blood of a parvenu.

Constant sprinted the remainder of the distance to the house.

An ancient butler in knee breeches opened the door for Malachi Constant of Hollywood. The butler was weeping for joy. He was pointing into a room that Constant could not see. The butler was trying to describe the thing that made him so happy and full of tears. He could not speak. His jaw was palsied, and all he could say to Constant was "Putt putt—putt putt putt."

The floor of the foyer was a mosaic, showing the signs of the zodiac encircling a golden sun.

Winston Niles Rumfoord, who had materialized only a minute before, came into the foyer and stood on the sun. He was much taller and heavier than Malachi Constant—and he was the first person who had ever made Constant think that there might actually be a person superior to himself. Winston Niles Rumfoord extended his soft hand, greeted Constant familiarly, almost singing his greeting in a glottal Groton tenor.

"Delighted, delighted, delighted, Mr. Constant," said Rumfoord. "How nice of you to commmmmmmmmme."

"My pleasure," said Constant.

"They tell me you are possibly the luckiest man who ever lived."

"That might be putting it a little too strong," said Constant.

"You won't deny you've had fantastically good luck financially," said Rumfoord.

Constant shook his head. "No. That would be hard to deny," he said.

"And to what do you attribute this wonderful luck of yours?" said Rumfoord.

Constant shrugged. "Who knows?" he said. "I guess somebody up there likes me," he said.

Rumfoord looked up at the ceiling. "What a charming concept—someone's liking you up there."

Constant, who had been shaking hands with Rumfoord during the conversation, thought of his own hand, suddenly, as small and clawlike.

Rumfoord's palm was callused, but not horny like the palm of a man doomed to a single trade for all of his days. The calluses were perfectly even, made by the thousand happy labours of an active leisure class.

For a moment, Constant forgot that the man whose hand he shook was simply one aspect, one node of a wave phenomenon extending all the way from the Sun to Betelguese. The handshake reminded Constant what it was that he was touching—for his hand tingled with a small but unmistakable electrical flow.

Constant had not been bullied into feeling inferior by the tone of Mrs. Rumfoord's invitation to the materialization. Constant was a male and Mrs. Rumfoord was a female, and

Constant imagined that he had the means of demonstrating, if given the opportunity, his unquestionable superiority.

Winston Niles Rumfoord was something else again—morally, spatially, socially, sexually, and electrically. Winston Niles Rumfoord's smile and handshake dismantled Constant's high opinion of himself as efficiently as carnival roustabouts might dismantle a Ferris wheel.

Constant, who had offered his services to God as a messenger, now panicked before the very moderate greatness of Rumfoord. Constant ransacked his memory for past proofs of his greatness. He ransacked his memory like a thief going through another man's billfold. Constant found his memory stuffed with rumpled, overexposed snapshots of all the women he had had, with preposterous credentials testifying to his ownership of even more preposterous enterprises, with testimonials that attributed to him virtues and strengths that only three billion dollars could have. There was even a silver medal with a red ribbon—awarded to Constant for placing second in the hop, skip, and jump in an intramural track meet at the University of Virginia.

Rumfoord's smile went on and on.

To follow the analogy of the thief who is going through another man's billfold: Constant ripped open the seams of his memory, hoping to find a secret compartment with something of value in it. There was no secret compartment —nothing of value. All that remained to Constant were the husks of his memory—unstitched, flaccid flaps.

The ancient butler looked adoringly at Rumfoord, went through the cringing contortions of an ugly old woman posing for a painting of the Madonna. "The mah-stuh—" he bleated. "The young mah-stuh."

"I can read your mind, you know," said Rumfoord.

"Can you?" said Constant humbly.

"Easiest thing in the world," said Rumfoord. His eyes twinkled. "You're not a bad sort, you know," he said, "particularly when you forget who you are." He touched Constant lightly on the arm. It was a politician's gesture—a vulgar public gesture by a man who in private, among his own kind, would take wincing pains never to touch anyone.

"If it's really so important to you, at this stage of our relationship, to feel superior to me in some way," he said to Constant pleasantly, "think of this: You can reproduce and I cannot."

He now turned his broad back to Constant, led the way through a series of very grand chambers.

He paused in one, insisted that Constant admire a huge oil painting of a little girl holding the reins of a pure white pony. The little girl wore a white bonnet, a white, starched dress, white gloves, white socks, and white shoes.

She was the cleanest, most frozen little girl that Malachi Constant had ever seen. There was a strange expression on her face, and Constant decided that she was worried about getting the least bit dirty.

"Nice picture," said Constant.

"Wouldn't it be too bad if she fell into a mud puddle?" said Rumfoord.

Constant smiled uncertainly.

"My wife as a child," said Rumfoord abruptly, and he led the way out of the room.

He led the way down a back corridor and into a tiny room hardly larger than a big broom closet. It was ten feet long, six feet wide, and had a ceiling, like the rest of the rooms in the mansion, twenty feet high. The room was like a chimney. There were two wing chairs in it.

"An architectural accident," said Rumfoord, closing the door and looked up at the ceiling.

"Pardon me?" said Constant.

"This room," said Rumfoord. With a limp right hand, he made the magical sign for spiral staircase. "It was one of the few things in life I ever really wanted with all my heart when I was a boy—this little room."

He nodded at shelves that ran six feet up the window wall. The shelves were beautifully made. Over the shelves was a driftwood plank that had written on it in blue paint: SKIP'S MUSEUM.

Skip's Museum was a museum of mortal remains—of endoskeletons and exoskeletons—of shells, coral, bone, cartilage, and chiton—of dottles and orts and residua of souls long gone. Most of the specimens were those that a child—presumably Skip—could find easily on the beaches and in the woods of Newport. Some were obviously expensive presents to a child extraordinarily interested in the science of biology.

Chief among these presents was the complete skeleton of an adult human male.

There was also the empty suit of armour of an armadillo,

a stuffed dodo, and the long spiral tusk of a narwhal, playfully labelled by Skip, *Unicorn Horn.*

"Who is Skip?" said Constant.

"I am Skip," said Rumfoord. "Was."

"I didn't know," said Constant.

"Just in the family, of course," said Rumfoord.

"Um," said Constant.

Rumfoord sat down in one of the wing chairs, motioned Constant to the other.

"Angels can't either, you know," said Rumfoord.

"Can't what?" said Constant.

"Reproduce," said Rumfoord. He offered Constant a cigarette, took one himself, and placed it in a long, bone cigarette holder. "I'm sorry my wife was too indisposed to come downstairs—to meet you," he said. "It isn't you she's avoiding—it's me."

"You?" said Constant.

"That's correct," said Rumfoord. "She hasn't seen me since my first materialization." He chuckled ruefully. "Once was enough."

"I—I'm sorry," said Constant. "I don't understand."

"She didn't like my fortunetelling," said Rumfoord. "She found it very upsetting, what little I told her about her future. She doesn't care to hear more." He sat back in his wing chair, inhaled deeply. "I tell you, Mr. Constant," he said genially, "it's a thankless job, telling people it's a hard, hard Universe they're in."

"She said you'd told her to invite me," said Constant.

"She got the message from the butler," said Rumfoord. "I dared her to invite you, or she wouldn't have done it. You might keep that in mind: the only way to get her to do anything is to tell her she hasn't got the courage to do it. Of course, it isn't an infallible technique. I could send her a message now, telling her that she doesn't have the courage to face the future, and she would send me back a message saying I was right."

"You—you really can see into the future?" said Constant. The skin of his face tightened, felt parched. His palms perspired.

"In a punctual way of speaking—yes," said Rumfoord. "When I ran my space ship into the chrono-synclastic infundibulum, it came to me in a flash that everything that ever has been always will be, and everything that ever will be always has been." He chuckled again. "Knowing that rather takes the glamour out of fortunetelling—makes it the simplest, most obvious thing imaginable."

"You told your wife everything that was going to happen to her?" said Constant. This was a glancing question. Constant had no interest in what was going to happen to Rumfoord's wife. He was ravenous for news of himself. In asking about Rumfoord's wife, he was being coy.

"Well—not everything," said Rumfoord. "She wouldn't let me tell her everything. What little I did tell her quite spoiled her appetite for more."

"I—I see," said Constant, not seeing at all.

"Yes," said Rumfoord genially, "I told her that you and she were to be married on Mars." He shrugged. "Not married exactly," he said, "but bred by the Martians—like farm animals."

Winston Niles Rumfoord was a member of the one true American class. The class was a true one because its limits had been clearly defined for at least two centuries—clearly defined for anyone with an eye for definitions. From Rumfoord's small class had come a tenth of America's presidents, a quarter of its explorers, a third of its Eastern Seaboard governors, a half of its full-time ornithologists, three-quarters of its great yachtsmen, and virtually all of its underwriters of the deficits of grand opera. It was a class singularly free of quacks, with the notable exception of political quacks. The political quackery was a means of gaining office—and was never carried into private life. Once in office, members of the class became, almost without exception, magnificently responsible.

If Rumfoord accused the Martians of breeding people as though people were no better than farm animals, he was accusing the Martians of doing no more than his own class had done. The strength of his class depended to some extent on sound money management—but depended to a much larger extent on marriages based cynically on the sorts of children likely to be produced.

Healthy, charming, wise children were the desiderata.

The most competent, if humourless, analysis of Rumfoord's class is, beyond question, Waltham Kittredge's *The American Philosopher Kings*. It was Kittredge who proved that the class was in fact a family, with its loose ends neatly turned back into a hard core of consanguinity through the agency of cousin marriages. Rumfoord and his wife, for instance, were third cousins, and detested each other.

And when Rumfoord's class was diagrammed by Kittredge, it resembled nothing so much as the hard, ball-like knot known as a *monkey's fist*.

Waltham Kittredge often floundered in his *The American Philosopher Kings*, trying to translate the atmosphere of Rumfoord's class into words. Like the college professor he was, Kittredge groped only for big words, and, finding no apt ones, he coined a lot of untranslatable new ones.

Of all Kittredge's jargon, only one term has ever found its way into conversation. The term is *un-neurotic courage*.

It was that sort of courage, of course, that carried Winston Niles Rumfoord out into space. It was pure courage— not only pure of lusts for fame and money, but pure of any drives that smack of the misfit or screwball.

There are, incidentally, two strong, common words that would have served handsomely, one or the other, in place of all of Kittredge's jargon. The words are *style* and *gallantry*.

When Rumfoord became the first person to own a private space ship, paying fifty-eight million dollars out of his own pocket for it—that was style.

When the governments of the earth suspended all space exploration because of the chrono-synclastic infundibula, and Rumfoord announced that he was going to Mars—that was style.

When Rumfoord announced that he was taking a perfectly tremendous dog along, as though a space ship were nothing more than a sophisticated sports car, as though a trip to Mars were little more than a spin down the Connecticut Turnpike—that was style.

When it was unknown what would happen if a space ship went into chrono-synclastic infundibulum, and Rumfoord steered a course straight for the middle of one—that was gallantry indeed.

To contrast Malachi Constant of Hollywood with Winston Niles Rumfoord of Newport and Eternity:

Everything Rumfoord did he did *with* style, making all mankind look good.

Everything Constant did he did *in* style—aggressively,

loudly, childishly, wastefully—making himself and mankind look bad.

Constant bristled with courage—but it was anything but un-neurotic. Every courageous thing he had ever done had been motivated by spitefulness and by goads from childhood that made fear seem puny indeed.

Constant, having just heard from Rumfoord that he was to be mated to Rumfoord's wife on Mars, looked away from Rumfoord to the museum of remains along one wall. Constant's hands were clasped together, tightening on each other pulsingly.

Constant cleared his throat several times. Then he whistled thinly between his tongue and the roof of his mouth. In all, he was behaving like a man who was waiting for a terrible pain to pass. He closed his eyes and sucked in air between his teeth. "Loo dee doo, Mr. Rumfoord," he said softly. He opened his eyes. "Mars?" he said.

"Mars," said Rumfoord. "Of course, that isn't your ultimate destination or Mercury either."

"Mercury," said Constant. He made an unbecoming quack of that lovely name.

"Your destination is Titan," said Rumfoord, "but you visit Mars, Mercury, and Earth again before you get there."

It is crucial to understand at what point in the history of punctual space exploration it was that Malachi Constant received the news of his prospective visits to Mars, Mercury, Earth, and Titan. The state of mind on Earth with regard to space exploration was much like the state of mind in Europe with regard to exploration of the Atlantic before Christopher Columbus set out.

There were these important differences, however, the monsters between space explorers and their goals were not imaginary, but numerous, hideous, various, and uniformly cataclysmic; the cost of even a small expedition was enough to ruin most nations; and it was a virtual certainty that no expedition could increase the wealth of its sponsors.

In short, on the basis of horse sense and the best scientific information, there was nothing good to be said for the exploration of space.

The time was long past when one nation could seem more glorious than another by hurling some heavy object into nothingness. Galactic Spacecraft, a corporation controlled by Malachi Constant, had, as a matter of fact, received the very last order for such a showpiece, a rocket three hundred feet high and thirty-six feet in diameter. It had actually been built, but the fire order had never come.

The ship was called simply *The Whale*, and was fitted with living quarters for five passengers.

What had brought everything to such an abrupt halt was the discovery of the chrono-synclastic infundibula. They had been discovered mathematically, on the basis of bizarre flight patterns of unmanned ships sent out, supposedly, in advance of men.

The discovery of the chrono-synclasic infundibula said to mankind in effect: "*What makes you think you're going anywhere?*"

It was a situation made to order for American fundamentalist preachers. They were quicker than philosophers or historians or anybody to talk sense about the truncated Age of Space. Two hours after the firing of *The Whale* was called off indefinitely, the Reverend Bobby Denton shouted at his Love Crusade in Wheeling, West Virginia:

" 'And the Lord came down to see the city and the tower, which the children of men builded. And the Lord said, "Behold, the people is one, and they have all one language; and this they begin to do; and now *nothing will be restrained from them, which they have imagined to do*. Go to, let us go go down, and there confound their language, that they may not understand one another's speech." So the Lord scattered them abroad from thence upon the face of all the earth; and they left off to build the city. Therefore is the name of it called Babel; because the Lord did there confound the language of all the earth: and from thence did the Lord scatter them abroad upon the face of the earth.' "

Bobby Denton spitted his audience on a bright and loving gaze, and proceeded to roast it whole over the coals of its own iniquity. "Are these not Bible times?" he said. "Have we not builded of steel and pride an abomination far taller than the Tower of Babel of old? And did we not mean, like those builders of old, to get right into Heaven with it? And haven't we heard it said many times that the language of scientists is international? They all use the same Latin and Greek words for things, and they all talk the language of numbers." This seemed a particularly damning piece of evidence to Denton, and the Love Crusaders agreed bleakly without quite understanding why.

"So why should we cry out in surprise and pain now when God says to us what He said to the people who built the Tower of Babel: 'No! Get away from there! You aren't going to Heaven or anywhere else with that thing! Scatter, you hear? Quit talking the language of science to each other! Nothing will be restrained from you which you have imagined to do, if you all keep on talking the language of science to each other, and I don't want that! I, your Lord God on High, *want* things restrained from you, so you will quit thinking about crazy towers and rockets to Heaven, and start thinking about how to be better neighbours and husbands and wives and daughters and sons! Don't look to rockets for salvation—look to your homes and churches!'"

Bobby Denton's voice grew hoarse and hushed. "You want to fly through space? God has already given you the most wonderful space ship in all creation! Yes! Speed? You want speed? The space ship God has given you goes sixty-six thousand miles an hour—and will keep on running at that speed for all eternity, if God wills it. You want a space ship that will carry men in comfort? You've got it! It won't carry just a rich man and his dog, or just five men or ten men. No! God is no piker! He's given you a space ship that will carry billions of men, women, and children! Yes! And they don't have to stay strapped in chairs or wear fishbowls over their heads. No! Not on God's space ship. The people on God's space ship can go swimming, and walk in the sunshine and play baseball and go ice skating and go for family rides in the family automobile on Sunday after church and a family chicken dinner!"

Bobby Denton nodded. "Yes!" he said. "And if anybody thinks his God is mean for putting things out in space to stop us from flying out there, just let him remember the space ship God already gave us. And we don't have to buy the fuel for it, and worry and fret over what kind of fuel to use. No! God worries about all that.

"God told us what *we* had to do on this wonderful space ship. He wrote the rules so anybody could understand them. You don't have to be a physicist or a great chemist or an Albert Einstein to understand them. No! And He didn't make a whole lot of rules, either. They tell me that if they were to fire *The Whale*, they would have to make eleven thousand separate checks before they could be sure it was ready to go: Is this valve open, is that valve closed, is that wire tight, is that tank full? — and on and on and on to eleven thousand things to check. Here on God's space ship, God only gives us ten things to check—and not for any little trip to some big, dead poisonous stones out in space, but for a trip to the Kingdom of Heaven! Think of it! Where would you rather be tomorrow—on Mars or in the Kingdom of Heaven?

"You know what the check list is on God's round, green space ship? Do I have to tell you? You want to hear God's countdown?"

The Love Crusaders shouted back that they did.

"Ten!" said Bobby Denton. "Do you covet thy neighbour's house, or his manservant, or his maidservant, or his ox, or his ass, or anything that is thy neighbour's?"

"No!" cried the Love Crusaders.

"Nine!" said Bobby Denton. "Do you bear false witness against thy neighbour?"

"No!" cried the Love Crusaders.

"Eight!" said Bobby Denton. "Do you steal?"

"No!" cried the Love Crusaders.

"Seven!" said Bobby Denton. "Do you commit adultery?"

"No!" cried the Love Crusaders.

"Six!" said Bobby Denton. "Do you kill?"

"No!" cried the Love Crusaders.

"Five!" said Bobby Denton. "Do you honour thy father and thy mother?"

"Yes!" cried the Love Crusaders.

"Four!" said Bobby Denton. "Do you remember the Sabbath day, and keep it holy?"

"Yes!" cried the Love Crusaders.

"Three!" said Bobby Denton. "Do you take the name of the Lord thy God in vain?"

"No!" cried the Love Crusaders.

"Two!" said Bobby Denton. "Do you make any graven images?"

"No!" cried the Love Crusaders.

"One!" cried Bobby Denton. "Do you put any gods before the one true Lord thy God?"

"No!" cried the Love Crusaders.

"Blast off!" shouted Bobby Denton joyfully. "Paradise, here we come! Blast off, children, and Amen!"

"Well," murmured Malachi Constant, there in the chimneylike room under the staircase in Newport, "it looks like the messenger is finally going to be used."

"What was that?" said Rumfoord.

"My name—it means *faithful messenger*," said Constant. "What's the message?"

"Sorry," said Rumfoord, "I know nothing about any message." He cocked his head quizzically. "Somebody said something to you about a message?"

Constant turned his palms upward. "I mean—what am I going to go to all this trouble to get to Triton for?"

"Titan," Rumfoord corrected him.

"Titan, Triton," said Constant. "What the blast would I go there for?" Blast was a weak, prissy, Eagle-Scoutish word for Constant to use—and it took him a moment to realize why he had used it. Blast was what space cadets on television said when a meteorite carried away a control surface, or the navigator turned out to be a space pirate from the planet Zircon. He stood. "Why the hell should I go there?"

"You do—I promise you," said Rumfoord.

Constant went over to the window, some of his arrogant strength returning. "I tell you right now," he said, "I'm not going."

"Sorry to hear that," said Rumfoord.

"I'm supposed to do something for you when I get there?" said Constant.

"No," said Rumfoord.

"Then why are you sorry?" said Constant. "What's it to you?"

"Nothing," said Rumfoord. "I'm only sorry for you. You'll really be missing something."

"Like what?" said Constant.

"Well—the most pleasant climate imaginable, for one thing," said Rumfoord.

"Climate!" said Constant contemptuously. "With houses in Hollywood, the Vale of Kashmir, Acapulco, Manitoba, Tahiti, Paris, Bermuda, Rome, New York, and Capetown, I should leave Earth in search of happier climes?"

"There's more to Titan than just climate," said Rumfoord. "The women, for instance, are the most beautiful creaures between the Sun and Betelgeuse."

Constant guffawed bitterly. "Women!" he said. "You think I'm having trouble getting beautiful women? You think I'm love starved, and the only way I'll ever get close to a beautiful woman is to climb on a rocket ship and head for one of Saturn's moons? Are you kidding? I've had women so beautiful, anybody between the Sun and Betelgeuse would sit down and cry if the women said as much as hello to 'em!"

He took out his billfold, and slipped from it a photograph of his most recent conquest. There was no question about it —the girl in the photograph was staggeringly beautiful. She was Miss Canal Zone, a runner-up in the Miss Universe Contest—and in fact far more beautiful than the winner of the contest. Her beauty had frightened the judges.

Constant handed Rumfoord the photograph. "They got anything like that on Titan?" he said.

Rumfoord studied the photograph respectfully, handed it back. "No," he said, "nothing like that on Titan."

"O.K.," said Constant, feeling very much in control of his own destiny again, "climate, beautiful women—what else?"

"Nothing else," said Rumfoord mildly. He shrugged. "Oh —art objects, if you like art."

"I've got the biggest private art collection in the world," said Constant.

Constant had inherited this famous art collection. The collection had been made by his father—or, rather, by agents of his father. It was scattered through museums all over the world, each piece plainly marked as a part of the Constant Collection. The collection had been made and then deployed in this manner on the recommendation of the Director of Public Relations of Magnum Opus, Incorporated, the corporation whose sole purpose was to manage the Constant affairs.

The purpose of the collection had been to prove how generous and useful and sensitive billionaires could be. The collection had turned out to be a perfectly gorgeous investment, as well.

"That takes care of art," said Rumfoord.

Constant was about to return the photograph of Miss Canal Zone to his billfold, when he felt that he held not one photograph but two. There was a photograph behind that of Miss Canal Zone. He supposed that that was a photograph of Miss Canal Zone's predecessor, and he thought that he might as well show Rumfoord her, too—show Rumfoord what a celestial lulu he had given the gate to.

"There—there's another one," said Constant, holding out the second photograph to Rumfoord.

Rumfoord made no move to take the photograph. He didn't even bother to look at it. He looked instead into Constant's eyes and grinned roguishly.

Constant looked down at the photograph that had been ignored. He found that it was not a photograph of Miss Canal Zone's predecessor. It was a photograph that Rumfoord had slipped to him. It was no ordinary photograph, though its surface was glossy and its margins white.

Within the margins lay shimmering depths. The effect was much like that of a rectangular glass window in the surface of a clear, shallow, coral bay. At the bottom of that seeming coral bay were three women—one white, one gold, one brown. They looked up at Constant, begging him to come to them, to make them whole with love.

Their beauty was to the beauty of Miss Canal Zone as the glory of the Sun was to the glory of a lightning bug.

Constant sank into a wing chair again. He had to look away from all that beauty in order to keep from bursting into tears.

"You can keep that picture, if you like," said Rumfoord. "It's wallet size."

Constant could think of nothing to say.

"My wife will still be with you when you get to Titan," said Rumfoord, "but she won't interfere if you want to frolic with these three young ladies. Your son will be with you, too, but he'll be quite as broadminded as Beatrice."

"Son?" said Constant. He had no son.

"Yes—a fine boy named Chrono," said Rumfoord.

"Chrono?" said Constant.

"A Martian name," said Rumfoord. "He's born on Mars —by you, out of Beatrice."

"Beatrice?" said Constant.

"My wife," said Rumfoord. He had become quite transparent. His voice was becoming tinny, too, as though coming from a cheap radio. "Things fly this way and that, my boy," he said, "with or without messages. It's chaos, and no mistake, for the Universe is just being born. It's the great becoming that makes the light and the heat and the motion, and bangs you from hither to yon.

28

"Predictions, predictions, predictions," said Rumfoord musingly. "Is there anything else I should tell you? Ohhhhh —yes, yes, yes. This child of yours, this boy named Chrono—

"Chrono will pick up a little strip of metal on Mars," said Rumfoord, "and he will call it his 'good-luck piece.' Keep your eye on that good-luck piece, Mr. Constant. It's unbelievably important."

Winston Niles Rumfoord vanished slowly, beginning with the ends of his fingers, and ending with his grin. The grin remained some time after the rest of him had gone.

"See you on Titan," said the grin. And then it was gone.

"Is it all over, Moncrief?" Mrs. Winston Niles Rumfoord called down to the butler from the top of the spiral staircase.

"Yes, Mum—he's left," said the butler, "and the dog, too."

"And that Mr. Constant?" said Mrs. Rumfoord—said Beatrice. She was behaving like an invalid—tottering, blinking hard, making her voice like wind in the treetops. She wore a long white dressing gown whose soft folds formed a counter-clockwise spiral in harmony with the white staircase. The train of the gown cascaded down the top riser, making Beatrice continuous with the architecture of the mansion.

It was her tall, straight figure that mattered most in the display. The details of her face were insignificant. A cannonball, substituted for her head, would have suited the grand composition as well.

But Beatrice did have a face—and an interesting one. It could be said that she looked like a buck-toothed Indian brave. But anyone who said that would have to add quickly that she looked marvellous. Her face, like the face of Malachi Constant, was a one-of-a-kind, of surprising variation on a familiar theme—a variation that made observers think, *Yes—that would be another very nice way for people to look*. What Beatrice had done with her face, actually, was what any plain girl could do. She had overlaid it with dignity, suffering, intelligence, and a piquant dash of bitchiness.

"Yes," said Constant from below, "that Mr. Constant is still here." He was in plain view, leaning against a column in the arch that opened on to the foyer. But he was so low in

29

the composition, so lost in architectural details as to be almost invisible.

"Oh!" said Beatrice. "How do you do." It was a very empty greeting.

"How do *you* do," said Constant.

"I can only appeal to your gentlemanly instincts," said Beatrice, "in asking you not to spread the story of your meeting with my husband far and wide. I can well understand how tremendous the temptation to do so must be."

"Yes," said Constant, "I could sell my story for a lot of money, pay off the mortgage on the homestead, and become an internationally famous figure. I could hob-nob with the great and near-great, and perform before the crowned heads of Europe."

"You'll pardon me," said Beatrice, "if I fail to appreciate sarcasm and all the other brilliant nuances of your no doubt famous wit, Mr. Constant. These visits of my husband's make me ill."

"You never see him any more, do you?" said Constant.

"I saw him the first time he materialized," said Beatrice, "and that was enough to make me ill for the rest of my days."

"I liked him very much," said Constant.

"The insane, on occasion, are not without their charms," said Beatrice.

"Insane?" said Constant.

"As a man of the world, Mr. Constant," said Beatrice, "wouldn't you say that any person who made complicated and highly improbable prophecies was mad?"

"Well," said Constant, "is it really very crazy to tell a man who has access to the biggest space ship ever built that he's going out into space?"

This bit of news, about the accessibility of a space ship to Constant, startled Beatrice. It startled her so much that she took a step back from the head of the staircase, separated herself from the rising spiral. The small step backward transformed her into what she was—a frightened, lonely woman in a tremendous house.

"You have a space ship, do you?" she said.

"A company I control has custody of one," said Constant. "You've heard of *The Whale*?"

"Yes," said Beatrice.

"My company sold it to the Government," said Constant.

"I think they'd be delighted if someone would buy it back at five cents on the dollar."

"Much luck to you on your expedition," said Beatrice.

Constant bowed. "Much luck to *you* on *yours*," he said.

He left without another word. In crossing the bright zodiac on the foyer floor, he sensed that the spiral staircase now swept down rather than up. Constant became the bottommost point in a whirlpool of fate. As he walked out the door, he was delightfully aware of pulling the aplomb of the Rumfoord mansion right out with him.

Since it was foreordained that he and Beatrice were to come together again, to produce a child named Chrono, Constant was under no compunction to seek and woo her, to send her so much as a get-well card. He could go about his business, he thought, and the haughty Beatrice would have to damn well come to him — like any other bimbo.

He was laughing when he put on his dark glasses and false beard and let himself out through the little iron door in the wall.

The limousine was back, and so was the crowd.

The police held open a narrow path to the limousine door. Constant scuttled down it, reached the limousine. The path closed like the Red Sea behind the Children of Israel. The cries of the crowd, taken together, were a collective cry of indignation and pain. The crowd, having been promised nothing, felt cheated, having received nothing.

Men and boys began to rock Constant's limousine.

The chauffeur put the limousine in gear, made it creep through the sea of raging flesh.

A bald man made an attempt on Constant's life with a hot dog, stabbed at the window glass with it, splayed the bun, broke the frankfurter — left a sickly sunburst of mustard and relish.

"Yah, yah, yah!" yelled a pretty young woman, and she showed Constant what she had probably never showed any other man. She showed him that her two upper front teeth were false. She let those two front teeth fall out of place. She shrieked like a witch.

A boy climbed on the hood, blocking the chauffeur's view. He ripped off the windshield wipers, threw them to the crowd. It took the limousine three-quarters of an hour to reach a fringe of the crowd. And on the fringe were not the lunatics but the nearly sane.

Only on the fringe did the shouts become coherent.

"Tell us!" shouted a man, and he was merely fed up—not enraged.

"We've got a right!" shouted a woman. She showed her two fine children to Constant.

Another woman told Constant what it was the crowd felt it had a right to. "We've got a right to know what's going on!" she cried.

The riot, then, was an exercise in science and theology—a seeking after clues by the living as to what life was all about.

The chauffeur, seeing at last a clear road before him, pressed the accelerator to the floor. The limousine zoomed away.

A huge billboard flashed by. LET'S TAKE A FRIEND TO THE CHURCH OF OUR CHOICE ON SUNDAY! it said.

CHAPTER TWO

CHEERS IN THE WIREHOUSE

"Sometimes I think it is a great mistake to have matter that can think and feel. It complains so. By the same token, though, I suppose that boulders and mountains and moons could be accused of being a little too phlegmatic."
—WINSTON NILES RUMFOORD

THE limousine zoomed north out of Newport, turned down a gravel road, kept a rendezvous with a helicopter that was waiting in a pasture.

The purpose of Malachi Constant's switch from the limousine to the helicopter was to prevent anyone's following him, to prevent anyone's discovering who the bearded and bespectacled visitor to the Rumfoord estate had been.

No one knew where Constant was.

Neither the chauffeur nor the pilot knew the true identity of their passenger. Constant was Mr. Jonah K. Rowley to both.

"Mist' Rowley, suh—?" said the chauffeur, as Constant stepped out of the limousine.

"Yes?" said Constant.

"Wasn't you scared, suh?" said the chauffeur.

"Scared?" said Constant, sincerely puzzled by the question. "Of what?"

"Of what?" said the chauffeur incredulously. "Why, of all them crazy people who liked to lynch us."

Constant smiled and shook his head. Not once in the midst of the violence had he expected to be hurt. "It hardly helps to panic, do you think?" he said. In his own words he recognized Rumfoord's phrasing—even a little of Rumfoord's aristocratic yodel.

"Man—you must have some kind of guardian angel—lets you keep cool as a cucumber, no matter what," said the chauffeur admiringly.

This comment interested Constant, for it described well his attitude in the midst of the mob. He took the comment

33

at first as an analogy—as a poetic description of his mood. A man who had a guardian angel would certainly have felt just as Constant had.

"Yes, suh!" said the chauffeur. "Sumpin' sure must be lookin' out for *you*!"

Then it hit Constant: *This was exactly the case.*

Until that moment of truth, Constant had looked upon his Newport adventure as one more drug-induced hallucination—as one more peyotl party—vivid, novel, entertaining, and of no consequence whatsoever.

The little door had been a dreamy touch . . . the dry fountain another . . . and the huge painting of the all white touch-me-not little girl with the all white pony . . . and the chimney-like room under the spiral staircase . . . and the photograph of the three sirens on Titan . . . and Rumfoord's prophecies . . . and the discomfiture of Beatrice Rumfoord at the top of the stairs . . .

Malachi Constant broke into a cold sweat. His knees threatened to buckle and his eyelids came unhinged. He was finally understanding that every bit of it had been real! He had been calm in the midst of the mob because he knew he wasn't going to die on Earth.

Something was looking out for him, all right.

And whatever it was, it was saving his skin for—

Constant quaked as he counted on his fingers the points of interest on the itinerary Rumfoord had promised him.

Mars.

Then Mercury.

Then Earth again.

Then Titan.

Since the itinerary ended on Titan, presumably that was where Malachi Constant was going to die. He was going to *die* there!

What had Rumfoord been so cheerful about?

Constant shuffled over to the helicopter, rocked the great, ramshackle bird as he climbed inside.

"You Rowley?" said the pilot.

"That's right," said Constant.

"Unusual first name you got, Mr. Rowley," said the pilot.

"Beg your pardon?" said Constant nauseously. He was looking through the plastic dome of the cockpit cover—looking up into the evening sky. He was wondering if there

34

could possibly be eyes up there, eyes that could see everything he did. And if there were eyes up there, and they
wanted him to do certain things, go certain places—how
could they make him?

Oh God—but it looked thin and cold up there!

"I said you've got an unusual first name," said the pilot.

"What name's that?" said Constant, who had forgotten
the foolish first name he had chosen for his disguise.

"Jonah," said the pilot.

Fifty-nine days later, Winston Niles Rumfoord and his
loyal dog Kazak materialized again. A lot had happened
since their last visit.

For one thing, Malachi Constant had sold out all his holdings in Galactic Spacecraft, the corporation that had the
custody of the great rocket ship called *The Whale*. He had
done this to destroy every connection between himself and
the only known means of getting to Mars. He had put the
proceeds of the sale into MoonMist Tobacco.

For another thing, Beatrice Rumfoord had liquidated her
diversified portfolio of securities, and had put the proceeds
into shares of Galactic Spacecraft, intending thereby to get
a leather-lunged voice in whatever was done with *The
Whale*.

For another thing, Malachi Constant had taken to writing
Beatrice Rumfoord offensive letters, in order to keep her
away—in order to make himself absolutely and permanently
intolerable to her. To see one of these letters was to see them
all. The most recent one went like this, written on stationery
of Magnum Opus, Inc., the corporation whose sole purpose
was to manage the financial affairs of Malachi Constant.

*Hello from sunny California, Space Baby! Gee, I am sure
looking forward to jazzing a high-class dame like you under
the twin moons of Mars. You're the only kind of dame I
never had, and I'll bet your kind is the greatest. Love and
kisses for a starter. Mal.*

For another thing, Beatrice had bought a capsule of cya-
nide—more deadly, surely, than Cleopatra's asp. It was
Beatrice's intention to swallow it if ever she had to share so
much as the same time zone with Malachi Constant.

For another thing, the stock market had crashed, wiping

35

out Beatrice Rumfoord, among others. She had bought Galactic Spacecraft shares at prices ranging from 151½ to 169. The stock had fallen to 6 in ten trading sessions, and now lay there, trembling fractional points. Since Beatrice had bought on margin as well as for cash, she had lost everything, including her Newport home. She had nothing left but her clothes, her good name, and her finishing school education.

For another thing, Malachi Constant had thrown a party two days after returning to Hollywood—and only now, fifty-six days later, was it petering out.

For another thing, a genuinely bearded young man named Martin Koradubian had identified himself as the bearded stranger who had been invited into the Rumfoord estate to see a materialization. He was a repairer of solar watches in Boston, and a charming liar.

A magazine had bought his story for three thousand dollars.

Sitting in Skip's Museum under the spiral staircase, Winston Niles Rumfoord read Koradubian's magazine story with delight and admiration. Koradubian claimed in his story that Rumfoord had told him about the year Ten Million A.D.

In the year Ten Million, according to Koradubian, there would be a tremendous house-cleaning. All records relating to the period between the death of Christ and the year One Million A.D. would be hauled to dumps and burned. This would be done, said Koradubian, because museums and archives would be crowding the living right off the earth.

The million-year period to which the burned junk related would be summed up in history books in one sentence, according to Koradubian: *Following the death of Jesus Christ, there was a period of readjustment that lasted for approximately one million years.*

Winston Niles Rumfoord laughed and laid Koradubian's article aside. Rumfoord loved nothing more than a thumping good fraud. "Ten million A.D.," he said out loud, "a great year for fireworks and parades and world fairs. A merry time for cracking open cornerstones and digging up time capsules."

Rumfoord wasn't talking to himself. There was someone else in Skip's Museum with him.

36

The other person was his wife Beatrice.

Beatrice was sitting in the facing wing chair. She had come downstairs to ask her husband's help in a time of great need.

Rumfoord blandly changed the subject.

Beatrice, already ghostly in a white peignoir, turned the colour of lead.

"What an optimistic animal man is!" said Rumfoord rosily. "Imagine expecting the species to last for ten million more years—as though people were as well-designed as turtles!" He shrugged. "Well—who knows—maybe human beings will last that long, just on the basis of pure cussedness. What's your guess?"

"What?" said Beatrice.

"Guess how long the human race will be around," said Rumfoord.

From between Beatrice's clenched teeth came a frail, keen, sustained note so high as to be almost above the range of the human ear. The sound bore the same ghastly promise as the whistle of fins on a falling bomb.

Then the explosion came. Beatrice capsized her chair, attacked the skeleton, threw it crashing into a corner. She cleaned off the shelves of Skip's Museum, bouncing specimens off the walls, trampling them on the floor.

Rumfoord was flabbergasted. "Good God," he said, "what made you do that?"

"Don't you know everything?" said Beatrice hysterically. "Does anybody have to tell you anything? Just read my mind!"

Rumfoord put his palms to his temples, his eyes wide. "Static—all I get is static," he said.

"What else *would* there be but static!" said Beatrice. "I'm going to be thrown right out in the street, without even the price of a meal—and my husband laughs and wants me to play guessing games!"

"It wasn't any *ordinary* guessing game," said Rumfoord. "It was about how long the human race was going to last. I thought that might sort of give you more perspective about your own problems."

"The hell with the human race!" said Beatrice.

"You're a member of it, you know," said Rumfoord.

"Then I'd like to put in for a transfer to the chimpanzees!" said Beatrice. "No chimpanzee husband would stand by while his wife lost all her coconuts. No chimpanzee hus-band would try to make his wife into a space whore for Malachi Constant of Hollywood, California!"

Having said this ghastly thing, Beatrice subsided some. She wagged her head tiredly. "How long *is* the human race going to be around, Master?"

"I don't know," said Rumfoord.

"I thought you knew everything," said Beatrice. "Just take a look at the future."

"I look at the future," said Rumfoord, "and I find that I shall not be in the Solar System when the human race dies out. So the end is as much a mystery to me as to you."

In Hollywood, California, the chimes of the blue tele-phone in the rhinestone phone booth by Malachi Constant's swimming pool were ringing.

It is always pitiful when any human being falls into a con-dition hardly more respectable than that of an animal. How much more pitiful it is when the person who falls has had all the advantages!

Malachi Constant lay in the wide gutter of his kidney-shaped swimming pool, sleeping the sleep of a drunkard. There was a quarter of an inch of warm water in the gutter. Constant was fully dressed in blue-green evening shorts and a dinner jacket of gold brocade. His clothes were soaked.

He was all alone.

The pool had once been covered uniformly by an undu-lating blanket of gardenias. But a persistent morning breeze had moved the blooms to one end of the pool, as though folding a blanket to the foot of a bed. In folding back the blanket, the breeze revealed a pool bottom paved with broken glass, cherries, twists of lemon peel, peyotl buttons, slices of orange, stuffed olives, sour onions, a television set, a hypodermic syringe, and the ruins of a white grand piano. Cigar butts and cigarette butts, some of them marijuana, littered the surface.

The swimming pool looked less like a facility for sport than like a punchbowl in hell.

One of Constant's arms dangled in the pool itself. From the wrist underwater came the glint of his solar watch. The watch had stopped.

The telephone chimes persisted.

Constant mumbled but did not move.

The chimes stopped. Then, after twenty seconds, the chimes began again.

Constant groaned, sat up, groaned.

From the inside of the house came a brisk, efficient sound, high heels on the tile floor. A ravishing, brassy blonde woman crossed from the house to the phone booth, giving Constant a look of haughty contempt.

She was chewing gum.

"Yah?" she said into the telephone. "Oh—it's you again. Yah—he's awake. Hey!" she yelled at Constant. She had a voice like a grackle. "Hey, space cadet!" she yelled.

"Hm?" said Constant.

"The guy who's president of that company you own wants to talk to you."

"Which company?" said Constant.

"Which company *you* president of?" said the woman into the telephone. She got her answer. "Magnum Opus," she said. "Ransom K. Fern of Magnum Opus," she said.

"Tell him—tell him I'll call him back," said Constant.

The woman told Fern, got another message to relay to Constant. "He says he's quitting."

Constant stood unsteadily, rubbing his face with his hands. "Quitting?" he said dully. "Old Ransom K. Fern quitting?"

"Yah," said the woman. She smiled hatefully. "He says you can't afford to pay his salary any more. He says you better come in and talk to him before he goes home." She laughed. "He says you're broke."

Back in Newport, the racket of Beatrice Rumfoord's outburst had attracted Moncrief the butler to Skip's Museum. "You called, Mum?" he said.

"It was more of a scream, Moncrief," said Beatrice.

"She doesn't want anything, thank you," said Rumfoord. "We were simply having a spirited discussion."

"How *dare* you say whether I want something or not?" said Beatrice hotly to Rumfoord. "I'm beginning to catch on that you're not *nearly* as omniscient as you pretend to be. It so happens I want something very much. I want a *number of things* very much."

"Mum?" said the butler.

"I'd like you to let the dog in, please," said Beatrice. "I'd like to pet him before he goes. I would like to find out if a chrono-synclastic infundibula kills love in a dog the way it kills love in a man."

The butler bowed and left.

"That was a pretty scene to play before a servant," said Rumfoord.

"By and large," said Beatrice, "my contribution to the dignity of the family has been somewhat greater than yours."

Rumfoord hung his head. "I've failed you in some way? Is that what you're saying?"

"In *some* way?" said Beatrice. "In *every* way!"

"What would you have me do?" said Rumfoord.

"You could have told me this stock-market crash was coming!" said Beatrice. "You could have spared me what I'm going through now."

Rumfoord's hands worked in air, unhappily trying on various lines of argument for size.

"Well?" said Beatrice.

"I just wish we could go out to the chrono-synclastic infundibula together," said Rumfoord. "So you could see for once what I was talking about. All I can say is that my failure to warn you about the stock-market crash is as much a part of the natural order as Halley's Comet—and it makes an equal amount of sense to rage against either one."

"You're saying you have no character, and no sense of responsibility toward me," said Beatrice. "I'm sorry to put it that way, but it's the truth."

Rumfoord rocked his head back and forth. "A truth—but, oh God, what a punctual truth," he said.

Rumfoord retreated into his magazine again. The magazine opened naturally to the centre spread, which was a colour ad for MoonMist Cigarettes. MoonMist Tobacco, Ltd., had been bought recently by Malachi Constant.

Pleasure in Depth! said the headline on the ad. The picture that went with it was the picture of the three sirens of Titan. There they were—the white girl, the golden girl, and the brown girl.

The fingers of the golden girl were fortuitously spread as they rested on her left breast, permitting an artist to paint in a MoonMist Cigarette between two of them. The smoke from her cigarette passed beneath the nostrils of the brown and white girls, and their space-annihilating concupiscence seemed centred on mentholated smoke alone.

Rumfoord had known that Constant would try to debase

the picture by using it in commerce. Constant's father had done a similar thing when he found he could not buy Leonardo's "Mona Lisa" at any price. The old man had punished Mona Lisa by having her used in an advertising campaign for suppositories. It was the free-enterprise way of handling beauty that threatened to get the upper hand.

Rumfoord made a buzzing sound on his lips, which was a sound he made when he approached compassion. The compassion he approached was for Malachi Constant, who was having a far worse time of it than Beatrice.

"Have I heard your whole defence?" said Beatrice, coming behind Rumfoord's chair. Her arms were folded, and Rumfoord, reading her mind, knew that she thought of her sharp, projected elbows as bull-fighter's swords.

"I beg your pardon?" said Rumfoord.

"This silence—this hiding in the magazine—this is the sum and total of your rebuttal?" said Beatrice.

"Rebuttal—a punctual word if there ever was one," said Rumfoord. "I say this, and then you rebut me, then I rebut you, then somebody else comes in and rebuts us both." He shuddered. "What a nightmare where everybody gets in line to rebut each other."

"Couldn't you, this very moment," said Beatrice, "give me stock-market tips that would enable me to gain back everything I lost and more? If you had one shred of concern for me, couldn't you tell me exactly how Malachi Constant of Hollywood is going to try to trick me into going to Mars, so I could outwit him?"

"Look," said Rumfoord, "life for a punctual person is like a roller coaster." He turned to shiver his hands in her face. "All kinds of things are going to happen to you! Sure," he said, "I can see the whole roller coaster you're on. And sure —I could give you a piece of paper that would tell you about every dip and turn, warn you about every bogeyman that was going to pop out at you in the tunnels. But that wouldn't help you any."

"I don't see why not," said Beatrice.

"Because you'd still have to take the roller coaster ride," said Rumfoord. "I didn't design the roller coaster, I don't own it, and I don't say who rides and who doesn't. I just know what it's shaped like."

"And Malachi Constant is part of the roller coaster?"

"Yes," said Rumfoord.

"And there's no avoiding him?" said Beatrice.

"No," said Rumfoord.

"Well—suppose you tell me then, just what steps bring us together," said Beatrice, "and let me do what little I can."

Rumfoord shrugged. "All right—if you wish," he said. "If it would make you feel better, at this very moment," he said, "the President of the United States is announcing a New Age of Space to relieve unemployment. Billions of dollars are going to be spent on unmanned space ships, just to make work. The opening episode in this New Age of Space will be the firing of *The Whale* next Tuesday. *The Whale* will be renamed *The Rumfoord* in my honour, will be loaded with organ-grinder monkeys, and will be fired in the general direction of Mars. You and Constant will both take part in the ceremonies. You will go on board for a ceremonial inspection, and a faulty switch will send you on your way with the monkeys."

It is worth stopping the narrative at this point to say that this cock-and-bull story told to Beatrice is one of the few known instances of Winston Niles Rumfoord's having told a lie.

This much of Rumfoord's story was true: *The Whale* was going to be renamed and fired on Tuesday, and the President of the United States *was* announcing a New Age of Space.

Some of the President's comments at the time bear repeating—and it should be remembered that the President gave the word "progress" a special flavour by pronouncing it *prog-erse*. He also flavoured the words "chair" and "warehouse," pronouncing them *cheer* and *wirehouse*.

"Now, some people are going around saying the American economy is old and sick," said the President, "and I frankly can't understand how they can say such a thing, because there is now more opportunity for progerse on all fronts than at any time in human history.

"And there is one frontier we can make particular progerse on and that is the great frontier of space. We have been turned back by space once, but it isn't the American way to take no for an answer where progerse is concerned.

"Now, people of faint heart come to see me every day at the White House," said the President, "and they weep and wail and say, 'Oh, Mr. President, the wirehouses are all full of automobiles and airplanes and kitchen appliances and various other products,' and they say, 'Oh, Mr. President, there is nothing more that anybody wants the factories to make because everybody already has two, three, and four of everything.'

"One man in particular, I remember, was a cheer manufacturer, and he had way overproduced, and all he could think about was all those cheers in the wirehouse. And I said to him, 'In the next twenty years, the population of the world is going to double, and all those billions of new people are going to need things to sit down on, so you just hang on to those cheers. Meanwhile, why don't you forget about those cheers in the wirehouse and think about progerse in space?'

"I said to him and I say to you and I say to everybody, 'Space can absorb the productivity of a trillion planets the size of earth. We could build and fire rockets forever, and never fill up space and never learn all there is to know about it.

"Now, these same people who like to weep and wail so much say, 'Oh, but Mr. President, what about the chronosynclastic infundibula and what about this and what about that?' And I say to them, 'If people listened to people like you, there wouldn't ever be any progerse. There wouldn't be the telephone or anything. And besides,' I tell them and I tell you and I tell everybody, 'we don't have to put people in the rocket ships. We will use the lower animals only.'"

There was more to the speech.

Malachi Constant of Hollywood, California, came out of the rhinestone phone booth cold sober. His eyes felt like cinders. His mouth tasted like horseblanket purée.

He was positive that he had never seen the beautiful blonde woman before.

He asked her one of the standard questions for times of violent change. "Where is everybody?" he said.

"You threw 'em all out," said the woman.

"I did?" said Constant.

"Yah," said the woman. "You mean you drew a blank?"

Constant nodded weakly. During the fifty-six-day party he had reached a point where he could draw almost nothing else. His aim had been to make himself unworthy of any

43

destiny—incapable of any mission—far too ill to travel. He had succeeded to a shocking degree.

"Oh, it was quite a show," said the woman. "You were having as good a time as anybody, helping shove the piano in the pool. Then, when it finally went in, you got this big crying jag."

"Crying jag," echoed Constant. That was something new.

"Yah," said the woman. "You said you had a very unhappy childhood, and made everybody listen to how unhappy it was. How your father never even threw a ball to you once—any kind of ball. Half the time nobody could understand you, but every time somebody could understand you, it was about how there never was any kind of ball.

"Then you talked about your mother," said the woman, "and you said if she was a whore, then you were proud to be a son of a whore, if that's what a whore was. Then you said you'd give an oil well to any woman who'd come up to you and shake your hand and say real loud, so everybody could hear, 'I'm a whore, just like your mother was.' "

"What happened then?" said Constant.

"You gave an oil well to every woman at the party," said the woman. "And then you started crying worse than ever, and you picked me out, and you told everybody I was the only person in the whole Solar System you could trust. You said everybody else was just waiting for you to fall asleep, so they could put you on a rocket ship and shoot you at Mars. Then you made everybody go home but me. Servants and everybody.

"Then we flew down to Mexico and got married, and then we came back here," she said. "Now I find out you haven't got a pot to piss in or a window to throw it out of. You better go down to the office and find out what the hell is going on, on account of my boyfriend is a gangster, and he'll kill you if I tell him you aren't providing for me right.

"Hell," she said, "I had an unhappier childhood than you did. My mother was a whore and my father never came home, either—but we were *poor* besides. At least you had billions of dollars."

In Newport, Beatrice Rumfoord turned her back to her husband. She stood on the threshold of Skip's Museum, facing the corridor. Down the corridor came the sound of the butler's voice. The butler was standing in the front doorway, calling to Kazak, the hound of space.

"I know a little something about roller coasters, too," Beatrice said.

"That's good," said Rumfoord emptily.

"When I was ten years old," said Beatrice, "my father got it into his head that it would be fun for me to ride a roller coaster. We were summering on Cape Cod, and we drove over to an amusement park outside of Fall River.

"He bought two tickets on the roller coaster. He was going to ride with me.

"I took one look at the roller coaster," said Beatrice, "and it looked silly and dirty and dangerous, and I simply refused to get on. My own father couldn't make me get on," said Beatrice, "even though he was Chairman of the Board of the New York Central Railroad.

"We turned around and came home," said Beatrice proudly. Her eyes glittered, and she nodded abruptly. "That's the way to treat roller coasters," she said.

She stalked out of Skip's Museum, went to the foyer to await the arrival of Kazak.

In a moment, she felt the electric presence of her husband behind her.

"Bea," he said, "if I seem indifferent to your misfortunes, it's only because I know how well things are going to turn out in the end. If it seems crude of me not to hate the idea of your pairing off with Constant, it's only an humble admission on my part that he's going to make you a far better husband than I ever was or will be.

"Look forward to being really in love for the first time, Bea," said Rumfoord. "Look forward to behaving aristocratically without any outward proofs of your aristocracy. Look forward to having nothing but the dignity and intelligence and tenderness that God gave you—look forward to taking those materials and nothing else, and making something exquisite with them."

Rumfoord groaned tinnily. He was becoming insubstantial. "Oh, God," he said, "you talk about roller coasters, stop and think sometime about the roller coaster I'm on. Some day on Titan, it will be revealed to you just how ruthlessly I've been used, and by whom, and to what disgustingly paltry ends."

45

Kazak now flung himself into the house, flews flapping. He landed skidding on the polished floor.

He ran in place, trying to make a right-angle turn in Beatrice's direction. Faster and faster he ran, and still he could get no traction.

He became translucent.

He began to shrink, to fizz crazily on the foyer floor like a ping-pong ball in a frying pan.

Then he disappeared.

There was no dog any more.

Without looking behind, Beatrice knew that her husband had disappeared, too.

"Kazak?" she said faintly. She snapped her fingers, as though to attract a dog. Her fingers were too weak to make a sound.

"Nice doggy," she whispered.

CHAPTER THREE

UNITED HOTCAKE PREFERRED

"Son—they say there isn't any royalty in this country, but do you want me to tell you how to be king of the United States of America? Just fall through the hole in a privy and come out smelling like a rose." —NOEL CONSTANT

MAGNUM OPUS, the Los Angeles Corporation that managed Malachi Constant's financial affairs, was founded by Malachi's father. It had a thirty-one-story building for its home. While Magnum Opus owned the whole building, it used only the top three floors, renting out the rest to corporations it controlled.

Some of these corporations, having been sold recently by Magnum Opus, were moving out. Others, having been bought recently by Magnum Opus, were moving in.

Among the tenants were Galactic Spacecraft, MoonMist Tobacco, Fandango Petroleum, Lennox Monorail, Fry-Kwik, Sani-Maid Pharmaceuticals, Lewis and Marvin Sulfur, Dupree Electronics, Universal Piezo-electric, Psychokinesis Unlimited, Ed Muir Associates, Max-Mor Machine Tools, Wilkinson Paint and Varnish, American Levitation, Flo-Fast, King O'Leisure Shirts, and the Emblem Supreme Casualty and Life Assurance Company of California.

The Magnum Opus Building was a slender, prismatic, twelve-sided shaft, faced on all twelve sides with blue-green glass that shaded to rose at the base. The twelve sides were said by the architect to represent the twelve great religions of the world. So far, no one had asked the architect to name them.

That was lucky, because he couldn't have done it.

There was a private heliport on top.

The shadow and flutter of Constant's helicopter settling to the heliport seemed to many of the people below to be like the shadow and flutter of the Bright Angel of Death.

47

It seemed that way because of the stock-market crash, because money and jobs were so scarce.

And it seemed especially that way to them because the things that had crashed the hardest, that had pulled everything down with them, were the enterprises of Malachi Constant.

Constant was flying his own helicopter, since all his servants had quit the night before. Constant was flying it badly. He set it down with a crash that sent shivers through the building.

He was arriving for a conference with Ransom K. Fern, President of Magnum Opus.

Fern waited for Constant on the thirty-first floor—a single, vast room that was Constant's office.

The office was spookily furnished, since none of the furniture had legs. Everything was suspended magnetically at the proper height. The tables and the desk and the bar and the couches were floating slabs. The chairs were tilted, floating bowls. And most eerie of all, pencils and pads were scattered at random through the air ready to be snatched by anyone who had an idea worth writing down.

The carpet was as green as grass for the simple reason that it was grass—living grass as lush as any putting green.

Malachi Constant sank from the heliport deck to his office in a private elevator. When the elevator door whispered open, Constant was startled by the legless furnishings, by the floating pencils and pads. He had not been in his office for eight weeks. Somebody had refurnished the place.

Ransom K. Fern, aging President of Magnum Opus, stood at a floor-to-ceiling window, looking out over the city. He wore his black Homburg hat and his black Chesterfield coat. He carried his whangee walking stick at port arms. He was exceedingly thin—always had been.

"A butt like two beebees," Malachi Constant's father Noel had said of Fern. "Ransom K. Fern is like a camel who has burned up both his humps, and now he's burning up everything else but his hair and eyeballs."

According to figures released by the Bureau of Internal Revenue, Fern was the highest-paid executive in the country. He had a salary of a flat million dollars a year—plus stock-option plans and cost-of-living adjustments.

He had joined Magnum Opus when he was twenty-two years old. He was sixty now.

"Some—somebody's changed all the furniture," said Constant.

"Yes," said Fern, still looking out over the city, "somebody changed it."

"You?" said Constant.

Fern sniffed, took his time about answering. "I thought we ought to demonstrate our loyalty to some of our own products."

"I—I never saw anything like it," said Constant. "No legs—just floating in air."

"Magnetism, you know," said Fern.

"Why—why I think it looks wonderful, now that I'm getting used to it," said Constant. "And some company we own makes this stuff?"

"American Levitation Company," said Fern. "You said to buy it, so we bought it."

Ransom K. Fern turned away from the window. His face was a troubling combination of youth and age. There was no sign in the face of any intermediate stages in the aging process, no hint of the man of thirty or forty or fifty who had been left behind. Only adolescence and the age of sixty were represented. It was as though a seventeen-year-old had been withered and bleached by a blast of heat.

Fern read two books a day. It has been said that Aristotle was the last man to be familiar with the whole of his own culture. Ransom K. Fern had made an impressive attempt to equal Aristotle's achievement. He had been somewhat less successful than Aristotle in perceiving patterns in what he knew.

The intellectual mountain had laboured to produce a philosophical mouse—and Fern was the first to admit that it was a mouse, and a mangy mouse at that. As Fern expressed the philosophy conversationally, in its simplest terms:

"You go up to a man, and you say, 'How are things going, Joe?' And he says, 'Oh, fine, fine—couldn't be better.' And you look into his eyes, and you see things really couldn't be much worse. When you get right down to it, everybody's having a perfectly lousy time of it, and I mean everybody. And the hell of it is, nothing seems to help much."

This philosophy did not sadden him. It did not make him brood.

It made him heartlessly watchful.

It helped in business, too—for it let Fern assume automatically that the other fellow was far weaker and far more bored than he seemed.

Sometimes, too, people with strong stomachs found Fern's murmured asides funny.

His situation, working for Noel Constant and then Malachi, conspired nicely to make almost anything he might say bitterly funny—for he was superior to Constant *père* and *fils* in every respect but one, and the respect excepted was the only one that really mattered. The Constants—ignorant, vulgar, and brash—had copious quantities of dumb luck.

Or had had up to now.

Malachi Constant had still to get it through his head that his luck was gone—every bit of it. He had still to get it through his head, despite the hideous news Fern had given him on the telephone.

"Gee," said Constant ingenuously, "the more I look at this furniture, the more I like it. This stuff should sell like hotcakes." There was something pathetic and repellent about Malachi Constant's talking business. It had been the same with his father. Old Noel Constant had never known anything about business, and neither had his son—and what little charm the Constants had evaporated the instant they pretended that their success depended on their knowing their elbows from third base.

There was something obscene about a billionaire's being optimistic and aggressive and cunning.

"If you ask me," said Constant, "that was a pretty sound investment—a company that makes furniture like this."

"United Hotcake preferred," said Fern. United Hotcake preferred was a favourite joke of his. Whenever people came to him, begging for investment advice that would double their money in six weeks, he advised them gravely to invest in this fictitious stock. Some people actually tried to follow his advice.

"Sitting on an American Levitation couch is harder than standing up in a birchbark canoe," said Fern dryly. "Throw yourself into one of these so-called chairs, and it will bounce you off the wall like a stone out of a slingshot. Sit on the edge of your desk, and it will waltz you around the room like a Wright brother at Kitty Hawk."

Constant touched his desk ever so lightly. It shuddered nervously.

"Well—they still haven't got all of the bugs out of it, that's all," said Constant.

"Truer words were never spoken," said Fern.

Constant now made a plea that he had never had to make before. "A guy is entitled to a mistake now and then," he said.

"Now and then?" said Fern, raising his eyebrows. "For three months you have made nothing but wrong decisions, and you've done what I would have said was impossible. You've succeeded in more than wiping out the results of almost forty years of inspired guessing."

Ransom K. Fern took a pencil from the air and broke it in two. "Magnum Opus is no more. You and I are the last two people in the building. Everyone else has been paid off and sent home."

He bowed and moved toward the door. "The switchboard has been arranged so that all incoming calls will come directly to your desk here. And when you leave, Mr. Constant, sir, remember to turn out the lights and lock the front door."

A history of Magnum Opus, Inc., is perhaps in order at this point.

Magnum Opus began as an idea in the head of a Yankee travelling salesman of copper-bottomed cook-ware. That Yankee was Noel Constant, a native of New Bedford, Massachusetts. He was the father of Malachi.

The father of Noel, in turn, was Sylvanus Constant, a loom fixer in the New Bedford Mills of the Nattaweena Division of the Grand Republic Woolen Company. He was an anarchist, though he never got into any trouble about it, except with his wife.

The family could trace its line back through an illegitimacy to Benjamin Constant, who was a tribune under Napoleon from 1799 to 1801, and a lover of Anne Louise Germaine Necker, Baronne de Stael-Holstein, wife of the then Swedish ambassador to France.

One night in Los Angeles, at any rate, Noel Constant got it into his head to become a speculator. He was thirty-nine at the time, single, physically and morally unattractive, and a business failure. The idea of becoming a speculator came to him as he sat all alone on a narrow bed in Room 223 of the Wilburhampton Hotel.

The most valuable corporate structure ever to be owned by one man could not have had humbler headquarters in the beginning. Room 223 of the Wilburhampton was eleven feet long and eight feet wide, and had neither telephone nor desk.

What it did have was a bed, a three-drawer dresser, old newspapers lining the drawers, and, in the bottom drawer, a Gideon Bible. The newspaper page that lined the middle drawer was a page of stock-market quotations from fourteen years before.

There is a riddle about a man who is locked in a room with nothing but a bed and a calendar, and the question is: How does he survive?

That answer is: He eats dates from the calendar and drinks water from the springs of the bed.

This comes very close to describing the genesis of Magnum Opus. The materials with which Noel Constant built his fortune were hardly more nourishing in themselves than calendar dates and bedsprings.

Magnum Opus was built with a pen, a cheque book, some cheque-sized Government envelopes, a Gideon Bible, and a bank balance of eight thousand, two hundred and twelve dollars.

The bank balance was Noel Constant's share in the estate of his anarchist father. The estate had consisted principally of Government bonds.

And Noel Constant had an investment programme. It was simplicity itself. The Bible would be his investment counsellor.

There are those who have concluded, after studying Noel Constant's investment pattern, that he was either a genius or had a superb system of industrial spies.

He invariably picked the stock-market's most brilliant performers days or hours before their performances began. In twelve months, rarely leaving Room 223 in the Wilburhampton Hotel, he increased his fortune to a million and a quarter.

Noel Constant did it without genius and without spies.

His system was so idiotically simple that some people can't understand it, no matter how often it is explained. The people who can't understand it are people who have to believe, for their own peace of mind, that tremendous wealth can be produced only by tremendous cleverness.

This was Noel Constant's system:

He took the Gideon Bible that was in his room, and he started with the first sentence in Genesis.

The first sentence in Genesis, as some people may know, is: "In the beginning God created the heaven and the earth." Noel Constant wrote the sentence in capital letters, put periods between the letters, divided the letters into pairs, rendering the sentence as follows: "I.N., T.H., E.B., E.G., I.N., N.I., N.G., G.O., D.C., R.E., A.T., E.D., T.H., E.H., E.A., V.E., N.A., N.D., T.H., E.E., A.R., T.H."

And then he looked for corporations with those initials, and bought shares in them. His rule at the beginning was that he would own shares in only one corporation at a time, would invest his whole nest-egg in it, and would sell the instant the value of his shares had doubled.

His very first investment was International Nitrate. After that came Trowbridge Helicopter, Electra Bakeries, Eternity Granite, Indiana Novelty, Norwich Iron, National Gelatin, Granada Oil, Del-Mar Creations, Richmond Electroplating, Anderson Trailer, and Eagle Duplicating.

His programme for the next twelve months was this: Trowbridge Helicopter again, ELCO Hoist, Engineering Associates, Vickery Electronics, National Alum, National Dredging, Trowbridge Helicopter again.

The third time he bought Trowbridge Helicopter, he didn't buy a piece of it. He bought the whole thing—lock, stock, and barrel.

Two days after that, the company landed a long-term Government contract for intercontinental ballistic missiles, a contract that made the company worth, conservatively, fifty-nine million dollars. Noel Constant had bought the company for twenty-two million.

The only executive decision he ever made relative to the company was contained in an order written on a picture postcard of the Wilburhampton Hotel. The card was addressed to the president of the company, telling him to change the name of the company to Galactic Spacecraft, Inc., since the company had long since outgrown both Trowbridges and helicopters.

Small as this exercise of authority was, it was significant, for it showed that Constant had at last become interested in something he owned. And, though his holdings in the firm had more than doubled in value, he did not sell them all. He sold only forty-nine per cent of them.

Thereafter, he continued to take the advice of his Gideon Bible, but he kept big pieces of any firm he really liked.

During his first two years in Room 223 of the Wilbur-hampton, Noel Constant had only one visitor. That visitor did not know he was rich. His one visitor was a chamber-maid named Florence Whitehill, who spent one night out of ten with him for a small, flat fee.

Florence, like everyone else in Wilburhampton, believed him when he said he was a trader in stamps. Personal hygiene was not Noel Constant's strongest suit. It was easy to believe that his work brought him into regular contact with mucilage.

The only people who knew how rich he was were em-ployees of the Bureau of Internal Revenue and of the august accounting firm of Clough and Higgins.

Then after two years, Noel Constant received his second visitor in Room 223.

The second visitor was a thin and watchful blue-eyed man of twenty-two. He engaged Noel Constant's serious attention by announcing that he was from the United States Bureau of Internal Revenue.

Constant invited the young man into his room, motioned for him to sit on the bed. He himself remained standing.

"They sent a child, did they?" said Noel Constant.

The visitor was not offended. He turned the gibe to his own advantage, using it in an image of himself that was chilling indeed. "A child with a heart of stone and a mind as quick as a mongoose, Mr. Constant," he said. "I have also been to Harvard Business School."

"That may be so," said Constant, "but I don't think you can hurt me. I don't owe the Federal Government a dime."

The callow visitor nodded. "I know," he said. "I found everything in apple-pie order."

The young man looked around the room. He wasn't sur-prised by its squalor. He was worldly enough to have ex-pected something diseased.

"I've been over your income-tax reports for the past two years," he said, "and, by my calculations, you are the luckiest man who ever lived."

"Lucky?" said Noel Constant.

"I think so," said the young visitor. "Don't *you* think so?

For instance—what does ELCO Hoist Company manufacture?"

"ELCO Hoist?" said Noel Constant blankly.

"You owned fifty-three per cent of it for a period of two months," said the young visitor.

"Why—hoists—things for lifting various articles," said Noel Constant stuffily. "And various allied products."

The young visitor's smile made cat's whiskers under his nose. "For your information," he said, "ELCO Hoist Company was a name given by the Government in the last war to a top-secret laboratory that was developing underwater listening gear. After the war, it was sold to private enterprise, and the name was never changed—since the work was still top secret, and the only customer was still the Government.

"Suppose you tell me," said the young visitor, "what it was you learned about Indiana Novelty that made you think it was a shrewd investment? Did you think they made little party poppers with paper hats inside?"

"I have to answer these questions for the Bureau of Internal Revenue?" said Noel Constant. "I have to describe every company I owned in detail, or I can't keep the money?"

"I was simply asking for my own curiosity. From your reaction, I gather that you haven't the remotest idea what Indiana Novelty does. For your information, Indiana Novelty manufactures nothing, but holds certain key patents on tyre-recapping machinery."

"Suppose we get down to the Bureau of Internal Revenue business," said Noel Constant curtly.

"I'm no longer with the Bureau," said the young visitor. "I resigned my one-hundred-and-fourteen-dollar-a-week job this morning in order to take a job making two thousand dollars a week."

"Working for whom?" said Noel Constant.

"Working for you," said the young man. He stood, held out his hand. "Ransom K. Fern is the name," he said.

"I had a professor in the Harvard Business School," said young Fern to Noel Constant, "who kept telling me that I was smart, but that I would have to *find my boy*, if I was going to be rich. He wouldn't explain what he meant. He said I would catch on sooner or later. I asked him how I could go looking for my boy, and he suggested that I work for the Bureau of Internal Revenue for a year or so.

"When I went over your tax returns, Mr. Constant, it suddenly came to me what it was he meant. He meant I was shrewd and thorough, but I wasn't remarkably lucky. I had to find somebody who had luck in an astonishing degree— and so I have."

"Why should I pay you two thousand dollars a week?" said Noel Constant. "You see my facilities and my staff here, and you know what I've done with them."

"Yes," said Fern, "and I can show you where you should have made two hundred million where you made only fifty-nine. You know absolutely nothing about corporate law or tax law—or even commonsense business procedure."

Fern thereupon proved this to Noel Constant, father of Malachi—and Fern showed him an organizational plan that had the name Magnum Opus, Incorporated. It was a marvellous engine for doing violence to the spirit of thousands of laws without actually running afoul of so much as a city ordinance.

Noel Constant was so impressed by this monument to hypocrisy and sharp practice that he wanted to buy stock in it without even referring to his Bible.

"Mr. Constant, sir," said young Fern, "don't you understand? Magnum Opus is you, with you as chairman of the board, with me as president.

"Mr. Constant," he said, "right now you're as easy for the Bureau of Internal Revenue to watch as a man on a street corner selling apples and pears. But just imagine how hard you would be to watch if you had a whole office building jammed to the rafters with industrial bureaucrats—men who lose things and use the wrong forms and create new forms and demand everything in quintuplicate, and who understand perhaps a third of what is said to them; who habitually give misleading answers in order to gain time in which to think, who make decisions only when forced to, and who then cover their tracks; who make perfectly honest mistakes in addition and subtraction, who call meetings whenever they feel lonely, who write memos whenever they feel unloved; men who never throw anything away unless they think it could get them fired. A single industrial bureaucrat, if he is sufficiently vital and nervous, should be able to create a ton of meaningless papers a year for the Bureau of Internal

Revenue to examine. In the Magnum Opus Building, we will have thousands of them! And you and I can have the top two stories, and you can go on keeping track of what's really going on the way you do now." He looked around the room. "How do you keep track now, by the way—writing with a burnt match on the margins of a telephone directory?"

"In my head," said Noel Constant.

"There is one more advantage I have yet to point out," said Fern. "Some day your luck is going to run out. And then you're going to need the shrewdest, most thorough manager you can hire—or you'll crash all the way back to pots and pans."

"You're hired," said Noel Constant, father of Malachi.

"Now, where should we erect the building?" said Fern.

"I own this hotel, and this hotel owns the lot across the street," said Noel Constant. "Build it on the lot across the street." He held up an index finger as crooked as a crankshaft. "There's just one thing—"

"Yes, sir?" said Fern.

"I'm not moving into it," said Noel Constant. "I'm staying right here."

Those who want more detailed histories of Magnum Opus, Inc., can go to their public libraries and ask for either Lavina Waters' romantic *Too Wild a Dream?* or Crowther Gomburg's harsh *Primordial Scales*.

Miss Waters' volume, while fuddled as to business details, contains the better account of the chambermaid Florence Whitehill's discovery that she was pregnant by Noel Constant, and her discovery that Noel Constant was a multi-multi-millionaire.

Noel Constant married the chambermaid, gave her a mansion and a chequeing account with a million dollars in it. He told her to name the child Malachi if it was a boy, and Prudence if it was a girl. He asked her to please keep coming to see him once every ten days in Room 223 of the Wilburhampton Hotel, but not to bring the baby.

Gomburg's book, while first-rate on business details, suffers from Gomburg's central thesis, to the effect that Magnum Opus was a product of a complex of inabilities to love. Reading between the lines of Gomburg's book, it is increasingly clear that Gomburg is himself unloved and unable to love.

Neither Miss Waters nor Gomburg, incidentally, discovered Noel Constant's investment method. Ransom K. Fern never discovered it either, though he tried hard enough.

The only person Noel Constant ever told was his son Malachi, on Malachi's twenty-first birthday. That birthday party of two took place in Room 223 of the Wilburhampton. It was the first time father and son had ever met.

Malachi had come to see Noel by invitation.

Human emotions being what they are, young Malachi Constant paid more attention to a detail in the room's furnishings than he did to the secret of how to make millions or even billions of dollars.

The money-making secret was so simple-minded to begin with, that it didn't require much attention. The most complicated part of it had to do with the manner in which young Malachi was to pick up the torch of Magnum Opus when Noel had, at long last, laid it down. Young Malachi was to ask Ransom K. Fern for a chronological list of the investments of Magnum Opus, and, reading down the margin, young Malachi would learn just how far old Noel had gone in the Bible, and where young Malachi should begin.

The detail in the furnishings of Room 223 that interested young Malachi so was a photograph of himself. It was a photograph of himself at the age of three—a photograph of a sweet, pleasant, game little boy on an ocean beach.

It was thumbtacked to the wall.

It was the only picture in the room.

Old Noel saw young Malachi looking at the picture, and was confused and embarrassed by the whole thing about fathers and sons. He ransacked his mind for something good to say, and found almost nothing.

"My father gave me only two pieces of advice," he said, "and only one of them has stood the test of time. They were: 'Don't touch your principal,' and 'Keep the liquor bottle out of the bedroom.'" His embarrassment and confusion were now too great to be borne. "Good-bye," he said abruptly.

"Good-bye?" said young Malachi, startled. He moved toward the door.

"Keep the liquor bottle out of the bedroom," said the old man, and he turned his back.

"Yes, sir, I will," said young Malachi. "Good-bye, sir," he said, and left.

That was the first and last time that Malachi Constant ever saw his father.

His father lived for five more years, and the Bible never played him false.

Noel Constant died just as he reached the end of this sentence: "And God made two great lights: the greater light to rule the day, and the lesser light to rule the night: he made the stars also."

His last investment was in Sonnyboy Oil at 17¼.

The son took over where the father had left off, though Malachi Constant did not move into Room 223 in the Wilburhampton.

And, for five years, the luck of the son was as sensational as the luck of the father had been.

And now, suddenly, Magnum Opus lay in ruins.

There in his office, with the floating furniture and the grass carpet, Malachi Constant still could not believe that his luck had run out.

"Nothing left?" he said faintly. He managed to smile at Ransom K. Fern. "Come on, guy—I mean there's got to be something left."

"I thought so, too, at ten o'clock this morning," said Fern. "I was congratulating myself on having buttressed Magnum Opus against any conceivable blow. We were weathering the depression quite nicely—yes, and your mistakes, too.

"And then, at ten-fifteen, I was visited by a lawyer who was apparently at your party last night. You, apparently, were giving away oil wells last night, and the lawyer was thoughtful enough to draw up documents which, if signed by you, would be binding. They were signed by you. You gave away five hundred and thirty-one producing oil wells last night, which wiped out Fandango Petroleum.

"At eleven," said Fern, "the President of the United States announced that Galactic Spacecraft, which we had sold, was receiving a three-billion contract for the New Age of Space.

"At eleven-thirty," said Fern, "I was given a copy of *The Journal of the American Medical Association*, which was marked by our public relations director, 'FYI.' These three letters, as you would know if you had ever spent any time in your office, mean 'for your information.' I turned to the page referred to, and learned, for my information, that Moon-Mist Cigarettes were not *a* cause but the *principal* cause of

59

sterility in both sexes wherever MoonMist cigarettes were sold. This fact was discovered not by human beings but by a computing machine. Whenever data about cigarette smoking was fed into it, the machine grew tremendously excited, and no one could figure out why. The machine was obviously trying to tell its operators something. It did everything it could to express itself, and finally managed to get its operators to ask it the right questions.

"The right questions had to do with the relationship of MoonMist Cigarettes to human reproduction. The relationship was this:

"People who smoked MoonMist Cigarettes couldn't have children, even if they wanted them," said Fern.

"Doubtless," said Fern, "there are gigolos and party girls and New Yorkers who are grateful for this relief from biology. In the opinion of the Legal Department of Magnum Opus, before that department was liquidated, however, there are several million persons who can sue successfully—on the grounds that MoonMist Cigarettes did them out of something rather valuable. Pleasure in depth, indeed.

"There are approximately ten million ex-smokers of MoonMist in this country," said Fern, "all sterile. If one in ten sues you for damages beyond price, sues you for the modest sum of five thousand dollars—the bill will be five billion dollars, excluding legal fees. And you haven't got five billion dollars. Since the stock-market crash and your acquisition of such properties as American Levitation, you aren't worth even five hundred million.

"MoonMist Tobacco," said Fern, "that's you. Magnum Opus," said Fern, "that's you, too. All the things you are are going to be sued and sued successfully. And, while the litigants may not be able to get blood from turnips, they can certainly ruin the turnips in the process of trying."

Fern bowed again. "I now perform my last official duty, which is to inform you that your father wrote you a letter which was to be given to you only if your luck turned for the worse. My instructions were to place that letter under the pillow in Room 223 in the Wilburhampton, if your luck ever really turned sour. I placed the letter under the pillow an hour ago.

"And I will now, as an humble and loyal corporate servant, ask you for one small favour," said Fern. "If the letter seems to cast the vaguest light on what life might be about, I would appreciate your telephoning me at home."

Ransom K. Fern saluted by touching the shaft of his cane to his Homburg hat. "Good-bye, Mr. Magnum Opus, Jr. Good-bye."

The Wilburhampton Hotel was a frumpish, three-story Tudor structure across the street from the Magnum Opus Building, standing in relation to that building like an unmade bed at the feet of the Archangel Gabriel. Pine slats were stacked to the stucco exterior of the hotel, simulating half-timbered construction. The backbone of the roof had been broken intentionally, simulating great age. The eaves were plump and low, tucked under, simulated thatch. The windows were tiny, with diamond-shaped panes.

The hotel's small cocktail lounge was known as the Hear Ye Room.

In the Hear Ye Room were three people—a bartender and two customers. The two customers were a thin woman and a fat man—both seemingly old. Nobody in the Wilburhampton had ever seen them before, but it already seemed as though they had been sitting in the Hear Ye Room for years. Their protective colouration was perfect, for they looked half-timbered and broken-backed and thatched and little-windowed, too.

They claimed to be pensioned-off teachers from the same high school in the Middle West. The fat man introduced himself as George M. Helmholtz, a former bandmaster. The thin woman introduced herself as Roberta Wiley, a former teacher of algebra.

They had obviously discovered the consolations of alcohol and cynicism late in life. They never ordered the same drink twice, were avid to know what was in this bottle and what was in that one—to know what a golden dawn punch was, and a Helen Twelvetrees, and a *plui d'or*, and a merry widow fizz.

The bartender knew they weren't alcoholics. He was familiar with the type, and loved the type: they were simply two *Saturday Evening Post* characters at the end of the road.

When they weren't asking questions about the different things to drink, they were indistinguishable from millions of other American barflies on the first day of the New Age of Space. They sat solidly on their barstools, staring straight ahead at the ranks of bottles. Their lips moved constantly—experimenting dismayingly with irrelevant grins and grimaces and sneers.

Evangelist Bobby Denton's image of Earth as God's space ship was an apt one—particularly with reference to barflies. Helmholtz and Miss Wiley were behaving like pilot and co-pilot of an enormously pointless voyage through space that was expected to take forever. It was easy to believe that they had begun the voyage nattily, flushed with youth and technical training, and that the bottles before them were the instruments they had been watching for years and years and years.

It was easy to believe that each day had found the space boy and the space girl microscopically more slovenly than the day before, until now, when they were the shame of the Pan-Galactic Space Service.

Two buttons on Helmholtz's fly were open. There was shaving cream in his left ear. His socks did not match.

Miss Wiley was a crazy-looking little old lady with a lantern jaw. She wore a frizzy black wig that looked as though it had been nailed to a farmer's barn door for years.

"I see where the President has ordered a whole brand-new Age of Space to begin, to see if that won't help the unemployment picture some," said the bartender.

"Uh, huh," said Helmholtz and Miss Wiley simultaneously.

Only an observant and suspicious person would have noticed a false note in the behaviour of the two: Helmholtz and Miss Wiley were *too interested in time.* For people who had nothing much to do and nowhere much to go, they were extraordinarily interested in their watches—Miss Wiley in her mannish wrist watch, Mr. Helmholtz in his gold pocket watch.

The truth of the matter was that Helmholtz and Miss Wiley weren't retired school teachers at all. They were both males, both masters of disguise. They were crack agents for the Army of Mars, the eyes and ears for a Martian press gang that hovered in a flying saucer two hundred miles overhead.

Malachi Constant didn't know it, but they were waiting for him.

Helmholtz and Wiley did not accost Malachi Constant

when he crossed the street to the Wilburhampton. They gave no sign that he mattered to them. They let him cross the lobby and board the elevator without giving him a glance.

They did, however, glance at their watches again—and an observant and suspicious person would have noticed that Miss Wiley pressed a button on her watch, starting a stopwatch hand on its twitching rounds.

Helmholtz and Miss Wiley were not about to use violence on Malachi Constant. They had never used violence on anyone, and had still recruited fourteen thousand persons for Mars.

Their usual technique was to dress like civil engineers and offer not-quite-bright men and women nine dollars an hour, tax free, plus food and shelter and transportation, to work on a secret Government project in a remote part of the world for three years. It was a joke between Helmholtz and Miss Wiley that they had never specified *what* government was organizing the project, and that no recruit had ever thought to ask.

Ninety-nine per cent of the recruits were given amnesia upon arriving on Mars. Their memories were cleaned out by mental-health experts, and Martian surgeons installed radio antennas in their skulls in order that the recruits might be radio-controlled.

And then the recruits were given new names in the most haphazard fashion, and were assigned to the factories, the construction gangs, the administrative staff, or to the Army of Mars.

The few recruits who were not treated in this way were those who demonstrated ardently that they would serve Mars heroically without being doctored at all. Those lucky few were welcomed into the secret circle of those in command.

Secret agents Helmholtz and Wiley belonged to this circle. They were in full possession of their memories, and they were not radio-controlled. They adored their work, just as they were.

"What's that there Slivovitz like?" Helmholtz asked the bartender, squinting at a dusty bottle on the bottom row. He had just finished a sloe gin rickey.

"I didn't even know we had it," said the bartender. He

put the bottle on the bar, tilting it away from himself so he could read the label. "Prune brandy," he said.

"Believe I'll try that next," said Helmholtz.

Ever since the death of Noel Constant, Room 223 in the Wilburhampton had been left empty—as a memorial.

Malachi Constant now let himself into Room 223. He had not been in the room since the death of his father. He closed the door behind him, and found the letter under the pillow.

Nothing in the room had been changed but the linen. The picture of Malachi as a little boy on the beach was still the only picture on the wall.

The letter said:

Dear Son: Something big and bad has happened to you or you wouldn't be reading this letter. I am writing this letter to tell you to calm down about the bad things and kind of look around and see if something good or something important anyway happened on account of we got so rich and then lost the boodle again. What I want you to try and find out is, is there anything special going on or is it all just as crazy as it looked to me?

If I wasn't a very good father or a very good anything that was because I was as good as dead for a long time before I died. Nobody loved me and I wasn't very good at anything and I couldn't find any hobbies I liked and I was sick and tired of selling pots and pans and watching television so I was as good as dead and I was too far gone to ever come back.

That is when I started the business with the Bible and you know what happened after that. It looked as though somebody or something wanted me to own the whole planet even though I was as good as dead. I kept my eyes open for some kind of signal that would tell me what it was all about but there wasn't any signal. I just went on getting richer and richer.

And then your mother sent me that picture of you on the beach and the way you looked at me out of that picture made me think maybe you were what all the big money buildup was for. I decided I would die without ever seeing any sense to it and maybe you would be the one who would all of a sudden see everything clear as a bell. I tell you even

64

*a half-dead man hates to be alive and not be able to see any
sense to it.*

*The reason I told Ransom K. Fern to give you this letter
only if your luck turned bad is that nobody thinks or notices
anything as long as his luck is good. Why should he?*

*So have a look around for me, boy. And if you go broke
and somebody comes along with a crazy proposition my
advice is to take it. You might just learn something when
you're in a mood to learn something. The only thing I ever
learned was that some people are lucky and other people
aren't and not even a graduate of the Harvard Business
School can say why.*

Yours truly—your Pa

There was a knock on the door of Room 223.

The door opened before Constant could reply to the
knock.

Helmholtz and Miss Wiley let themselves in. They
entered at precisely the right instant, having been advised
by their superiors as to when, to the second, Malachi Constant would finish the letter. They had been told, too, precisely what to say to him.

Miss Wiley removed her wig, revealing herself to be a
scrawny man, and Helmholtz composed his features to reveal that he was fearless and used to command.

"Mr. Constant," said Helmholtz, "I am here to inform
you that the planet Mars is not only populated, but populated by a large and efficient and military and industrial
society. It has been recruited from Earth, with the recruits
being transferred to Mars by flying saucer. We are now
prepared to offer you a direct lieutenant-colonelcy in the
Army of Mars.

"Your situation on Earth is hopeless. Your wife is a beast.
Moreover, our intelligence informs us that here on Earth you
will not only be made penniless by civil suits, but that you
will be imprisoned for criminal negligence as well.

"In addition to a pay scale and privileges well above those
accorded lieutenant-colonels in Earthling armies, we can
offer you immunity from all Earthling legal harassment,
and an opportunity to see a new and interesting planet, and
an opportunity to think about your native planet from a
fresh and beautifully detached viewpoint."

65

"If you accept the commission," said Miss Wiley, "raise your left hand and repeat after me—"

On the following day, Malachi Constant's helicopter was found empty in the middle of the Mojave Desert. The footprints of a man led away from it for a distance of forty feet, then stopped.

It was as though Malachi Constant had walked forty feet, and had then dissolved into thin air.

On the following Tuesday, the space ship known as *The Whale* was rechristened *The Rumfoord* and was readied for firing.

Beatrice Rumfoord smugly watched the ceremonies on a television set two thousand miles away. She was still in Newport. *The Rumfoord* was going to be fired in exactly one minute. If destiny was going to get Beatrice Rumfoord on board, it was going to have to do it in one hell of a hurry.

Beatrice was feeling marvellous. She had proved so many good things. She had proved that she was mistress of her own fate, could say *no* whenever she pleased—and make it stick. She had proved that her husband's omniscient bullying was all a bluff—that he wasn't much better at forecasts than the United States Weather Bureau.

She had, moreover, worked out a plan that would enable her to live in modest comfort for the rest of her days, and would, at the same time, give her husband the treatment he deserved. The next time he materialized, he would find the estate teeming with gawkers. Beatrice was going to charge them five dollars a head to come in through the Alice-in-Wonderland door.

This was no pipe-dream. She had discussed it with two supposed representatives of the mortgage-holders on the estate—and they were enthusiastic.

They were with her now, watching the preparations for the firing of *The Rumfoord* on television. The television set was in the same room with the huge painting of Beatrice as an immaculate little girl in white, with a white pony all her own. Beatrice smiled up at the painting. The little girl had yet to get the least bit soiled.

The television announcer now began the last minute's countdown for the firing of *The Rumfoord*.

During the countdown, Beatrice's mood was bird-like. She

could not sit still and she could not keep quiet. Her restlessness was a result of happiness, not of supense. It was a matter of indifference to her whether *The Rumfoord* was a fizzle or not.

Her two visitors, on the other hand, seemed to take the firing very seriously—seemed to be praying for the success of the shot. They were a man and a woman, a Mr. George M. Helmholtz and his secretary, a Miss Roberta Wiley. Miss Wiley was a funny-looking little old thing, but very alert and witty.

The rocket went up with a roar.

It was a flawless shot.

Helmholtz sat back and heaved a manly sigh of relief. Then he smiled and beat his thick thighs exuberantly. "By glory," he said, "I'm proud to be an American—and proud to be living in the time I do."

"Would you like something to drink?" said Beatrice.

"Thank you very much," said Helmholtz, "but I daren't mix business with pleasure."

"Isn't the business all over?" said Beatrice. "Haven't we discussed everything?"

"Well—Miss Wiley and I had hoped to take an inventory of the larger buildings on the grounds," said Helmholtz, "but I'm afraid it's gotten quite dark. Are there floodlights?"

Beatrice shook her head. "Sorry," she said.

"Perhaps you have a powerful flashlight?" said Helmholtz.

"I can probably get you a flashlight," said Beatrice, "but I don't think it's really necessary for you to go out there. I can tell you what all the buildings are." She rang for the butler, told him to bring a flashlight. "There's the tennis house, the greenhouse, the gardener's cottage, what used to be the gate house, the carriage house, the guest house, the tool shed, the bath house, the kennel, and the old water tower."

"Which one is the new one?" said Helmholtz.

"The *new* one?" said Beatrice.

The butler returned with a flashlight, which Beatrice gave to Helmholtz.

"The metal one," said Miss Wiley.

"Metal?" said Beatrice puzzled. "There aren't any *metal* buildings. Maybe some of the weathered shingles have kind of a silvery look." She frowned. "Did somebody tell you there was a metal building here?"

"We saw it when we came in," said Helmholtz.

"Right by the path—in the undergrowth near the fountain," said Miss Wiley.

"I can't imagine," said Beatrice.

"Could we go out and have a look?" said Helmholtz.

"Yes—of course," said Beatrice, rising.

The party of three crossed the zodiac on the foyer floor, moved into the balmy dark.

The flashlight beam danced before them.

"Really," said Beatrice, "I'm as curious to find out what it is as you are."

"It looks like a kind of prefabricated thing made out of aluminium," said Miss Wiley.

"It looks like a mushroom-shaped water tank or something," said Helmholtz, "only it is squatting right on the ground."

"Really," said Beatrice.

"You know what I said it was, don't you?" said Miss Wiley.

"No," said Beatrice, "what *did* you say it was?"

"I have to whisper," said Miss Wiley playfully, "or somebody will want to lock me up in the crazy house." She put her hand to her mouth, directing her loud whisper to Beatrice. "Flying saucer," she said.

CHAPTER FOUR

TENT RENTALS

Rented a tent, a tent, a tent;
Rented a tent, a tent, a tent.
Rented a tent!
Rented a tent!
Rented a, rented a tent.
—SNARE DRUM ON MARS

THE men had marched to the parade ground to the sound of a snare drum. The snare drum had this to say to them:

Rented a tent, a tent, a tent;
Rented a tent, a tent, a tent.
Rented a tent!
Rented a tent!
Rented a, rented a tent.

They were an infantry division of ten thousand men, formed in a hollow square on a natural parade ground of solid iron one mile thick. The soldiers stood at attention on orange rust. They shivered rigidly, being as much like iron as they could be—both officers and men. Their uniforms were a rough-textured, frosty green—the colour of lichens.

The army had come to attention in utter silence. No audible or visible signal had been given. They had come to attention as a man, as though through a stupendous coincidence.

The third man in the second squad of the first platoon of the second company of the third battalion of the second regiment of the First Martian Assault Infantry Division was a private who had been broken from lieutenant-colonel three years before. He had been on Mars for eight years.

When a man in a modern army is broken from field grade to private, it is likely that he will be old for a private, and that his comrades in arms, once they get used to the fact that he isn't an officer any more, will, out of respect for his failing legs, eyes, and wind, call him something like *Pops*, or *Gramps*, or *Unk*.

The third man in the second squad of the first platoon of the second company in the third battalion of the second regiment of the First Martian Assault Infantry Division was called *Unk*. Unk was forty years old. Unk was a well-made man—a light heavyweight, dark-skinned, with poet's lips, with soft brown eyes in the shaded caves of a Cro-Magnon brow ridge. Incipient baldness had isolated a dramatic scalplock.

An illustrative anecdote about Unk:

One time, when Unk's platoon was taking a shower, Henry Brackman, Unk's platoon sergeant, asked a sergeant from another regiment to pick out the best soldier in the platoon. The visiting sergeant, without any hesitation, picked Unk, because Unk was a compact, nicely muscled, intelligent man among boys.

Brackman rolled his eyes. "Jesus—you'd think so, wouldn't you?" he said. "That's the platoon f—kup."

"You kidding me?" said the visiting sergeant.

"Hell no, I ain't kidding you," said Brackman. "Look at him—been standing there for ten minutes, and hasn't touched a piece of soap yet. Unk! Wake up, Unk!"

Unk shuddered, stopped dreaming under the tepid drizzle of the shower head. He looked questioningly at Brackman, bleakly co-operative.

"Use some soap, Unk!" said Brackman. "For Chrissakes, use some soap!"

Now, on the iron parade ground, Unk stood at attention in the hollow square like all the rest.

In the middle of the hollow square was a stone post with iron rings fixed to it. Chains had been drawn rattling through the rings—had been drawn tight around a red-haired soldier standing against a post. The soldier was a clean soldier—but he was not a neat soldier, for all the badges and decorations had been stripped off his uniform, and he had no belt, no necktie, no snow-white puttees.

Everybody else, including Unk, was all spiffed up. Everybody else looked very nice indeed.

Something painful was going to happen to the man at the stake—something from which the man would want to escape very much, something from which he was not going to escape, because of the chains.

And all the soldiers were going to watch.

The event was being given great importance.

Even the man at the stake was standing at attention, being the best soldier he knew how to be, under the circumstances.

Again—no audible or visible order was given, but the ten thousand soldiers executed the movement of *parade rest* as a man.

So did the man at the stake.

Then the soldiers relaxed in ranks, as though given the order *at ease*. Their obligations under this order were to relax, but to keep their feet in place, and to keep silent. The soldiers were free to think a little now, and to look around and to send messages with their eyes, if they had messages and could find receivers.

The man at the stake tugged against his chains, craned his neck to judge the height of the stake to which he was chained. It was as though he thought he might escape by use of the scientific method, if only he could find out how high the stake was and what it was made of.

The stake was nineteen feet, six and five thirty-seconds inches high, not counting the twelve feet, two and one-eighth inches of it embedded in the iron. The stake had a mean diameter of two feet, five and eleven thirty-seconds inches, varying from this mean, however, by as much as seven and one thirty-second inches. The stake was composed of quartz, alkali, feldspar, mica, and traces of tourmaline and hornblende. For the information of the man at the stake: He was one hundred and forty-two million, three hundred and forty-six thousand, nine hundred and eleven miles from the Sun, and help was not on its way.

The red-haired man at the stake made no sound, because soldiers at ease were not permitted to make sounds. He sent a message with his eyes, however, to the effect that he would like to scream. He sent the message to anyone whose eyes would meet his. He was hoping to get the message to one person in particular, to his best friend—to Unk. He was looking for Unk.

He couldn't find Unk's face.

If he had found Unk's face, there wouldn't have been any blooming of recognition and pity on Unk's face. Unk had just come out of the base hospital, where he had been treated for mental illness, and Unk's mind was almost a blank. Unk

71

didn't recognize his best friend at the stake. Unk didn't recognize anybody. Unk wouldn't have even known his own name was Unk, wouldn't even have known he was a soldier, if they hadn't told him so when they discharged him from the hospital.

He had gone straight from the hospital to the formation he was in now.

At the hospital they told him again and again and again that he was the best soldier in the best squad in the best platoon in the best company in the best battalion in the best regiment in the best division in the best army.

Unk guessed that was something to be proud of.

At the hospital they told him he had been a pretty sick boy, but he was fully recovered now.

That seemed like good news.

At the hospital they told him what his sergeant's name was, and what a sergeant was, and what all the symbols of ranks and grades and specialties were.

They had blanked out so much of Unk's memory that they even had to teach him the foot movements and the manual of arms all over again.

At the hospital they even had to explain to Unk what Combat Respiratory Rations or CRR's or goofballs were—had to tell him to take one every six hours or suffocate. These were oxygen pills that made up for the fact that there wasn't any oxygen in the Martian atmosphere.

At the hospital they even had to explain to Unk that there was a radio antenna under the crown of his skull, and that it would hurt him whenever he did something a good soldier wouldn't ever do. The antenna also would give him orders and furnish drum music to march to. They said that not just Unk but everybody had an antenna like that—doctors and nurses and four-star generals included. It was a very democratic army, they said.

Unk guessed that was a good way for an army to be.

At the hospital they gave Unk a small sample of the pain his antenna would stick him with if he ever did anything wrong.

The pain was horrible.

Unk was bound to admit that a soldier would be crazy not to do his duty at all times.

At the hospital they had said the most important rule of

all was this one: Always obey a direct order without a moment's hesitation.

Standing there in formation on the iron parade ground, Unk realized that he had a lot to relearn. At the hospital they hadn't taught him everything there was to know about living.

The antenna in his head brought him to attention again and his mind went blank. Then the antenna put Unk at parade rest again, then at attention again, then made him give a rifle salute, then put him at ease again.

His thinking began again. He caught another glimpse of the world around him.

Life was like that, Unk told himself tentatively—blanks and glimpses, and now and then maybe that awful flash of pain for doing something wrong.

A small, low-flying, fast-flying moon sailed in the violet sky overhead. Unk didn't know why he thought so, but he thought the moon was moving too fast. It didn't seem right. And the sky, he thought, should be blue instead of violet.

Unk felt cold, too, and he longed for more warmth. The unending cold seemed as wrong, as unfair, somehow, as the fast moon and the violet sky.

Unk's divisional commander was now talking to Unk's regimental commander. Unk's regimental commander spoke to Unk's battalion commander. Unk's battalion commander spoke to Unk's company commander. Unk's company commander spoke to Unk's platoon leader, who was Sergeant Brackman.

Brackman came up to Unk and ordered him to march up to the man at the stake in a military manner and strangle him until he was dead.

Brackman told Unk it was a direct order.

So Unk did it.

He marched up to the man at the stake. He marched in time to the dry, tinny music of one snare drum. The sound of the snare drum was really just in his head, coming from his antenna:

> *Rented a tent, a tent, a tent;*
> *Rented a tent, a tent, a tent.*
> *Rented a tent!*
> *Rented a tent!*
> *Rented a, rented a tent.*

73

When Unk got to the man at the stake, Unk hesitated for just a second—because the red-haired man at the stake looked so unhappy. Then there was a tiny warning pain in Unk's head, like the first deep nip of a dentist's drill.

Unk put his thumbs on the red-haired man's windpipe, and the pain stopped right away. Unk didn't press with his thumbs, because the man was trying to tell him something. Unk was puzzled by the man's silence—and then realized that the man's antenna must be keeping him silent, just as antennas were keeping all of the soldiers silent.

Heroically, the man at the stake now overcame the will of his antenna, spoke rapidly, writhingly. "Unk . . . Unk . . . Unk . . ." he said, and the spasms of the fight between his own will and the will of the antenna made him repeat the name idiotically. *"Blue stone, Unk,"* he said. *"Barrack twelve . . . letter."*

The warning pain nagged in Unk's head again. Dutifully, Unk strangled the man at the stake—choked him until the man's face was purple and his tongue stuck out.

Unk stepped back, came to attention, did a smart about-face and returned to his place in the ranks—again accompanied by the snare drum in his head:

> *Rented a tent, a tent, a tent;*
> *Rented a tent, a tent, a tent.*
> *Rented a tent!*
> *Rented a tent!*
> *Rented a, rented a tent.*

Sergeant Brackman nodded at Unk, winked affectionately.

Again the ten thousand came to attention.

Horribly, the dead man at the stake struggled to come to attention, too, rattling his chains. He failed—failed to be a perfect soldier—not because he didn't want to be one but because he was dead.

Now the great formation broke up into rectangular components. These marched mindlessly away, each man hearing a snare drum in his head. An observer would have heard nothing but the tread of boots.

An observer would have been at a loss as to who was really in charge, since even the generals moved like marionettes, keeping time to the idiotic words:

Rented a tent, a tent, a tent;
Rented a tent, rented a tent.
Rented a tent!
Rented a tent!
Rented a, rented a tent.

CHAPTER FIVE

LETTER FROM AN UNKNOWN HERO

"We can make the centre of a man's memory virtually as sterile as a scalpel fresh from the auto-clave. But grains of new experience begin to accumulate on it at once. These grains in turn form themselves into patterns not necessarily favourable to military thinking. Unfortunately, this problem of recontamination seems insoluble."

—DR. MORRIS N. CASTLE,
Director of Mental Health, Mars

UNK's formation halted before a granite barrack, before a barrack in a perspective of thousands, a perspective that ran to seeming infinity on the iron plain. Before every tenth barrack was a flagpole with a banner snapping in the keen wind.

The banners were all different.

The banner that fluttered like a guardian angel over Unk's company area was very gay—red and white stripes, and many white stars on a field of blue. It was Old Glory, the flag of the United States of America on Earth.

Down the line was the red banner of the Union of Soviet Socialist Republics.

Past that was a wonderful green, orange, yellow, and purple banner, showing a lion holding a sword. It was the flag of Ceylon.

And past that was a red ball on a white field, the flag of Japan.

The banners signified the countries that the various Martian units would attack and paralyze when the war between Mars and Earth began.

Unk saw no banners until his antenna let his shoulders sag, let his joints loosen—let him fall out. He gawked at the long perspective of barracks and flagpoles. The barrack before which he stood had a large number painted over the door. The number was 576.

Some part of Unk found the number fascinating, made Unk study it. Then he remembered the execution—remem-

bered that the red-headed man he had killed had told him
something about a blue stone and barrack twelve.

Inside barrack 576, Unk cleaned his rifle, found it an
extremely pleasant thing to do. He found, moreover, that he
still knew how to take the weapon apart. That much of his
memory, at any rate, had not been wiped out at the hospital.
It made him furtively happy to suspect that there were
probably other parts of his memory that had been missed as
well. Why this suspicion should make him furtively happy
he didn't know.

He swabbed away at his rifle's bore. His weapon was an
11-millimeter German Mauser, single shot, a type of rifle
that made its reputation when used by the Spaniards in the
Earthling Spanish-American War. All of the Martian
Army's rifles were of about the same vintage. Martian
agents, working quietly on Earth, had been able to buy up
huge quantities of Mausers and British Enfields and American Springfields for next to nothing.

Unk's squadmates were swabbing their bores, too. The oil
smelled good, and the oily patches, twisting through the
rifling, resisted the thrust of the cleaning rod just enough to
be interesting. There was hardly any talk.

No one seemed to have taken particular notice of the execution. If there had been a lesson in the execution for Unk's
squadmates, they were finding the lesson as digestible as
Pablum.

There had been only one comment on Unk's participation
in the execution, and that had come from Sergeant Brackman. "You done all right, Unk," said Brackman.

"Thanks," said Unk.

"This man done all right, didn't he?" Brackman asked
Unk's squadmates.

There had been some nods, but Unk had the impression
that his squadmates would have nodded in response to any
positive question, would have shaken their heads in response
to any negative one.

Unk withdrew the rod and patch, slipped his thumb under
the open breech, caught the sunlight on his oily thumbnail.
The thumbnail sent the sunlight up the bore. Unk put his eye
to the muzzle and was thrilled by perfect beauty. He could
have stared happily at the immaculate spiral of the rifling
for hours, dreaming of the happy land whose round gate he

saw at the other end of the bore. The pink under his oily thumbnail at the far end of the barrel made that far end seem a rosy paradise indeed. Some day he was going to crawl down the barrel to that paradise.

It would be warm there—and there would be only one moon, Unk thought, and the moon would be fat, stately, and slow. Something else about the pink paradise at the end of the barrel came to Unk, and Unk was puzzled by the clarity of the vision. There were three beautiful women in that paradise, and Unk knew exactly what they looked like! One was white, one was gold, and one was brown. The golden girl was smoking a cigarette in Unk's vision. Unk was further surprised to find that he even knew what kind of cigarette the golden girl was smoking.

It was a MoonMist Cigarette.

"Sell MoonMist," Unk said out loud. It felt good to say that—felt authoritative, shrewd.

"Huh?" said a young coloured soldier, cleaning his rifle next to Unk. "What's that you say, Unk?" he said. He was twenty-three years old. His name was stitched in yellow on a black patch over his left breast pocket.

Boaz was his name.

If suspicions had been permitted in the Army of Mars, Boaz would have been a person to suspect. His rank was only Private, First Class, but his uniform, though regulation lichen green, was made of far finer stuff, and was much better tailored than the uniform of anyone around him—including the uniform of Sergeant Brackman.

Everyone else's uniform was coarse, scratchy—held together by clumsy stitches of thick thread. And everyone else's uniform looked good only when the wearer stood at attention. In any other position, an ordinary soldier found that his uniform tended to bunch and crackle, as though made of paper.

Boaz's uniform followed his every movement with silken grace. The stitches were numerous and tiny. And most puzzling of all: Boaz's shoes had a deep, rich, ruby lustre—a lustre that other soldiers could not achieve no matter how much they might polish their shoes. Unlike the shoes of anyone else in the company area, the shoes of Boaz were genuine leather from Earth.

"You say sell something, Unk?" said Boaz.

"Dump MoonMist. Get rid of it," murmured Unk. The

words made no sense to him. He had let them out simply because they had wanted out so badly. "Sell," he said.

Boaz smiled—ruefully amused. "Sell it, eh?" he said. "O.K., Unk—we sell it." He raised an eyebrow. "What we gonna sell, Unk?" There was something particularly bright and piercing about the pupils of his eyes.

Unk found this yellow brightness, this sharpness of Boaz's eyes disquieting—increasingly so, as Boaz continued to stare. Unk looked away, looked by chance into the eyes of some of his other squadmates—found their eyes to be uniformly dull. Even the eyes of Sergeant Brackman were dull.

Boaz's eyes continued to bite into Unk. Unk felt compelled to meet their gaze again. The pupils were seeming diamonds.

"You don't remember me, Unk?" said Boaz.

The question alarmed Unk. For some reason, it was important that he should not remember Boaz. He was grateful that he really didn't remember him.

"Boaz, Unk," said the coloured man. "I'm Boaz."

Unk nodded. "How do you do?" he said.

"Oh—I don't do what you'd call real bad," said Boaz. He shook his head. "You don't remember nothing about me, Unk?"

"No," said Unk. His memory was nagging him a little now—telling him that he might remember something about Boaz, if he tried as hard as he could. He shushed his memory. "Sorry," said Unk. "My mind's a blank."

"You and me—we're buddies," said Boaz. "Boaz and Unk."

"Um," said Unk.

"You remember what the buddy system is, Unk?" said Boaz.

"No," said Unk.

"Ever' man in ever' squad," said Boaz, "he got a buddy. Buddies share the same foxhole, stick right close to each other in attacks, cover each other. One buddy get in trouble in hand-to-hand, other buddy come up and help, slip a knife in."

"Um," said Unk.

"Funny," said Boaz, "what a man'll forget in the hospital and what he'll still remember, no matter what they do. You and me—we trained as buddies for a whole year, and you

79

done forgot that. And then you say that thing 'bout cigarettes. What kind cigarettes, Unk?"

"I—I forget," said Unk.

"Try and remember now," said Boaz. "You had it once." He frowned and squinted, as though trying to help Unk remember. "I think it's *so* interesting what a man can remember after he's been to the hospital. Try and remember everything you can."

There was a certain effeminacy about Boaz—in the nature of a cunning bully's chucking a sissy under the chin, talking baby-talk to him.

But Boaz liked Unk—that was in his manner, too.

Unk had the eerie feeling that he and Boaz were the only real people in the stone building—that the rest were glass-eyed robots, and not very well-made robots at that. Sergeant Brackman, supposedly in command, seemed no more alert, no more responsible, no more in command than a bag of wet feathers.

"Let's hear all you can remember, Unk," wheedled Boaz. "Old buddy," he said, "just remember all you can."

Before Unk could remember anything, the head pain that had made him get on with the execution hurt him again. The pain did not stop, however, with the warning nip. While Boaz watched expressionlessly, the pain in Unk's head became a whanging, flashing thing.

Unk stood, dropped his rifle, clawed at his head, reeled, screamed, fainted.

When Unk came to on the barrack floor, his buddy Boaz was daubing Unk's temples with a cold washrag.

Unk's squadmates stood in a circle around Unk and Boaz. The faces of the squadmates were unsurprised, unsympathetic. Their attitude was that Unk had done something stupid and unsoldierly, and so deserved what he got.

They looked as though Unk had done something as militarily stupid as silhouetting himself against the sky or cleaning a loaded weapon, as sneezing on patrol or contracting and not reporting a venereal disease, as refusing a direct order or sleeping through reveille, as being drunk on guard or drawing to an inside straight, as keeping a book or a live hand grenade in his foot-locker, as asking who had started the Army anyway and why . . .

Boaz was the only one who looked sorry about what had happened to Unk. "It was all my fault, Unk," he said.

Sergeant Brackman now pushed through the circle, stood over Unk and Boaz. "Wha'd he do, Boaz?" said Brackman.

"I was kidding him, Sergeant," said Boaz earnestly. "I told him to try an' remember back as far as he could. I never dreamed he'd go and do it."

"Oughta have more sense than to kid a man just back from the hospital," said Brackman gruffly.

"Oh, I know it—I know it," said Boaz, full of remorse, "My buddy," he said. "God *damn* me!"

"Unk," said Brackman, "didn't they tell you about remembering at the hospital?"

Unk shook his head vaguely. "Maybe," he said. "They told me a lot."

"That's the worst thing you can *do*, Unk—remembering back," said Brackman. "That's what they put you in the hospital for in the first place—on account of you remembered too much." He made cups of his stubby hands, held in them the heart-breaking problem Unk had been. "Holy smokes," he said, "you were remembering so much, Unk, you weren't worth a nickel as a soldier."

Unk sat up, laid his hand on his breast, found that the front of his blouse was wet with tears. He thought of explaining to Brackman that he hadn't really tried to remember back, that he'd known instinctively that that was a bad thing to do—but that the pain had hit him *anyway*. He didn't tell Brackman that for fear that the pain would come again.

Unk groaned and blinked away the last of the tears. He wasn't going to do anything he wasn't ordered to do.

"As for you, Boaz," said Brackman. "I don't know but what a week's latrine duty would maybe teach you something about horseplay with people just out of the hospital."

Something formless in Unk's memory told Unk to watch the by-play between Brackman and Boaz closely. It was somehow important.

"A week, Sergeant?" said Boaz.

"Yes, by God," said Brackman, and then he shuddered and closed his eyes. Plainly, his antenna had just given him a little stab of pain.

"A whole week, Sarge?" asked Boaz innocently.

81

"A day," said Brackman, and it was less a threat than a question. Again Brackman reacted to pain in his head.

"Starting when, Sarge?" asked Boaz.

Brackman fluttered his stubby hands. "Never mind," he said. He looked rattled, betrayed—haunted. He lowered his head, as though better to fight the pain if it came again. "No more horseplay, damn it," he said, his voice deep in his throat. And he hurried away, hurried into his room at the end of the barrack, slammed the door.

The company commander, a Captain Arnold Burch, came into the barrack for a surprise inspection.

Boaz was the first to see him. Boaz did what a soldier was supposed to do under such circumstances. Boaz shouted, "*Attennnn-hut!*" Boaz did this, though he had no rank at all. It is a freak of military custom that the lowliest private can command his equals and noncommissioned superiors to attention, if he is the first to detect the presence of a commissioned officer in any roofed-over structure not in a combat area.

The antennas of the enlisted men responded instantly, straightened the men's backs, locked their joints, hauled in their guts, tucked in their butts—made their minds go blank. Unk sprang up from the floor, stood stiff and shivering.

Only one man was slow about coming to attention. That man was Boaz. And when he did come to attention, there was something insolent and loose and leering about the way he did it.

Captain Burch, finding Boaz's attitude profoundly offensive, was about to speak to Boaz about it. But the Captain no sooner got his mouth open than pain hit him between the eyes.

The captain closed his mouth without having made a sound.

Under the baleful gaze of Boaz, he came smartly to attention, did an about-face, heard a snare drum in his head, and marched out of the barrack in step with the drum.

When the captain was gone, Boaz did not put his squadmates at ease again, though it was in his power to do so. He had a small control box in his right front trouser pocket that could make his squadmates do just about anything. The box was the size of a one-pint hip flask. Like a hip flask, the box was curved to fit a body curve. Boaz chose to carry it on the hard, curved face of his thigh.

The control box had six buttons and four knobs on it. By manipulating these, Boaz could control anybody who had an antenna in his skull. Boaz could administer pain in any amount to that anybody—could bring him to attention, could make him hear a snare drum, could make him march, halt, fall in, fall out, salute, attack, retreat, hop, skip, jump. . . .

Boaz had no antenna in his own skull.

As free as it wanted to be—that's how free the free will of Boaz was.

Boaz was one of the real commanders of the Army of Mars. He was in command of one-tenth of the force that was to attack the United States of America when the attack on Earth was mounted. Down the line were units training to attack Russia, Switzerland, Japan, Australia, Mexico, China, Nepal, Uruguay. . . .

To the best of Boaz's knowledge, there were eight hundred real commanders of the Army of Mars—not one of them with an apparent rank above buck sergeant. The nominal commander of the entire Army, General of the Armies, Borders M. Pulsifer, was in fact controlled at all times by his orderly, Corporal Bert Wright. Corporal Wright, the perfect orderly, carried aspirin for the General's almost chronic headaches.

The advantages of a system of secret commanders are obvious. Any rebellion within the Army of Mars would be directed against the wrong people. And, in time of war, the enemy could exterminate the entire Martian officer class without disturbing the Army of Mars in the least.

"Seven hundred and ninety-nine," said Boaz out loud, correcting his own understanding of the number of real commanders. One of the real commanders was dead, having been strangled at the stake by Unk. The strangled man had been Private Stony Stevenson, former real commander of a British attack unit. Stony had become so fascinated by Unk's struggles to understand what was going on that he had begun, unconsciously, to help Unk think.

Stevenson had suffered the ultimate humiliation for this. An antenna had been installed in his skull, and he had been

83

forced by it to march to the stake like a good soldier—there to await murder by his protégé.

Boaz let his squadmates go on standing at attention—let them go on quivering, thinking nothing, seeing nothing. Boaz went to Unk's cot, lay down on it with his big, lustrous shoes on the brown blanket. He folded his hands behind his head —arched his body like a bow.

"Awwwww," said Boaz, somewhere between a yawn and a groan. "Awwwww—now, men, men, men," he said, letting his mind idle. "God damn, now, men," he said. It was lazy, nonsense talk. Boaz was a little bored with his toys. It occurred to him to have them fight each other—but the penalty for doing that, if he got caught, was the same penalty Stony Stevenson had paid.

"Awwwww—now, men. Really now, men," said Boaz languidly.

"God damn it now, men," he said. "I got it *made*. You men got to admit that. Old Boaz is doing how you might say real fine."

He rolled off the bed, landed on all fours, sprang to his feet with pantherlike grace. He smiled dazzlingly. He was doing everything he could to enjoy the fortunate position in life that was his. "You boys ain't got it so bad," he said to his rigid squadmates. "You oughta see how we treat the generals, if you think you's bad off." He chuckled and cooed. "Two night ago us real commanders got ourselves in a argument about which general could run the fastest. Next thing you know, we got all twenty-three generals out of bed, all bare-ass naked, and we lined 'em up like they was race horses, and then we put our money down and laid the odds, and then we sent them generals off like the devil was after 'em. General Stover, he done placed first, with General Harrison right behind him, and with General Mosher behind *him*. Next morning, ever' general in the Army was stiff as a board. Not one of 'em could remember a thing about the night before."

Boaz chuckled and cooed again, and then he decided that his fortunate position in life would look a lot better if he treated it seriously—showed what a load it was, showed how honoured he felt to have a load like that. He reared back judiciously, hooked his thumbs under his belt and scowled. "Oh," he said, "it ain't all play by any means." He sauntered over to Unk, stood inches away from him, looked him up and down. "Unk, boy," he said, "I'd hate to tell you how much time I've spent thinking about you—worrying about you, Unk."

Boaz rocked on his feet. "You *will* try an' puzzle things out, won't you! You know how many times they had you in the hospital, trying to clean out that memory of yours? Seven times, Unk! You know how many times they usually have to send a man to have his memory cleaned out? Once, Unk. One time!" Boaz snapped his finger under Unk's nose. "And that does it, Unk. One time, and the man never bothers hisself about anything ever after." He shook his head wonderingly. "Not *you*, though, Unk."

Unk shuddered.

"I keeping you at attention too long, Unk?" said Boaz. He gritted his teeth. He couldn't forbear torturing Unk from time to time.

For one thing, Unk had had everything back on Earth, and Boaz had had nothing.

For another thing. Boaz was wretchedly dependent on Unk—or would be when they hit Earth. Boaz was an orphan who had been recruited when he was only fourteen—and he didn't have the haziest notion as to how to have a good time on Earth.

He was counting on Unk to show him how.

"You want to know who you are—where you come from —what you were?" said Boaz to Unk. Unk was still at attention, thinking nothing, unable to profit from whatever Boaz might tell him. Boaz wasn't talking for Unk's benefit anyway. Boaz was reassuring himself about the buddy who was going to be by his side when they hit Earth.

"Man," said Boaz, scowling at Unk, "you are one of the luckiest men ever lived. Back there on Earth, man, you were King!"

Like most pieces of information on Mars, Boaz's pieces of information about Unk were underdeveloped. He could not say from where, exactly, the pieces had come. He had picked them out of the general background noises of army life.

And he was too good a soldier to go around asking questions, trying to round out his knowledge.

A soldier's knowledge wasn't supposed to be round.

So that Boaz didn't really know anything about Unk except that he had been very lucky once. He embroidered on this.

"I mean," said Boaz, "there wasn't anything you couldn't have, wasn't anything you couldn't do, wasn't no place you couldn't go!"

And while Boaz stressed the marvel of Unk's good luck on Earth, he was expressing a deep concern for another marvel—his superstitious conviction that his own luck on Earth was sure to be rotten.

Boaz now used three magical words that seemed to describe the maximum happiness a person could achieve on Earth: *Hollywood night clubs*. He had never seen Hollywood, had never seen a night club. "Man," he said, "you were in and out of Hollywood night clubs all day and all night long.

"Man," said Boaz to uncomprehending Unk, "you had everything a man needs to really lead hisself a life on Earth, and you knowed how to *do* it, too.

"Man," said Boaz to Unk, trying to conceal the pathetic formlessness of his aspirations. "We're going to go into some fine places and order us up some fine things, and circulate and carry on with some fine people, and just generally have us a good whoop-dee-doo." He seized Unk's arm, rocked him. "Buddies—that's us, buddy. Boy—we're going to be a famous pair—going everywhere, doing everything.

" 'Here comes lucky old Unk and his buddy Boaz!' " said Boaz, saying what he hoped Earthlings would be saying after the conquest. " 'And there they go, happy as two birds!' " He chuckled and cooed about the happy, birdlike pair.

His smile withered.

His smiles never lasted very long. Somewhere deep inside Boaz was worried sick. He was worried sick about losing his job. It had never been clear to him how he had landed the job—the great privilege. He didn't even know who had given him the swell job.

Boaz didn't even know who was in command of the real commanders.

He had never received an order—not from anyone who was superior to the real commanders. Boaz based his actions, as did all the real commanders, on what could be best described as conversational tidbits—tidbits circulated on the real-commander level.

Whenever the real commanders got together late at night, the tidbits were passed around with the beer and the crackers and cheese.

There would be a tidbit, for instance, about waste in the supply rooms, and another about the desirability of soldiers' actually getting hurt and mad during jujitsu training, another about soldiers' shabby tendency to skip loops in lacing up their puttees. Boaz himself would pass these on, without any idea as to their point of origin—and he would base his actions on them.

The execution of Stony Stevenson by Unk had also been announced in this way. Suddenly, it had been the topic of conversation.

Suddenly, the real commanders had placed Stony under arrest.

Boaz now fingered the control box in his pocket, without actually touching a control. He took his place among the men he controlled, came to attention voluntarily, pressed a button, and relaxed as his squadmates relaxed.

He wanted a drink of hard liquor very much. And he was entitled to liquor, too, whenever he wanted it. Unlimited supplies of all kinds of liquor were flown in from Earth regularly for the real commanders. And the officers could have all the liquor they wanted, too, though they couldn't get the good stuff. What the officers drank was a lethal green liquor made locally out of fermented lichens.

But Boaz never drank. One reason he didn't drink was that he was afraid that alcohol would impair his efficiency as a soldier. Another reason he didn't drink was that he was afraid that he would forget himself and offer an enlisted man a drink.

The penalty for a real commander who offered an enlisted man an alcoholic beverage was death.

"Yes, Lord," said Boaz, adding his voice to the hubbub of the relaxing men.

Ten minutes later, Sergeant Brackman declared a recreation period, during which everyone was supposed to go out and play German batball, the chief sport of the Army of Mars.

Unk stole away.

Unk stole away to barrack 12 to look for the letter under the blue rock—the letter that his red-headed victim had told him about.

The barracks in the area were empty.

The banner at the head of the mast before them was thin air.

The empty barracks had been the home of a battalion of Martian Imperial Commandos. The Commandos had disappeared quietly in the dead of night a month before. They had taken off in their space ships, their faces blackened, their dog tags taped so as not to clink—their destination secret.

The Martian Imperial Commandos were experts at killing sentries with loops of piano wire.

Their secret destination was the Earthling moon. They were going to start the war there.

Unk found a big blue stone outside the furnace room of barrack twelve. The stone was a turquoise. Turquoises are very common on Mars. The turquoise Unk found was a flagstone a foot across.

Unk looked under it. He found an aluminium cylinder with a screw cap. Inside the cylinder was a very long letter written in pencil.

Unk did not know who had written it. He was in poor shape for guessing, since he knew the names of only three people—Sergeant Brackman, Boaz, and Unk.

Unk went into the furnace room and closed the door.

He was excited, though he didn't know why. He began to read by the light from the dusty window.

Dear Unk:—the letter began.

Dear Unk:—the letter began: *They aren't much, God knows—but here are the things I know for sure, and at the end you will find a list of questions you should do your best to find answers to. The questions are important. I have thought harder about them than I have about the answers I already have. That is the first thing I know for sure: (1.) If the questions don't make sense, neither will the answers.*

All the things that the writer knew for sure were numbered, as though to emphasize the painful, step-by-step nature of the game of finding things out for sure. There were one hundred and fifty-eight things the writer knew for sure. There had once been one hundred and eighty-five, but twenty-seven had been crossed off.

The second item was, (2.) *I am a thing called alive.*

The third was, (3.) *I am in a place called Mars.*

The fourth was, (4.) *I am in a part of a thing called an army.*

The fifth was, (5.) *The army plans to kill other things called alive in a place called Earth.*

Of the first eighty-one items, not one was crossed out. And, in the first eighty-one items, the writer progressed to subtler and subtler matters, and mistakes grew more numerous.

Boaz was explained and dismissed by the writer very early in the game.

(46.) *Watch out for Boaz, Unk. He is not what he seems.*

(47.) *Boaz has something in his right-hand pocket that hurts people in the head when they do something Boaz doesn't like.*

(48.) *Some other people have things that can hurt you in the head too. You can't tell by looking who has one, so be sweet to everybody.*

(71.) *Unk, old friend—almost everything I know for sure has come from fighting the pain from my antenna,* said the letter to Unk. *Whenever I start to turn my head and look at something, and the pain comes, I keep turning my head anyway, because I know I am going to see something I'm not supposed to see. Whenever I ask a question, and the pain comes, I know I have asked a really good question. Then I break the question into little pieces, and I ask the pieces of the questions. Then I get answers to the pieces, and then I put the answers all together and get an answer to the big question.*

(72.) *The more pain I train myself to stand, the more I learn. You are afraid of the pain now, Unk, but you won't learn anything if you don't invite the pain. And the more you learn, the gladder you will be to stand the pain.*

There in the furnace room of the empty barrack, Unk laid the letter aside for a moment. He felt like crying, for the heroic writer's faith in Unk was misplaced. Unk knew he couldn't stand a fraction of the pain the writer had stood— couldn't possibly love knowledge that much.

Even the little sample twinge they had given him in the hospital had been excruciating. He gulped air now, like a fish dying on a riverbank, remembering the big pain Boaz had slammed him with in the barrack. He would rather die than risk another pain like that.

His eyes watered.

If he had tried to speak, he would have sobbed.

Poor Unk didn't want any trouble from anybody ever again. Whatever information he gained from the letter—information gained by another man's heroism—he would use to avoid any more pain.

Unk wondered if there were people who could stand more pain than others. He supposed this was the case. He supposed tearfully that he was especially sensitive in this regard. Without wishing the writer any harm, Unk wished the writer could feel, just once, the pains as Unk felt them.

Then maybe the writer would address his letters to someone else.

Unk had no way of judging the quality of the information contained in the letter. He accepted it all hungrily, uncritically. And, in accepting it, Unk gained an understanding of life that was identical with the writer's understanding of life. Unk wolfed down a philosophy.

And mixed in with the philosophy were gossip, history, astronomy, biology, theology, geography, psychology, medicine—and even a short story.

Some random examples:

Gossip: (*22.*) *General Borders is drunk all the time. He is so drunk he can't even tie his shoelaces so they will stay tied. Officers are as mixed up and unhappy as anybody. You used to be one, Unk, with a battalion all your own.*

History: (*26.*) *Everybody on Mars came from Earth. They thought they would be better off on Mars. Nobody can remember what was so bad about Earth.*

Astronomy: (*11.*) *Everything in the whole sky revolves around Mars once a day.*

Biology: (*58.*) *New people come out of women when men and women sleep together. New people hardly ever come out of women on Mars because the men and the women sleep in different places.*

Theology: (*15*) *Somebody made everything for some reason.*

Geography: (*16.*) *Mars is round. The only city on it is called Phoebe. Nobody knows why it is called Phoebe.*

Psychology: (*103.*) *Unk, the big trouble with dumb bastards is that they are too dumb to believe there is such a thing as being smart.*

Medicine: (*73.*) *When they clean out a man's memory on this place called Mars, they don't really clean it completely. They just clean out the middle of it, sort of. They always*

90

leave a lot of stuff in the corners. There is a story around about how they tried cleaning out a few memories completely. The poor people who had that done to them couldn't walk, couldn't talk, couldn't do anything. The only thing anybody could think of to do with them was to housebreak them, teach them a basic vocabulary of a thousand words, and give them jobs in military or industrial public relations.

The short story: (89.) *Unk, your best friend is Stony Stevenson. Stony is a big, happy, strong man, and he drinks a quart of whisky a day. Stony doesn't have an antenna in his head, and he can remember everything that ever happened to him. He pretends to be an intelligence scout, but he is one of the real commanders. He radio-controls a company of assault infantrymen who are going to attack a place on Earth called England. Stony is from England. Stony likes the Army of Mars because there is so much to laugh about. Stony laughs all the time. He heard what an eightball you were, Unk, so he came over to your barrack to have a look at you. He pretended he was a friend of yours, so he could hear you talk. After a while, you got to trust him, Unk, and you told him some of your secret theories about what life on Mars was all about. Stony tried to laugh, but then he realized that you had turned up some things that he didn't know anything about. He couldn't get over it, because he was supposed to know everything, and you weren't supposed to know anything. And then you told Stony a lot of the big questions you wanted answered, and Stony knew the answers to only about half of them. And Stony went back to his barrack, and the questions he didn't know the answers to kept going around and around in his head. He couldn't sleep that night, even though he drank and drank and drank. He was catching on that somebody was using him, and he didn't have any idea who it was. He didn't even know why there had to be an Army of Mars in the first place. He didn't even know why Mars was going to attack Earth. And the more he remembered about Earth, the more he realized that the Army of Mars didn't have the chance of a snowball in hell. The big attack on Earth would be suicide for sure. Stony wondered who he could talk to about this, and there just wasn't anybody but you, Unk. So Stony staggered out of bed about an hour before sunrise, and he sneaked in your barrack, Unk, and he woke you up. He told you everything about Mars he knew. And he said that from now on he*

*would tell you every bloody thing he found out, and you
were supposed to tell him every bloody thing you found out.
And every so often you two would get off somewhere and
try to fit things together. And he gave you a bottle of whisky.
And you both drank from it, and Stony said you were his
best bloody friend. He said you were the only bloody friend
he had ever had on Mars, even though he laughed all the
time, and he cried, and almost woke up people around your
bunk. He told you to watch out for Boaz, and then he went
back to his barrack and slept like a baby.*

The letter, from the point of the short story on, was proof
of the effectiveness of the secret observation team of Stony
Stevenson and Unk. From that point on, the things known
for sure in the letter were almost all introduced by phrases
like: *Stony says*—and *You found out*—and *Stony told you*
—and *You told Stony*—and *You and Stony got roaring
drunk out on the rifle range one night, and you two crazy
bums decided*—

The most important thing that the two crazy bums decided was that the man who was in actual command of
everything on Mars was a big, genial, smiling, yodelling man
who always had a big dog with him. The man and his dog,
according to the letter to Unk, appeared at secret meetings
of the real commanders of the Army of Mars about once
every hundred days.

The letter said nothing about it, because the writer knew
nothing about it, but this man and his dog were Winston
Niles Rumfoord and Kazak, the hound of space. And their
appearances on Mars were not irregular. Being chrono-
synclastic infundibulated, Rumfoord and Kazak appeared as
predictably as Halley's Comet. They appeared on Mars
once every one hundred and eleven days.

As the letter to Unk said, (*155.*) *According to Stony, this
big guy and his dog show up at the meetings, and just snow
everybody under. He is a big charm boy, and by the time a
meeting is over everybody is trying to think just exactly the
way he thinks. Every idea anybody has comes from him. He
just smiles and smiles and yodels and yodels in that fancy
voice of his, and fills everybody up with new ideas. And
then all the people at the meeting pass around the ideas as
though they had thought them up themselves. He is crazy
about the game of German batball. Nobody knows what his*

name is. He just laughs, if anybody asks him. He usually wears the uniform of the Parachute Ski Marines, but the real commanders of the Parachute Ski Marines swear they've never seen him anywhere but at the secret meetings.

(156.) Unk, old pal, said the letter to Unk, *every time you and Stony find out something new, add it on to this letter. Keep this letter well hidden. And every time you change its hiding place, be sure to tell Stony where you put it. That way, even if you go to the hospital to have your memory cleaned out, Stony can tell you where to go to have your memory filled up again.*

(157.) Unk—you know why you keep on going? You keep on going because you have a mate and a child. Almost nobody on Mars has either one. Your mate's name is Bee. She is an instructress at the Schliemann Breathing School in Phoebe. Your son's name is Chrono. He lives in the grade school in Phoebe. According to Stony Stevenson, Chrono is the best German batball player in the school. Like everybody else on Mars, Bee and Chrono have learned to get along all alone. They don't miss you. They never think of you. But you have to prove to them that they need you in the biggest way possible.

(158.) Unk, you crazy son-of-a-bitch, I love you. I think you are the cat's pyjamas. When you get this little family of yours together, swipe a space ship and go flying away to somewhere peaceful and beautiful, some place where you don't have to take goofballs all the time to stay alive. Take Stony with you. And when you get settled down, all of you spend a lot of time trying to figure out why whoever made everything went and made it.

All that remained for Unk to read of the letter was the signature.

The signature was on a separate page.

Before turning to the signature, Unk tried to imagine the character and appearance of the writer. The writer was fearless. The writer was such a lover of truth that he would expose himself to any amount of pain in order to add to his store of truth. He was superior to Unk and Stony. He watched and recorded their subversive activities with love, amusement, and detachment.

93

Unk imagined the writer as being a marvellous old man with a white beard and the build of a blacksmith.

Unk turned the page and read the signature.

I remain faithfully yours—was the sentiment expressed above the signature.

The signature itself filled almost the whole page. It was three block letters, six inches high and two inches wide. The letters were executed clumsily, with a smeary black kindergarten exuberance.

This was the signature:

The signature was Unk's.

Unk was the hero who had written the letter.

Unk had written the letter to himself before having his memory cleaned out. It was literature in its finest sense, since it made Unk courageous, watchful, and secretly free. It made him his own hero in very trying times.

Unk did not know that the man he had murdered at the stake was his best friend, was Stony Stevenson. Had he known that, he might have killed himself. But Fate spared him that awful knowledge for many years.

When Unk got back to his barrack, jungle knives and bayonets were being honed with harsh *screescraws*. Everyone was sharpening a blade.

And everywhere were sheepish smiles of a peculiar sort. The smiles spoke of sheep who, under proper conditions, could commit murder gladly.

Orders had just been received that the regiment was to proceed with all possible haste to its space ships.

The war with Earth had begun.

Advance units of the Martian Imperial Commandos had already obliterated Earthling installations on the Earthling moon. The Commando rocket batteries, firing from the moon, were now giving every major city a taste of hell.

And, as dinner music for those tasting hell, Martian radios were beaming this message to Earth in a maddening sing-song:

Brown man, white man, yellow man—surrender or die.
Brown man, white man, yellow man—surrender or die.

CHAPTER SIX

A DESERTER IN TIME OF WAR

"I am at a loss to understand why German bat-ball is not an event, possibly a key event, in the Olympic Games."
— WINSTON NILES RUMFOORD

IT was a six-mile march from the army camp to the plain where the invasion fleet lay. And the route of the march cut across the northwest corner of Phoebe, the only city on Mars.

The population of Phoebe at its height, according to Winston Niles Rumfoord's *Pocket History of Mars*, was eighty-seven thousand. Every soul and every structure in Phoebe was directly related to the war effort. The mass of Phoebe's workers were controlled just as the soldiers were controlled, by antennas under their skulls.

Unk's company was now marching through the north-west corner of Phoebe, on its way in the midst of its regiment to the fleet. It was thought unnecessary now to keep the soldiers moving and in ranks by means of twinges from their antennas. War fever had them now.

They chanted as they marched, and set their iron-heeled boots down hard on the iron street. Their chant was bloody:

> *Terror, grief, and desolation—*
> *Hut, tup, thrup, fo!—*
> *Come to every Earthling nation!*
> *Hut, tup, thrup, fo!—*
> *Earth eat fire! Earth wear chains!*
> *Hut, tup, thrup, fo!*
> *Break Earth's spirit, spill Earth's brains!*
> *Hut, tup, thrup, fo!*
> *Scream! Tup, thrup, fo!*
> *Die! Tup, thrup, fo!*
> *Dooooooooooommmmmmmmm.*

The factories of Phoebe were still going full blast. No one was idling in the streets to watch the chanting heroes pass. Windows winked as dazzling torches inside went off and on. A doorway vomited spattering, smoking yellow light as metal was poured. The screams of grinding wheels cut through the soldiers' chant.

Three flying saucers, blue scout ships, skimmed low over the city, making sweet cooing sounds like singing tops. "Toodleoo," they seemed to sing, and they skimmed away in a flat course while the surface of Mars curved away beneath them. In two shakes of a lamb's tail, they were twinkling in space eternal.

"*Terror, grief and desolation—*" chanted the troops.

But one soldier was moving his lips without making a sound. The soldier was Unk.

Unk was in the first file of the next to the last rank of his company.

Boaz was right behind him, his eyes making the back of Unk's neck itch. Boaz and Unk, moreover, were made Siamese twins by the song tube of a six-inch siege mortar which they were carrying between them.

"*Bleed! Tup, thrup, fo!*" chanted the troops. "*Die! Tup, thrup, fo! Doooooooooommmmmmmmmmm.*"

"Unk, old buddy—" said Boaz.

"Yes, old buddy?" said Unk absently. He was holding, amid the confusion of his soldier's harness, a live hand grenade. The pin had been pulled. To make it go off in three seconds, Unk had only to let go of it.

"I done fixed us up with a good assignment, old buddy," said Boaz. "Old Boaz—he takes care of his buddy, don't he, buddy?"

"That's right, buddy," said Unk.

Boaz had arranged things so that he and Unk would be on board the company mother ship for the invasion. The company mother ship, though it would, through a logistical fluke, be carrying the tube of the siege mortar, was essentially a noncombat ship. It was meant to carry only two men, the rest of the space being taken up by candy, sporting goods, recorded music, canned hamburgers, board games, goofballs, soft drinks, Bibles, note paper, barber kits, ironing boards, and other morale-builders.

"That's a lucky start, ain't it, old buddy—getting on the mother ship?"

"Lucky us, old buddy," said Unk. He had just chucked the grenade into a sewer as he passed.

97

There was a spout and roar from the throat of the sewer. The soldiers hurled themselves to the street.

Boaz, as the real commander of the company, was the first to raise his head. He saw the smoke coming from the sewer, supposed that it was sewer gas that had exploded.

Boaz slipped his hand into his pocket, pressed a button, fed to his company the signal that would make them stand up again.

As they stood, Boaz stood, too. "God damn, buddy," he said, "I guess we done had a baptism of fire."

He picked up his end of the siege mortar's tube.

There was nobody to pick up the other end.

Unk had gone in search of his wife and son and his best friend.

Unk had gone over the hill on flat, flat, flat, flat Mars.

The son that Unk was looking for was named Chrono.

Chrono was, by Earthling reckoning, eight years old.

He was named after the month in which he had been born. The Martian year was divided into twenty-one months, twelve with thirty days, and nine with thirty-one. These months were named January, February, March, April, May, June, July, August, September, October, November, December, Winston, Niles, Rumfoord, Kazak, Newport, Chrono, Synclastic, Infundibulum, and Salo.

Mnemonically:

> *Thirty days have Salo, Niles, June, and September,*
> *Winston, Chrono, Kazak, and November,*
> *April, Rumfoord, Newport, and Infundibulum.*
> *All the rest, baby mine, have thirty-one.*

The month of Salo was named after a creature Winston Niles Rumfoord knew on Titan. Titan, of course, is an extremely pleasant moon of Saturn.

Salo, Rumfoord's crony on Titan, was a messenger from another galaxy who was forced down on Titan by the failure of a part in his space ship's power plant. He was waiting for a replacement part.

He had been waiting patiently for two hundred thousand years.

His ship was powered, and the Martian war effort was powered, by a phenomenon known as UWTB, or the Universal Will to Become. UWTB is what makes universes out of nothingness—that makes nothingness insist on becoming somethingness.

Many Earthlings are glad that Earth does not have UWTB.

As the popular doggerel has it:

Willy found some Universal Will to Become,
Mixed it with his bubble gum.
Cosmic piddling seldom pays:
Poor Willy's six new Milky Ways.

Unk's son Chrono was, at eight years old, a wonderful player of a game called German batball. German batball was all that he cared about. German batball was the major sport on Mars—in the grammar school, in the Army, and in the factory worker's recreation areas.

Since there were only fifty-two children on Mars, Mars got along with just one grammar school, right in the middle of Phoebe. None of the fifty-two children there had been conceived on Mars. All had been conceived either on Earth or, as in Chrono's case, on a space ship bringing new recruits to Mars.

The children in the school studied very little, since the society of Mars had no particular use for them. They spent most of their time playing German batball.

The game of German batball is played with a flabby ball the size of a big honeydew melon. The ball is no more lively than a ten-gallon hat filled with rain water. The game is something like baseball, with a batter striking the ball into a field of opposing players and running around bases; and with the fielders attempting to catch the ball and frustrate the runner. There are, however, only three bases in German batball—first, second, and home. And the batter is not pitched to. He places the ball on one fist and strikes the ball with his other fist. And if a fielder succeeds in striking the runner with the ball when the runner is between bases, the runner is deemed *out*, and must leave the playing field at once.

The person responsible for the heavy emphasis on German batball on Mars was, of course, Winston Niles Rumfoord, who was responsible for everything on Mars.

Howard W. Sams proves in his *Winston Niles Rumfoord,*

Benjamin Franklin, and Leonardo da Vinci that German batball was the only team sport with which Rumfoord was at all familiar as a child. Sams shows that Rumfoord was taught the game, when a child, by his governess, a Miss Joyce MacKenzie.

Back in Rumfoord's childhood in Newport, a team composed of Rumfoord, Miss MacKenzie, and Earl Moncrief the butler, used to play German batball regularly against a team composed of Watanabe Wataru the Japanese gardener, Beverly June Wataru the gardener's daughter, and Edward Seward Darlington the half-wit stable boy. Rumfoord's team invariably won.

Unk, the only deserter in the history of the Army of Mars, now crouched panting behind a turquoise boulder and watched the school children playing German batball on the iron playground. Behind the boulder with Unk was a bicycle he had stolen from a gas-mask factory's bicycle rack. Unk did not know which child was his son, which child was Chrono.

Unk's plans were nebulous. His dream was to gather together his wife, his son, and his best friend, to steal a space ship, and to fly away to some place where they could all live happily ever after.

"Hey, Chrono!" cried a child on the playground. "You're up to bat!"

Unk peered around the boulder at home plate. The child who came up to bat there would be Chrono, would be his son.

Chrono, Unk's son, came up to bat.

He was small for his age, but surprisingly manly through the shoulders. The child's hair was jet black, bristly—and the black bristles grew in a violently counter-clockwise swirl.

The child was left-handed. The ball rested on his right fist, and he prepared to hit it with his left.

His eyes were deep-set, like his father's eyes. And his eyes were luminous under their black-thatched eaves. They glowed with an unshared rage.

Those rage-filled eyes flicked this way, then that. Their movements rattled the fielders, drawing them away from their positions, convincing them that the slow, stupid ball was going to come at them with terrible speed, was going to tear them to pieces if they dared to get in the way.

The alarm inspired by the boy at bat was felt by the teacher, too. She was in the traditional position for an umpire in German batball, between first and second base, and she was terrified. She was a frail old lady named Isabel Fenstermaker. She was seventy-three, and had been a Jehovah's Witness before having her memory cleaned out. She had been shanghaied while trying to sell a copy of *The Watchtower* to a Martian agent in Duluth.

"Now, Chrono," she said simperingly, "it's only a game, you know."

The sky was suddenly blackened by a formation of a hundred flying saucers, the blood-red ships of the Martian Parachute Ski Marines. The combined cooing of the ships was a melodious thunder that rattled the schoolhouse windowpanes.

But, as a measure of the importance young Chrono gave to German batball when he came to bat, not a single child looked up at the sky.

Young Chrono, having brought the fielders and Miss Fenstermaker to the brink of nervous collapse, now put the ball down by his feet, took from his pocket a short strip of metal that was his good-luck piece. He kissed the strip for luck, returned the strip to his pocket.

Then he suddenly picked up the ball again, hit it a mighty *bloop*, and went scrambling around the bases.

The fielders and Miss Fenstermaker dodged the ball as though it were a red-hot cannonball. When the ball came to a stop of its own accord, the fielders went after it with a sort of ritual clumsiness. Clearly, the point of their efforts was not to hit Chrono with the ball, was not to put him out. The fielders were all conspiring to increase the glory of Chrono by making a show of helpless opposition.

Clearly, Chrono was the most glorious thing that the children had ever seen on Mars, and any glory they themselves had came from their association with him. They would do anything to make his glory grow.

Young Chrono slid into home in a cloud of rust.

A fielder hurled the ball at him—too late, too late, much too late. The fielder ritually cursed his luck.

Young Chrono stood, dusted himself off, and again kissed his good-luck piece, thanked it for another home run. He believed firmly that all his powers came from the good-luck piece, and so did his schoolmates, and so, secretly, did Miss Fenstermaker.

The history of the good-luck piece was this:

One day the school children were taken by Miss Fenstermaker on an educational tour of the flame-thrower factory. The factory manager explained to the children all the steps in the manufacture of flame-throwers, and hoped that some of the children, when they grew up, would want to come to work for him. At the end of the tour, in the packaging department, the manager's ankle became snarled in a spiral of steel strapping, a type of strapping that was used for binding shut the packaged flame-throwers.

The spiral was a piece of jagged-ended scrap that had been cast into the factory aisle by a careless workman. The manager scratched his ankle and tore his pants before he got free of the spiral. He thereupon put on the first really comprehensible demonstration that the children had seen that day. Comprehensibly, he blew up at the spiral.

He stamped on it.

Then, when it nipped him again, he snatched it up and chopped it into four-inch lengths with great shears.

The children were edified, thrilled, and satisfied. And, as they were leaving the packaging department, young Chrono picked up one of the four-inch pieces and slipped it into his pocket. The piece he picked up differed from all the rest in having two holes drilled in it.

This was Chrono's good-luck piece. It became as much a part of him as his right hand. His nervous system, so to speak, extended itself into the metal strip. Touch it and you touched Chrono.

Unk, the deserter, stood up behind his turquoise boulder, walked vigorously and officiously into the school yard. He had stripped his uniform of all insignia. This gave him a rather official, warlike look, without binding him to any particular enterprise. Of all the equipment he had been carrying before he deserted, he retained only a jungle knife, his single-shot Mauser, and one grenade. These three weapons he left cached behind the boulder, along with the stolen bicycle.

Unk marched up to Miss Fenstermaker. He told her that he wished to interview young Chrono on official business at once—privately. He did not tell her that he was the boy's father. Being the boy's father entitled him to nothing. Being an official investigator entitled him to anything he might care to ask for.

Poor Miss Fenstermaker was easily fooled. She agreed to let Unk interview the boy in her own office.

Her office was crammed with ungraded school papers, some of them dating back five years. She was far behind in her work—so far behind that she had declared a moratorium on school work until she could catch up on her grading. Some of the stacks of paper had tumbled, forming glaciers that sent fingers under her desk, into the hallway, and into her private lavatory.

There was an open, two-drawer filing cabinet filled with her rock collection.

Nobody ever checked up on Miss Fenstermaker. Nobody cared. She had a teaching certificate from the State of Minnesota, U.S.A., Earth, Solar System, Milky Way, and that was all that mattered.

For his interview with his son, Unk sat behind her desk while his son Chrono stood before him. It was Chrono's wish to remain standing.

Unk, in planning the things he would say, idly opened Miss Fenstermaker's desk drawers, found that they were filled with rocks, too.

Young Chrono was shrewd and hostile, and he thought of something to say before Unk did. "Baloney," he said.

"What?" said Unk.

"Whatever you say—it's baloney," said the eight-year-old.

"What makes you think so?" said Unk.

"Everything anybody says is baloney," said Chrono. "What you care what I think anyway? When I'm fourteen, you put a thing in my head and I do whatever you want anyway."

He was referring to the fact that antennas were not installed in the skulls of children until their fourteenth year. This was a matter of skull size. When a child reached his fourteenth birthday, he was sent to the hospital for the operation. His hair was shaved off, and the doctors and nurses joshed him about having entered adulthood. Before the child was wheeled into the operating room he was asked to name his favourite kind of ice cream. When the child awoke after the operation, a big dish of that kind of ice cream was waiting for him—maple walnut, butter-crunch, chocolate chip, anything.

"Is your mother full of baloney?" said Unk.

"She is since she came back from the hospital this last time," said Chrono.

"What about your father?" said Unk.

"I don't know anything about him," said Chrono. "I don't care. He's full of baloney like everybody else."

"Who isn't full of baloney?" said Unk.

"I'm not full of baloney," said Chrono. "I'm the only one."

"Come closer," said Unk.

"Why should I?" said Chrono.

"Because I'm going to whisper something very important."

"I doubt it," said Chrono.

Unk got up from the desk, went around to Chrono, and whispered in his ear, "I'm your father, boy!" When Unk said those words, his heart went off like a burglar alarm.

Chrono was unmoved. "So what?" he said stonily. He had never received any instructions, had never seen an example in life, that would make him think a father was of any importance. On Mars, the word was emotionally meaningless.

"I've come to get you," said Unk. "Somehow we're going to get away from here." He shook the boy gently, trying to make him bubble a little.

Chrono peeled his father's hand from his arm as though the hand were a leech. "And do what?" he said.

"Live!" said Unk.

The boy looked over his father dispassionately, seeking one good reason why he should throw in his lot with this stranger. Chrono took his good-luck piece from his pocket, and rubbed it between his palms.

The imagined strength he got from the good-luck piece made him strong enough to trust nobody, to go on as he had for so long, angry and alone. "I'm living," he said. "I'm all right," he said. "Go to hell."

Unk took a step backward. The corners of his mouth pulled down. "Go to hell?" he whispered.

"I tell everybody to go to hell," said the boy. He was trying to be kind, but he wearied of the effort at once. "Can I go out and play batball now?"

"You'd tell your own father to go to hell?" murmured Unk. The question echoed back through Unk's emptied memory to an untouched corner where bits of his own strange childhood still lived. His own strange childhood had been spent in daydreams of at last seeing and loving a father who did not want to see him, who did not want to be loved by him.

"I—I deserted from the Army to come here—to find you," said Unk.

Interest flickered in the boy's eyes, then died. "They'll get you," he said. "They get everybody."

"I'll steal a space ship," said Unk. "And you and your mother and I will get on it, and we'll fly away!"

"To where?" said the boy.

"Some place good!" said Unk.

"Tell me about some place good," said Chrono.

"I don't know. We'll have to look!" said Unk.

Chrono shook his head pityingly. "I'm sorry," he said. "I don't think you know what you're talking about. You'd just get a lot of people killed."

"You want to stay here?" said Unk.

"I'm all right here," said Chrono. "Can I go out and play batball now?"

Unk wept.

His weeping appalled the boy. He had never seen a man weep before. He never wept himself. "I'm going out to play!" he cried wildly, and ran out of the office.

Unk went to the window of the office. He looked out at the iron playground. Young Chrono's team was in the field now. Young Chrono joined his teammates, faced a batter whose back was to Unk.

Chrono kissed his good-luck piece, put it in his pocket. "Easy out, you guys," he yelled hoarsely. "Come on, you guys—let's *kill* him!"

Unk's mate, the mother of young Chrono, was an instructress in the Schliemann Breathing School for Recruits. Schliemann breathing, of course, is a technique that enables human beings to survive in a vacuum or in an inhospitable atmosphere without the use of helmets or other cumbersome respiratory gear.

It consists, essentially, of taking a pill rich in oxygen. The bloodstream takes on this oxygen through the wall of the small intestine rather than through the lungs. On Mars, the pills were known officially as Combat Respiratory Rations, in popular parlance as *goofballs*.

Schliemann Breathing is at its simplest in a benign but useless atmosphere like that of Mars. The breather goes on breathing and talking in a normal manner, though there is no oxygen for his lungs to take in from the atmosphere. All he has to remember is to take his goofballs regularly.

The school in which Unk's mate was an instructress taught recruits the more difficult techniques necessary in a vacuum or in a harmful atmosphere. This involves not only pill-taking, but plugging one's ears and nostrils, and keeping one's mouth shut as well. Any effort to speak or to breathe would result in haemorrhages and probably death.

Unk's mate was one of six instructresses at the Schliemann Breathing School for Recruits. Her classroom was a bare, windowless, whitewashed room, thirty feet square. Ranged around the walls were benches.

On a table in the middle was a bowl of goofballs, a bowl of nose and ear plugs, a roll of adhesive plaster, scissors, and a small tape recorder. Purpose of the tape recorder was to play music during the long periods in which there was nothing to do but sit and wait patiently for nature to take its course.

Such a period had been reached now. The class had just been dosed with goofballs. Now the students had to sit quietly on the benches and listen to music and wait for the goofballs to reach their small intestines.

The tune being played had been pirated recently from an Earthling broadcast. It was a big hit on Earth—a trio composed for a boy, a girl, and cathedral bells. It was called "God is Our Interior Decorator." The boy and girl sang alternate lines of the verses, and joined in close harmony on the choruses.

The cathedral bells whanged and clanged whenever anything of a religious nature was mentioned.

There were seventeen recruits. They were all in their newly issued lichen-green undershorts. The purpose of having them strip was to permit the instructress to see at a glance their external bodily reactions to Schliemann breathing.

The recruits were fresh from amnesia treatments and antenna installations at the Reception Centre Hospital.

Their hair had been shaved off, and each recruit had a strip of adhesive plaster running from the crown of his head to the nape of his neck.

The adhesive plaster showed where the antenna had been put in.

The recruits' eyes were as empty as the windows of abandoned textile mills.

So were the eyes of the instructress, since she, too, had recently had her memory cleaned out.

When they released her from the hospital, they told her what her name was, and where she lived, and how to teach Schliemann breathing—and that was about all the factual information they gave her. There was one other item: they told her she had an eight-year-old son named Chrono, and that she could visit him at his school on Tuesday evenings, if she liked.

The name of the instructress, of Chrono's mother, of Unk's mate, was Bee. She wore a lichen-green sweatsuit, white gym shoes, and, around her neck, a whistle on a chain and a stethoscope.

There was a rebus of her name on her sweatshirt.

She looked at the clock on the wall. Enough time had passed for the slowest digestive system to carry a goofball to the small intestine. She stood, turned off the tape recorder, and blew her whistle.

"Fall in!" she said.

The recruits had not yet had basic military training, so they were incapable of falling in with precision. Painted on the floor were squares within which the recruits were to stand in order to form ranks and files pleasing to the eye. A game resembling musical chairs was now played, with several empty-eyed recruits shuffling for the same square. In time, each found a square of his own.

"All right," said Bee, "take your plugs and plug up your noses and ears, please."

The recruits had been carrying the plugs in their clammy fists. They plugged their noses and ears.

Bee now went from recruit to recruit, making certain that all ears and nostrils were sealed.

"All right," she said, when her inspection was done. "Very good," she said. She took from the table the roll of adhesive plaster. "Now I am going to prove to you that you don't need to use your lungs at all, as long as you have Combat Respiratory Rations—or, as you'll soon be calling them in the Army, goofballs." She moved through the ranks, snipping off lengths of adhesive, sealing mouths with them. No one objected. When she got through, no one had a suitable aperture through which to issue an objection.

She noted the time, and again turned on the music. For the next twenty minutes there would be nothing to do but watch the bare bodies for colour changes, for the dying spasms in the sealed and useless lungs. Ideally, the bodies would turn blue, then red, then natural again within the twenty minutes—and the rib cages would quake violently, give up, be still.

When the twenty-minute ordeal was over, every recruit would know how unnecessary lung-breathing was. Ideally, every recruit would be so confident in himself and goofballs, when his course of instruction was over, that he would be ready to spring out of a space ship on the Earthling moon or on the bottom of an Earthling ocean or anywhere, without wondering for a split second what he might be springing into.

Bee sat on a bench.

There were dark circles around her fine eyes. The circles had come after she left the hospital, and they had grown more sombre with each passing day. At the hospital, they had promised her that she would become more serene and efficient with each passing day. And they had told her that, if through some fluke she should not find this to be the case, she was to report back to the hospital for more help.

"We all need help from time to time," Dr. Morris N. Castle had said. "It's nothing to be ashamed of. Some day I may need *your* help, Bee, and I won't hesitate to ask for it."

She had been sent to the hospital after showing her supervisor this sonnet, which she had written about Schliemann breathing:

> Break every link with air and mist,
> Seal every open vent;
> Make throat as tight as miser's fist,
> Keep life within you pent
> Breath out, breathe in, no more, no more,
> For breathing's for the meek;
> And when in deathly space we soar,

Be careful not to speak.
If you with grief or joy are rapt,
Just signal with a tear;
To soul and heart within you trapped
Add speech and atmosphere.
Every man's an island as in
    lifeless space we roam.
Yes, every man's an island:
    island fortress, island home.

Bee, who had been sent to the hospital for writing this poem, had a strong face—high cheek-boned and haughty. She looked strikingly like an Indian brave. But whoever said so was under an obligation to add quickly that she was, all the same, quite beautiful.

Now there was a sharp knock on Bee's door. Bee went to the door and opened it. "Yes?" she said.

In the deserted corridor stood a red and sweating man in uniform. The uniform had no insignia. Slung on the man's back was a rifle. His eyes were deep-set and furtive. "Messenger," he said gruffly. "Message for Bee."

"I'm Bee," said Bee uneasily.

The messenger looked her up and down, made her feel naked. His body threw off heat, and the heat enveloped her suffocatingly.

"Do you recognize me?" he whispered.

"No," she said. His question relieved her a little. Apparently she had done business with him before. He and his visit, then, were routine—and, in the hospital, she had simply forgotten the man and his routine.

"I don't remember you, either," he whispered.

"I've been in the hospital," she said. "I had to have my memory cleaned."

"Whisper!" he said sharply.

"What?" said Bee.

"Whisper!" he said.

"Sorry," she whispered. Apparently whispering was part of the routine for dealing with this particular functionary. "I've forgotten so much."

"We *all* have!" he whispered angrily. He again looked up and down the corridor. "You are the mother of Chrono, aren't you?" he whispered.

"Yes," she whispered.

Now the strange messenger concentrated his gaze on her face. He breathed deeply, sighed, frowned—blinked frequently.

"What—what's the message?" whispered Bee.

"The message is this," whispered the messenger. "I am the father of Chrono. I have just deserted from the Army. My name is Unk. I am going to find some way for you, me, the boy, and my best friend to escape from here. I don't know how yet, but you've got to be ready to go at a moment's notice!" He gave her a hand grenade. "Hide this somewhere," he whispered. "When the times comes, you may need it."

Excited shouts came from the reception room at the far end of the corridor.

"*He said he was a confidential messenger!*" shouted a man.

"*In a pig's eye he's a messenger!*" shouted another. "*He's a deserter in time of war! Who'd he come to see?*"

"*He didn't say. He said it was top secret!*"

A whistle shrilled.

"*Six of you come with me!*" shouted a man. "*We'll search this place room by room. The rest of you surround the outside!*"

Unk shoved Bee and her hand grenade into the room, shut the door. He unslung his rifle, levelled it at the plugged and taped recruits. "One peep, one funny move out of any of you guys," he said, "and you'll all be dead."

The recruits, standing rigidly on their assigned squares on the floor, did not respond in any way.

They were pale blue.

Their rib cages were quaking.

The whole awareness of each man was concentrated in the region of a small, white, life-giving pill dissolving in the duodenum.

"Where can I hide?" said Unk. "How can I get out?"

It was unnecessary for Bee to reply. There was no place to hide. There was no way out save through the door to the corridor.

There was only one thing to do, and Unk did it. He stripped to his lichen-green undershorts, hid his rifle under a bench, put plugs in his ears and nostrils, taped his mouth, and stood among the recruits.

His head was shaved, just like the heads of the recruits.

And, like the recruits, Unk had a strip of adhesive plaster running from the crown of his head to the nape of his neck. He had been such a terrible soldier that the doctors had opened his head up at the hospital to see if he might not be suffering from malfunctioning antenna.

Bee surveyed the room with enchanted calm. She held the grenade that Unk had given her as though it were a vase with one perfect rose in it. Then she went to the place where Unk had hidden his rifle, and she put the grenade beside it —put it there neatly, with a decent respect for another's property.

Then she went back to her post at the table.

She neither stared at Unk nor avoided looking at him. As they told her at the hospital: she had been very, very sick, and she would be very, very sick again if she didn't keep her mind strictly on her work and let other people do the thinking and the worrying. At all costs, she was to keep calm.

The blustering false alarms of the men making the room-to-room search were approaching slowly.

Bee refused to worry about anything. Unk, by taking his place among the recruits, had reduced himself to a cipher. Considering him professionally, Bee saw that Unk's body was turning blue-green rather than pure blue. This might mean that he had not taken a goofball for several hours— in which case he would soon keel over.

To have him keel over would certainly be the most peaceful solution to the problem he presented, and Bee wanted peace above all else.

She didn't doubt that Unk was the father of her child. Life was like that. She didn't remember him, and she didn't bother now to study him in order to recognize him the next time—if there was going to be a next time. She had no use for him.

She noted that Unk's body was now predominantly green. Her diagnosis had been correct, then. He would keel over at any minute.

Bee daydreamed. She daydreamed of a little girl in a starched white dress and white gloves and white shoes, and with a white pony all her own. Bee envied that little girl who had kept so clean.

Bee wondered who the little girl was.

Unk fell noiselessly, as limp as a bag of eels.

Unk awoke, found himself on his back in a bunk in a space ship. The cabin lights were dazzling. Unk started to yell, but a sick headache shushed him.

He struggled to his feet, clung drunkenly to the pipe supports of the bunk. He was all alone. Someone had put his uniform back on him.

He thought at first that he had been launched into space eternal.

But then he saw that the airlock was open to the outside and that outside was solid ground.

Unk lurched out through the airlock and threw up.

He raised his watering eyes, and saw that he was seemingly still on Mars, or on something a lot like Mars.

It was night time.

The iron plain was studded with ranks and files of space ships.

As Unk watched, a file of ships five miles long arose from the formation, sailed melodiously off into space.

A dog barked, barked with a voice like a great bronze gong.

And out of the night loped the dog—as big and terrible as a tiger.

"Kazak!" cried a man in the dark.

The dog stopped at the command, but he held Unk at bay, kept Unk flattened against the space ship with the threat of his long, wet fangs.

The dog's master appeared, the beam of a flashlight dancing before him. When he got within a few yards of Unk, he placed the flashlight under his chin. The contrasting beam and shadows made his face look like the face of a demon.

"Hello, Unk," he said. He turned the flashlight off, stepped to one side so that he was illuminated by the light spilling from the space ship. He was big, vaguely soft, marvellously self-assured. He wore the blood-red uniform and square-toed boots of a Parachute Ski Marine. He was unarmed save for a black and gold swaggerstick one foot long.

"Long time no see," he said. He gave a very small, V-shaped smile. His voice was a glottal tenor, a yodel.

Unk had no recollection of the man, but the man obviously knew Unk well—knew him warmly.

"Who am I, Unk," said the man gaily.

Unk gasped. This had to be Stony Stevenson, had to be Unk's fearless best friend. "Stony?" he whispered.

"Stony?" said the man. He laughed. "Oh, God," he said, "many's the time I've wished I was Stony, and many's the time I'll wish it again."

The ground shook. There was a whirlwind rush in the air. Neighbouring space ships on all sides had leaped into the air, were gone.

Unk's ship now had its sector of the iron plain all to itself. The nearest ships on the ground were perhaps half a mile away.

"There goes your regiment, Unk," said the man, "and you are not with them. Aren't you ashamed?"

"Who are you?" said Unk.

"What do names matter in wartime?" said the man. He put his big hand on Unk's shoulder. "Oh, Unk, Unk, Unk," he said, "what a time you've had."

"Who brought me here?" said Unk.

"The military police, bless them," said the man.

Unk shook his head. Tears ran down his cheeks. He was defeated. There was no reason for secrecy any more, even in the presence of someone who might have the power of life and death over him. As to life and death, poor Unk was indifferent. "I—I tried to bring my family together," he said. "That's all."

"Mars is a very bad place for love, a very bad place for a family man, Unk," said the man.

The man was, of course, Winston Niles Rumfoord. He was commander-in-chief of everything Martian. He was not actually a practising Parachute Ski Marine. But he was free to wear any uniform that caught his fancy, regardless of how much hell anybody else had to go through for the privilege.

"Unk," said Rumfoord, "the very saddest love story I ever hope to hear took place on Mars. Would you like to hear it?"

"Once upon a time," said Rumfoord, "there was a man being carried from Earth to Mars in a flying saucer. He had volunteered for the Army of Mars, and already wore the dashing uniform of a lieutenant-colonel in the Assault Infantry of that service. He felt elegant, indeed, having been rather underprivileged spiritually on Earth, and assumed, as spiritually underprivileged persons will, that the uniform said lovely things about him.

"His memory hadn't been cleaned out yet, and his antenna had yet to be installed—but he was so patently a loyal Martian that he was given the run of the space ship. The recruiters have a saying about a male recruit like that—that he has named his balls Deimos and Phobus," said Rumfoord, "Deimos and Phobus being the two moons of Mars.

"This lieutenant-colonel, with no military training whatsoever, was having the experience known on Earth as *finding himself*. Ignorant as he was of the enterprise in which he was ensnarled, he was issuing orders to the other recruits, and having them obeyed."

Rumfoord held up a finger, and Unk was startled to see that it was quite translucent. "There was one locked stateroom that the man was not permitted to enter," said Rumfoord. "The crew carefully explained to him that the stateroom contained the most beautiful woman ever taken to Mars, and that any man who saw her was certain to fall in love with her. Love, they said, would destroy the value of any but the most professional soldier.

"The new lieutenant-colonel was offended by the suggestion that he was not a professional soldier, and he regaled the crew with stories of his amatory exploits with gorgeous women—all of which had left his heart absolutely untouched. The crew remained sceptical, pretending to the opinion that the lieutenant-colonel had never, for all his lascivious questing, exposed himself to an intelligent, haughty beauty such as the one in the locked stateroom.

"The crew's seeming respect for the lieutenant-colonel was now subtly withdrawn. The other recruits sensed this withdrawal, and withdrew their own. The lieutenant-colonel in his gaudy uniform was made to feel like what he really was, after all—a strutting clown. The manner in which he could win back his dignity was never stated, but was obvious to one and all. He could win it back by making a conquest of the beauty locked in the stateroom. He was fully prepared to do this—was desperately prepared—

"But the crew," said Rumfoord, "continued to protect him from supposed amatory failure and a broken heart. His ego fizzed, it sizzled, it snapped, it crackled, it popped.

"There was a drinking party in the officers' mess," said Rumfoord, "and the lieutenant-colonel became quite drunk and loud. He bragged again of his heartless lewdnesses on Earth. And then he saw that someone had placed in the bottom of his glass a stateroom key.

"The lieutenant-colonel sneaked away to the locked stateroom forthwith, let himself in, and closed the door behind him," said Rumfoord. "The stateroom was dark, but the inside of the lieutenant-colonel's head was illuminated by liquor and by the triumphant words of the announcement he would make at breakfast the next morning.

"He took the woman in the dark easily, for she was weak with terror and sedatives," said Rumfoord. "It was a joyless union, satisfactory to no one but Mother Nature at her most callous.

"The lieutenant-colonel did not feel marvellous. He felt wretched. Foolishly, he turned on the light, hoping to find in the woman's appearance some cause for pride in his brutishness," said Rumfoord sadly. "Huddled on the bunk was a rather plain woman past thirty. Her eyes were red and her face was puffy with weeping, despair.

"The lieutenant-colonel, moreover, knew her. She was a woman that a fortune teller had promised him would one day bear his child," said Rumfoord. "She had been so high and proud the last time he saw her, and was now so crushed, that even the heartless lieutenant-colonel was moved.

"The lieutenant-colonel realized for the first time what most people never realize about themselves—that he was not only a victim of outrageous fortune, but one of outrageous fortune's cruellest agents as well. The woman had regarded him as a pig when they met before. He had now proved beyond question that he was a pig.

"As the crew had predicted," said Rumfoord, "the lieutenant-colonel was spoiled forever as a soldier. He became hopelessly engrossed in the intricate tactics of causing less rather than more pain. Proof of his success would be his winning of the woman's forgiveness and understanding.

"When the space ship reached Mars, he learned from loose talk in the Reception Centre Hospital that he was about to have his memory taken away. He thereupon wrote himself the first of a series of letters that listed all the things he did not want to forget. The first letter was all about the woman he had wronged.

"He looked for her after his amnesia treatment, and found that she had no recollection of him. Not only that, she was pregnant, carrying his child. His problem, thereupon, became to win her love, and through her, to win the love of her child.

"This he attempted to do, Unk," said Rumfoord, "not once, but many times. He was consistently defeated. But it remained the central problem of his life—probably because he himself had come from a shattered family.

"What defeated him, Unk," said Rumfoord, "was a congenital coldness on the part of the woman, and a system of psychiatry that took the ideals of Martian society as noble common sense. Each time the man wobbled his mate, utterly humourless psychiatry straightened her out—made her an efficient citizen again.

"Both the man and his mate were frequent visitors to the psychiatric wards of their respective hospitals. And it is perhaps food for thought," said Rumfoord, "that this supremely frustrated man was the only Martian to write a philosophy, and that this supremely self-frustrating woman was the only Martian to write a poem."

Boaz arrived at the company mother ship from the town of Phoebe, where he had gone to look for Unk. "God damn," he said to Rumfoord, "everybody go and leave without us?" He was on a bicycle.

He saw Unk. "God damn, buddy," he said to Unk, "boy —you ever put your buddy through hell. I mean! How you get here?"

"Military police," said Unk.

"The way everybody gets everywhere," said Rumfoord lightly.

"We got to catch up, buddy," said Boaz. "Them boys ain't going to attack, if they don't have a mother ship along. What they going to fight for?"

"For the privilege of being the first army that ever died in a good cause," said Rumfoord.

"How's that?" said Boaz.

"Never mind," said Rumfoord. "You boys just get on board, close the airlock, push the *on* button. You'll catch up before you know it. Everything's all fully automatic."

Unk and Boaz got on board.

Rumfoord held open the outer door of the airlock. "Boaz," he said, "that red button on the centre shaft there, that's the *on* button."

"I know," said Boaz.

"Unk," said Rumfoord.

"Yes?" said Unk emptily.

"That story I told you—the love story? I left out one thing."

"That so?" said Unk.

"The woman in the love story—the woman who had that man's baby?" said Rumfoord. "The woman who was the only poet on Mars?"

"What about her?" said Unk. He didn't care much about her. He hadn't caught on that the woman in Rumfoord's story was Bee, was his own mate.

"She'd been married for several years before she got to Mars," said Rumfoord. "But when the hot-shot lieutenant-colonel got to her there in the space ship bound for Mars, she was still a virgin."

Winston Niles Rumfoord winked at Unk before shutting the outside door of the airlock. "Pretty good joke on her husband, eh, Unk?" he said.

CHAPTER SEVEN

VICTORY

"There is no reason why good cannot triumph
as often as evil. The triumph of anything is a
matter of organization. If there are such things as
angels, I hope that they are organized along the
lines of the Mafia."
—WINSTON NILES RUMFOORD

IT has been said that Earthling civilization, so far, has
created ten thousand wars, but only three intelligent commentaries on war—the commentaries of Thucydides, of
Julius Caesar, and of Winston Niles Rumfoord.

Winston Niles Rumfoord chose 75,000 words so well for
his *Pocket History of Mars* that nothing remains to be said,
or to be said better, about the war between Earth and Mars.
Anyone who finds himself obliged, in the course of a history,
to describe the war between Earth and Mars is humbled by
the realization that the tale has already been told to glorious
perfection by Rumfoord.

The usual course for such a discomfited historian is to
describe the war in the barest, flattest, most telegraphic
terms, and to recommend that the reader go at once to
Rumfoord's masterpiece.

Such a course is followed here.

The war between Mars and Earth lasted 67 Earthling
days.

Every nation on Earth was attacked.

Earth's casualties were 461 killed, 223 wounded, none
captured, and 216 missing.

Mars' casualties were 149,315 killed, 446 wounded, 11
captured, and 46,634 missing.

At the end of the war, every Martian had been killed,
wounded, captured, or missing.

Not a soul was left on Mars. Not a building was left
standing on Mars.

The last waves of Martians to attack Earth were, to the

horror of the Earthlings who pot-shotted them, old men, women, and a few little children.

The Martians arrived in the most brilliantly-conceived space vehicles ever known in the Solar System. And, as long as the Martian troops had their real commanders to radio-control them, they fought with a steadfastness, selflessness, and a will to close with the enemy that won the grudging admiration of everyone who fought them.

It was frequently the case, however, that the troops lost their real commanders, either in the air or on the ground. When that happened, the troops became sluggish at once.

Their biggest trouble, however, was that they were scarcely better armed than a big-city police department. They fought with firearms, grenades, knives, mortars, and small rocket-launchers. They had no nuclear weapons, no tanks, no medium or heavy artillery, no air cover, and no transport once they hit the ground.

The Martian troops, moreover, had no control over where their ships were to land. Their ships were controlled by fully automatic pilot-navigators, and these electronic devices were set by technicians on Mars so as to make the ships land at particular points on Earth, regardless of how awful the military situation might be down there.

The only controls available to those on board were two push-buttons on the centre post of the cabin—one labelled *on* and one labelled *off*. The *on* button simply started a flight from Mars. The *off* button was connected to nothing. It was installed at the insistence of Martian mental-health experts, who said that human beings were always happier with machinery they thought they could turn off.

The war between Earth and Mars began when 500 Martian Imperial Commandos took possession of the Earthling moon on April 23. They were unopposed. The only Earthlings on the moon at the time were 18 Americans in the Jefferson Observatory, 53 Russians in the Lenin Observatory, and four Danish geologists at large in the Mare Imbrium.

The Martians announced their presence by radio to Earth, demanding Earth's surrender. And they gave Earth what they described as "a taste of hell."

This taste, to Earth's considerable amusement, turned out to be a very light shower of rockets carrying twelve pounds apiece of TNT.

After giving Earth this taste of hell, the Martians told Earth that Earth's situation was hopeless.

Earth thought otherwise.

In the next twenty-four hours, Earth fired 617 thermo-nuclear devices at the Martian bridgehead on the moon. Of these 276 were hits. These hits not only vaporized the bridgehead—they rendered the moon unfit for human occupation for at least ten million years.

And, in a freak of war, one wild shot missed the moon and hit an incoming formation of space ships that carried 15,671 Martian Imperial Commandos. That took care of all the Martian Imperial Commandos there were.

They wore knee spikes, and glossy black uniforms, and carried 14-inch, saw-toothed knives in their boots. Their insignia was a skull and crossbones.

Their motto was *Per aspera ad astra*, the same as the motto of Kansas, U.S.A., Earth, Solar System, Milky Way.

There was then a lull of thirty-two days, the length of time it took for the main Martian striking force to cross the void between the two planets. This hammer blow consisted of 81,932 troops in 2,311 ships. Every military unit, save for the Martian Imperial Commandos, was represented. Earth was spared suspense as to when this terrible armada might arrive. The Martian broadcasters on the moon, before being vaporized, had promised the arrival of this irresistible force in thirty-two days.

In thirty-two days, four hours, and fifteen minutes, the Martian Armada flew into a radar-directed thermo-nuclear barrage. The official estimate of the number of thermo-nuclear anti-aircraft rockets fired at the Martian armada is 2,542,670. The actual number of rockets fired is of little interest when one can express the power of that barrage in another way, in a way that happens to be both poetry and truth. The barrage turned the skies of Earth from heavenly blue to a hellish burnt orange. The skies remained burnt orange for a year and a half.

Of the mighty Martian Armada, only 761 ships carrying 26,635 troops survived the barrage and landed on Earth.

Had all these ships landed at one point, the survivors might have made a stand. But the electronic pilot-navigators of the ships had other ideas. The pilot-navigators scattered the remnants of the armada far and wide over the surface of the Earth. Squads, platoons, and companies emerged from the ships everywhere demanding that nations of millions give in.

A single, badly scorched man named Krishna Garu attacked all of India with a double-barrelled shotgun. Though there was no one to radio-control him, he did not surrender until his gun blew up.

The only Martian military success was the capture of a meat market in Basel, Switzerland, by seventeen Parachute Ski Marines.

Everywhere else the Martians were butchered promptly, before they could even dig in.

As much butchering was done by amateurs as by professionals. At the Battle of Boca Raton, in Florida, U.S.A., for instance, Mrs. Lyman R. Peterson shot four members of the Martian Assault Infantry with her son's .22 calibre rifle. She picked them off as they came out of their space ship, which had landed in her back yard.

She was awarded the Congressional Medal of Honour posthumously.

The Martians who attacked Boca Raton, incidentally, were the remains of Unk's and Boaz's company. Without Boaz, their real commander, to radio-control them, they fought listlessly, to say the least.

When American troops arrived at Boca Raton to fight the Martians, there was nothing left to fight. The civilians, flushed and proud, had taken care of everything nicely. Twenty-three Martians had been hanged from lamp posts in the business district, eleven had been shot dead, and one, Sergeant Brackman, was a grievously wounded prisoner in the jail.

The total attacking force had been thirty-five.

"Send us more Martians," said Ross L. McSwann, the Mayor of Boca Raton.

He later became a United States Senator.

And everywhere the Martians were killed and killed and killed, until the only Martians left free and standing on the face of the Earth were the Parachute Ski Marines carousing in the meat market in Basel, Switzerland. They were told by loudspeaker that their situation was hopeless, that bombers were overhead, that all streets were blocked by tanks and crack infantry, and that fifty artillery pieces were trained on the meat market. They were told to come out with their hands up, or the meat market would be blown to bits.

"Nuts!" yelled the real commander of the Parachute Ski Marines.

There was another lull.

A single Martian scout ship far out in space broadcast to Earth that another attack was on its way, an attack more terrible than anything ever known in the annals of war.

Earth laughed and got ready. All around the globe there was the cheerful popping away of amateurs familiarizing themselves with small arms.

Fresh stocks of thermo-nuclear devices were delivered to the launching pads, and nine tremendous rockets were fired at Mars itself. One hit Mars, wiped the town of Phoebe and the Army camp off the face of the planet. Two others disappeared in a chrono-synclastic infundibulum. The rest became space derelicts.

It did not matter that Mars was hit.

There was no one there any more—not a soul.

The last of the Martians were on their way to Earth.

The last of the Martians were coming in three waves.

In the first wave came the Army reserves, the last of the trained troops—26,119 men in 721 ships.

A half an Earthling day behind them came 86,912 recently-armed male civilians in 1,738 ships. They had no uniforms, had fired their rifles only once, and had no training at all in the use of any other weapons.

A half an Earthling day behind these wretched irregulars, came 1,391 unarmed women and 52 children in 46 ships.

That was all the people and all the ships that Mars had left.

The mastermind behind the Martian suicide was Winston Niles Rumfoord.

The elaborate suicide of Mars was financed by capital gains on investments in land, securities, Broadway shows, and inventions. Since Rumfoord could see into the future, it was easy as pie for him to make money grow.

The Martian treasury was kept in Swiss banks, in accounts identified only by code numbers.

The man who managed the Martian investments, headed the Martian Procurement Programme and the Martian Secret Service on Earth, the man who took orders directly from Rumfoord, was Earl Moncrief, the ancient Rumfoord butler. Moncrief, given the opportunity at the very close of his servile life, became Rumfoord's ruthless, effective, and even brilliant Prime Minister of Earthling Affairs.

Moncrief's façade remained unchanged.

Moncrief died of old age in his bed in the servants' wing of the Rumfoord mansion two weeks after the war ended.

The person chiefly responsible for the technological triumphs of the Martian suicide was Salo, Rumfoord's friend on Titan. Salo was a messenger from the planet Tralfamadore in the Small Magellanic Cloud. Salo had technological know-how from a civilization that was millions of Earthling years old. Salo had a space ship that was crippled—but, even in its crippled condition, it was by far the most marvellous space ship that the Solar System had ever seen. His crippled ship, stripped of luxury features, was the prototype of all the ships of Mars. While Salo himself was not a very good engineer, he was none the less able to measure every part of his ship, and to draw up the plans for its Martian descendants.

Most important of all—Salo had in his possession a quantity of the most powerful conceivable source of energy, UWTB, or the Universal Will to Become. Salo generously donated half of his supply of UWTB to the suicide of Mars.

Earl Moncrief, the butler, built his financial, procurement, and secret service organizations with the brute power of cash and a profound understanding of clever, malicious, discontented people who lived behind servile façades.

It was such people who took the Martian money and the Martian orders gladly. They asked no questions. They were grateful for the opportunity to work like termites on the sills of the established order.

They came from all walks of life.

The modified plans of Salo's space ship were broken down into plans for components. The plans for the components were taken by Moncrief's agents to manufacturers all over the world.

The manufacturers had no idea what the components were for. They knew only that the profits on making them were fine.

The first one hundred Martian ships were assembled by Moncrief's agents in secret depots right on Earth.

These ships were charged with UWTB given to Moncrief

by Rumfoord at Newport. They were put into service at once, shuttling the first machines and the first recruits to the iron plain on Mars where the city of Phoebe would rise.

When Phoebe did rise, every wheel was turned by Salo's UWTB.

It was Rumfoord's intention that Mars should lose the war—that Mars should lose it foolishly and horribly. As a seer of the future, Rumfoord knew for certain that this would be the case—and he was content.

He wished to change the World for the better by means of the great and unforgettable suicide of Mars.

As he says in his *Pocket History of Mars*: "Any man who would change the World in a significant way must have showmanship, a genial willingness to shed other people's blood, and a plausible new religion to introduce during the brief period of repentance and horror that usually follows bloodshed.

"Every failure of Earthling leadership has been traceable to a lack on the part of the leader," says Rumfoord, "of at least one of these three things.

"Enough of these fizzles of leadership, in which millions die for nothing or less!" says Rumfoord. "Let us have, for a change, a magnificently-led few who die for a great deal."

Rumfoord had that magnificently-led few on Mars—and he was their leader.

He had showmanship.

He was genially willing to shed the blood of others.

He had a plausible new religion to introduce at the war's end.

And he had methods for prolonging the period of repentance and horror that would follow the war. These methods were variations on one theme: That Earth's glorious victory over Mars had been a tawdry butchery of virtually unarmed saints, saints who had waged feeble war on Earth in order to weld the peoples of that planet into a monolithic Brotherhood of Man.

The woman called Bee and her son, Chrono, were in the very last wave of Martian ships to approach Earth. Theirs was a wavelet, really, composed, as it was, of only forty-six ships.

The rest of the fleet had already gone down to destruction.

This last incoming wave, or wavelet, was detected by Earth. But thermo-nuclear devices were not fired at it. There were no more thermo-nuclear devices to fire.

And the wavelet came in unscathed. It was scattered over the face of the Earth.

The few people who were lucky enough to have Martians to shoot at in this last wave fired away happily—fired away happily until they discovered that their targets were unarmed women and children.

The glorious war was over.

Shame, as Rumfoord had planned it, began to set in.

The ship carrying Bee and Chrono and twenty-two other women was not fired upon when it landed. It did not land in a civilized area.

It crashed into the Amazon Rain Forest in Brazil.

Only Bee and Chrono survived.

Chrono emerged, kissed his good-luck piece.

Unk and Boaz weren't fired upon either.

A very peculiar thing happened to them after they pressed the *on* button and took off from Mars. They expected to overtake their company, but they never did.

They never even saw another space ship.

The explanation was simple, though there was no one around to make it: Unk and Boaz weren't supposed to go to Earth—not right away.

Rumfoord had had their automatic pilot-navigator set so that the ship would carry Unk and Boaz to the planet Mercury first—and then from Mercury to Earth.

Rumfoord didn't want Unk killed in the war.

Rumfoord wanted Unk to stay in some safe place for about two years.

And then Rumfoord wanted Unk to appear on Earth, as though by a miracle.

Rumfoord was preserving Unk for a major part in a pageant Rumfoord wanted to stage for his new religion.

Unk and Boaz were very lonely and mystified out there in space. There wasn't much to see or do.

"God damn, Unk," said Boaz. "I wonder where the gang got to."

Most of the gang was hanging, at that moment, from lamp posts in the business district of Boca Raton.

Unk's and Boaz's automatic pilot-navigator, controlling the cabin lights, among other things, created an artificial cycle of Earthling nights and days, nights and days, nights and days.

The only things to read on board were two comic books left behind by the ship fitters. They were *Tweety* and *Sylvester*, which was about a canary that drove a cat crazy, and *The Miserable Ones*, which was about a man who stole some gold candlesticks from a priest who had been nice to him.

"What he take those candlesticks for, Unk?" said Boaz.

"Damn if I know," said Unk. "Damn if I care."

The pilot-navigator had just turned out the cabin lights, had just decreed that it be night inside.

"You don't give a damn for nothing, do you?" said Boaz in the dark.

"That's right," said Unk, "I don't even give a damn for that thing you've got in your pocket."

"What I got in my pocket?" said Boaz.

"A thing to hurt people with," said Unk. "A thing to make people do whatever you want 'em to do."

Unk heard Boaz grunt, then groan softly, there in the dark. And he knew that Boaz had just pressed a button on the thing in his pocket, a button that was supposed to knock Unk cold.

Unk didn't make a sound.

"Unk—?" said Boaz.

"Yeah?" said Unk.

"You *there*, buddy?" said Boaz, amazed.

"Where would I go?" said Unk. "You think you vaporized me?"

"You O.K., buddy?" said Boaz.

"Why wouldn't I be, buddy?" said Unk. "Last night, while you were asleep, old buddy, I took that fool thing out of your pocket, old buddy, and I opened it up, old buddy, and I tore the insides out of it, old buddy, and I stuffed it with toilet paper. And now I'm sitting on my bunk, old buddy, and I've got my rifle loaded, old buddy, and it's aimed in your direction, old buddy, and just what the hell do you think you're going to do about anything?"

Rumfoord materialized on Earth, in Newport, twice during the war between Mars and Earth—once just after the war started, and again on the day it ended. He and his dog had, at that time, no particular religious significance. They were merely tourist attractions.

The Rumfoord estate had been leased by the mortgage holders to a showman named Marlin T. Lapp. Lapp sold tickets to materializations for a dollar apiece.

Save for the appearance and then the disappearance of Rumfoord and his dog, it wasn't much of a show. Rumfoord wouldn't say a word to anyone but Moncrief, the butler, and he whispered to him. He would slouch broodingly in a wing chair in the room under the staircase, in Skip's Museum. And he would cover his eyes with one hand and twine the fingers of his other hand around Kazak's choke chain.

Rumfoord and Kazak were billed as ghosts.

There was a scaffolding outside the window of the little room, and the door to the corridor had been removed. Two lines of sightseers could file past for a peek at the chrono-synclastic infundibulated man and dog.

"I guess he don't feel much like talking today, folks," Marlin T. Lapp would say. "You got to realize he's got a lot to think about. He isn't just here, folks. Him and his dog are spread all the way from the Sun to Betelgeuse."

Until the last day of the war, all the action and all the noise was provided by Marlin T. Lapp. "I think it's wonderful of all you people, on this great day in the history of the world, to come and see this great cultural and educational and scientific exhibit," Lapp said on the last day of the war.

"If this ghost ever speaks," said Lapp, "he is going to tell us of wonders in the past and the future, and of things in the Universe as yet undreamed of. I just hope some of you are lucky enough to be here when he decides the time is ripe to tell us all he can."

"The time is ripe," said Rumfoord hollowly.

"The time is rotten-ripe," said Winston Niles Rumfoord.

"The war that ends so gloriously today was glorious only for the saints who lost it. Those saints were Earthlings like yourselves. They went to Mars, mounted their hopeless attacks, and died gladly, in order that Earthlings might at last become one people—joyful, fraternal, and proud.

"Their wish, when they died," said Rumfoord, "was not

for paradise for themselves, but that the brotherhood of mankind on Earth might be enduring.

"To that end, devoutly to be wished," said Rumfoord, "I bring you word of a new religion that can be received enthusiastically in every corner of every Earthling heart.

"National borders," said Rumfoord, "will disappear.

"The lust for war," said Rumfoord, "will die.

"All envy, all fear, all hate will die," said Rumfoord.

"The name of the new religion," said Rumfoord, "is The Church of God the Utterly Indifferent.

"The flag of that church will be blue and gold," said Rumfoord. "These words will be written on that flag in gold letters on a blue field: *Take Care of the People, and God Almighty Will Take Care of Himself.*

"The two chief teachings of this religion are these," said Rumfoord: "Puny man can do nothing at all to help or please God Almighty, and Luck is not the hand of God.

"Why should you believe in this religion, rather than any other?" said Rumfoord. "You should believe in it because I, as head of this religion, can work miracles, and the head of no other religion can. What miracles can I work? I can work the miracle of predicting, with absolute accuracy, the things that the future will bring."

Rumfoord thereupon predicted fifty future events in great detail.

These predictions were carefully recorded by those present.

Needless to say, they all came true eventually—came true in great detail.

"The teachings of this religion will seem subtle and confusing at first," said Rumfoord. "But they will become beautiful and crystal clear as time goes by.

"As a presently confusing beginning," said Rumfoord, "I shall tell you a parable:

"Once upon a time, luck arranged things so that a baby named Malachi Constant was born the richest child on Earth. On the same day, luck arranged things so that a blind grandmother stepped on a rollerskate at the head of a flight of cement stairs, a policeman's horse stepped on an organ grinder's monkey, and a paroled bank robber found a postage stamp worth nine hundred dollars in the bottom of a trunk in his attic. I ask you—is luck the hand of God?"

Rumfoord held up an index finger that was as translucent

as a Limoges teacup. "During my next visit with you, fellow-believers," he said, "I shall tell you a parable about people who do things that they think God Almighty wants done. In the meanwhile, you would do well, for background on this parable, to read everything that you can lay your hands on about the Spanish Inquisition.

"The next time I come to you," said Rumfoord, "I shall bring you a Bible, revised so as to be meaningful in modern times. And I shall bring you a short history of Mars, a true history of the saints who died in order that the world might be united as the Brotherhood of Man. This history will break the heart of every human being who has a heart that can be broken."

Rumfoord and his dog dematerialized abruptly.

On the space ship out of Mars and bound for Mercury, on the space ship carrying Unk and Boaz, the automatic pilot-navigator decreed that it be day in the cabin again.

It was the dawn following the night in which Unk had told Boaz that the thing in Boaz's pocket couldn't hurt anybody any more.

Unk was asleep on his bunk in a sitting position. His Mauser rifle, loaded and cocked, lay across his knees.

Boaz was not asleep. He was lying on his bunk across the cabin from Unk. Boaz had not slept a wink. He could now, if he wanted to, disarm and kill Unk easily.

But Boaz had decided that he needed a buddy far more than he needed a means of making people do exactly what he wanted them to. During the night, he had become very unsure of what he wanted people to do, anyway.

Not to be lonely, not to be scared—Boaz had decided that those were the important things in life. A real buddy could help more than anything.

The cabin was filled with a strange, rustling, coughing sound. It was laughter. It was Boaz's laughter. What made it so strange was that Boaz had never laughed in that particular way before—had never laughed before at the things he was laughing at now.

He was laughing at the ferocious mess he was in—at the way he had pretended all his army life that he had understood everything that was going on, and that everything that was going on was just fine.

He was laughing at the dumb way he had let himself be used—by God knows who for God knows what.

"Holy smokes, buddy," he said out loud, "what we doing way out here in space? What we doing in these here clothes? Who's steering this fool thing? How come we climbed into this tin can? How come we got to shoot somebody when we get to where we're going? How come he got to try and shoot us? How come?" said Boaz. "Buddy," he said, "you tell me how come?"

Unk woke up, swung the muzzle of his Mauser around to Boaz.

Boaz went right on laughing. He took the control box out of his pocket, and he threw it on the floor. "I don't want it, buddy," he said. "That's O.K. you went and tore its insides out. I don't want it."

And then he yelled, "I don't want *none* of this crap!"

CHAPTER EIGHT

IN A HOLLYWOOD NIGHT CLUB

HARMONIUM—The only known form of life on
the planet Mercury. The harmonium is a cave-
dweller. A more gracious creature would be hard
to imagine.

—*A Child's Cyclopedia
of Wonders and Things to do.*

THE PLANET Mercury sings like a crystal goblet.

It sings all the time.

One side of Mercury faces the Sun. That side has always
faced the Sun. That side is a sea of white-hot dust.

The other side faces the nothingness of space eternal.
That side has always faced the nothingness of space eternal.
That side is a forest of giant blue-white crystals, aching
cold.

It is the tension between the hot hemisphere of day-
without-end and the cold hemisphere of night-without-end
that makes Mercury sing.

Mercury has no atmosphere, so the song it sings is for
the sense of touch.

The song is a slow one. Mercury will hold a single note
in the song for as long as an Earthling millennium. There
are those who think that the song was quick, wild and brilliant once—excruciatingly various. Possibly so.

There are creatures in the deep caves of Mercury.

The song their planet sings is important to them, for
the creatures are nourished by vibrations. They feed on
mechanical energy.

The creatures cling to the singing walls of their caves.

In that way, they eat the song of Mercury.

The caves of Mercury are cozily warm in their depths.

The walls of the caves in their depths are phosphorescent.
They give off a jonquil-yellow light.

The creatures in the caves are translucent. When they
cling to the walls, light from the phosphorescent walls
comes right through them. The yellow light from the walls,

however, is turned, when passed through the bodies of the creatures, to a vivid aquamarine.

The creatures in the caves look very much like small and spineless kites. They are diamond-shaped, a foot high and eight inches wide when fully mature.

They have no more thickness than the skin of a toy balloon.

Each creature has four feeble suction cups—one at each of its corners. These cups enable it to creep, something like a measuring worm, and to cling, and to feel out the places where the song of Mercury is best.

Having found a place that promises a good meal, the creatures lay themselves against the wall like wet wall-paper.

There is no need for a circulatory system in the creatures. They are so thin that life-giving vibrations can make all their cells tingle without intermediaries.

The creatures do not excrete.

The creatures reproduce by flaking. The young, when shed by a parent, are indistinguishable from dandruff.

There is only one sex.

Every creature simply sheds flakes of his own kind, and his own kind is like everybody else's kind.

There is no childhood as such. Flakes begin flaking three Earthling hours after they themselves have been shed.

They do not reach maturity, then deteriorate and die. They reach maturity and stay in full bloom, so to speak, for as long as Mercury cares to sing.

There is no way in which one creature can harm another, and no motive for one's harming another.

Hunger, envy, ambition, fear, indignation, religion, and sexual lust are irrelevant and unknown.

The creatures have only one sense: touch.

They have weak powers of telepathy. The messages they are capable of transmitting and receiving are almost as monotonous as the song of Mercury. They have only two possible messages. The first is an automatic response to the second, and the second is an automatic response to the first.

The first is, *"Here I am, here I am, here I am."*

The second is, *"So glad you are, so glad you are, so glad are."*

There is one last characteristic of the creatures that has not been explained on utilitarian grounds: the creatures seem to like to arrange themselves in striking patterns on the phosphorescent walls.

Though blind and indifferent to anyone's watching, they often arrange themselves so as to present a regular and dazzling pattern of jonquil-yellow and vivid aquamarine diamonds. The yellow comes from the bare cave walls. The aquamarine is the light of the walls filtered through the bodies of the creatures.

Because of their love for music and their willingness to deploy themselves in the service of beauty, the creatures are given a lovely name by Earthlings.

They are called *harmoniums*.

Unk and Boaz came in for a landing on the dark side of Mercury, seventy-nine Earthling days out of Mars. They did not know that the planet on which they were landing was Mercury.

They thought the Sun was terrifyingly large.

But that didn't keep them from thinking that they were landing on Earth.

They blacked out during the period of sharp deceleration. Now they were regaining consciousness—were being treated to a cruel and lovely illusion.

It seemed to Unk and Boaz that their ship was settling slowly among Skyscrapers over which searchlights played.

"They aren't shooting," said Boaz. "Either the war's over, or it ain't begun."

The merry beams of light they saw were not from searchlights. The beams came from tall crystals on the borderline between the light and dark hemispheres of Mercury. Those crystals were catching beams from the sun, were bending them prismatically, playing them over the dark side. Other crystals on the dark side caught the beams and passed them on.

It was easy to believe that the searchlights were playing over a sophisticated civilization indeed. It was easy to mistake the dense forest of giant blue-white crystals for skyscrapers, stupendous and beautiful.

Unk, standing at a porthole, wept quietly. He was weeping for love, for family, for friendship, for truth, for civilization. The things he wept for were all abstractions, since his memory could furnish few faces or artifacts with which his imagination might fashion a passion play. Names rattled

in his head like dry bones. *Stony Stevenson, a friend . . .*
Bee, a wife . . . Chrono, a son . . . Unk, a father . . .

The name *Malachi Constant* came to him, and he didn't
know what to do with it.

Unk lapsed into a blank reverie, a blank respect for the
splendid people and the splendid lives that had produced
the majestic buildings that the searchlights swept. Here,
surely, faceless families and faceless friends and nameless
hopes could flourish like—

An apt image for flourishing eluded Unk.

He imagined a remarkable fountain, a cone described by
descending bowls of increasing diameters. It wouldn't do.
The fountain was bone dry, filled with the ruins of birds'
nests. Unk's fingertips tingled, as though abraded by a
climb up the dry bowls.

The image wouldn't do.

Unk imagined again the three beautiful girls who had
beckoned him to come down the oily bore of his Mauser
rifle.

"Man!" said Boaz, "everybody asleep—but not for
long!" He cooed, and his eyes flashed. "When old Boaz
and old Unk hits town," he said, "everybody going to wake
up and stay woke up for weeks on end!"

The ship was being controlled skillfully by its pilot-
navigator. The equipment was talking nervously to itself—
cycling, whirring, clicking, buzzing. It was sensing and
avoiding hazards to the sides, seeking an ideal landing
place below.

The designers of the pilot-navigator had purposely obsessed the equipment with one idea—and that idea was
to seek shelter for the precious troops and matériel it was
supposed to be carrying. The pilot-navigator was to set the
precious troops and matériel down in the deepest hole it
could find. The assumption was that the landing would be
in the face of hostile fire.

Twenty Earthling minutes later, the pilot-navigator was
still talking to itself finding as much to talk about as ever.

And the ship was still falling, and falling fast.

The seeming searchlights and skyscrapers outside were
no longer to be seen. There was only inky blackness.

Inside the ship, there was silence of a hardly lighter
shade. Unk and Boaz sensed what was happening to them—
found what was happening unspeakable.

They sensed correctly that they were being buried alive.

The ship lurched suddenly, throwing Boaz and Unk to the floor.

The violence brought violent relief.

"Home at last," yelled Boaz. "Welcome home!"

Then the ghastly feeling of the leaf-like fall began again. Twenty Earthling minutes later, the ship was still falling gently.

Its lurches were more frequent.

To protect themselves against the lurches, Boaz and Unk had gone to bed. They lay face down, their hands gripping the steel pipe supports of their bunks.

To make their misery complete, the pilot-navigator decreed that night should fall in the cabin.

A grinding noise passed over the dome of the ship, forced Unk and Boaz to turn their eyes from their pillows to the portholes. There was a pale yellow light outside now.

Unk and Boaz shouted for joy, ran to the portholes. They reached them just in time to be thrown to the floor again as the ship freed itself from an obstruction, began its fall again.

One Earthling minute later, the fall stopped.

There was a modest click from the pilot-navigator. Having delivered its cargo safely from Mars to Mercury, as instructed, it had shut itself off.

It had delivered its cargo to the floor of a cave one hundred and sixteen miles below the surface of Mercury. It had threaded its way down through a tortuous system of chimneys until it could go no deeper.

Boaz was the first to reach a porthole, to look out and see the gay welcome of yellow and aquamarine diamonds the harmoniums had made on the walls.

"Unk!" said Boaz. "God damn if it didn't go and set us down right in the middle of a Hollywood night club!"

A recapitulation of Schleimann breathing techniques is in order at this point, in order that what happened next can be fully understood. Unk and Boaz, in their pressurized cabin, had been getting their oxygen from goofballs in their small intestines. But, living in an atmosphere under pressure, there was no need for them to plug their ears and nostrils, and keep their mouths shut tight. This sealing off was necessary only in a vacuum or in a poisonous atmosphere.

Boaz was under the impression that outside the space ship was the wholesome atmosphere of his native Earth.

Actually, there was nothing out there but a vacuum.

Boaz threw open both the inner and outer doors of the airlock with a grand carelessness predicated on a friendly atmosphere outside.

He was rewarded with the explosion of the small atmosphere of the cabin into the vacuum outside.

He slammed shut the inner door, but not before he and Unk had haemorrhaged in the act of shouting for joy.

They collapsed, their respiratory systems bleeding profusely.

All that saved them from death was a fully automatic emergency system that answered the explosion with another, bringing the pressure of the cabin up to normal again.

"Mama," said Boaz, as he came to. "God damn, Mama— this sure as hell ain't Earth."

Unk and Boaz did not panic.

They restored their strength with food, rest, drink, and goofballs.

And they then plugged their ears and nostrils, shut their mouths, and explored the neighbourhood of the ship. They determined that their tomb was deep, tortuous, endless— airless, uninhabited by anything remotely human, and uninhabitable by anything remotely human.

They noted the presence of the harmoniums, but could find nothing encouraging in the presence of the creatures there. The creatures seemed ghastly.

Unk and Boaz didn't really believe they were in such a place. Not believing it was the thing that saved them from panic.

They returned to their ship.

"O.K.," said Boaz calmly. "There has been some mistake. We have wound up too deep in the ground. We got to fly back on up to where them buildings are. I tell you frankly, Unk, it don't seem like to me this is even Earth we're in. There's been some mistake, like I say, and we got to ask the folks in the buildings where we are."

"O.K." said Unk. He licked his lips.

"Just push that old *on* button," said Boaz, "and up we fly like a bird."

"O.K.," said Unk.

"I mean," said Boaz, "up there, the folks in the build-

136

ings may not even *know* about all this down here. Maybe we discovered something they'll be just *amazed* about."

"Sure," said Unk. His soul felt the pressure of the miles of rock above. And his soul felt the true nature of their predicament. On all sides and overhead were passages that branched and branched and branched. And the branches forked to twigs, and the twigs forked to passages no larger than a human pore.

Unk's soul was right in feeling that not one branch in ten thousand led all the way to the surface.

The space ship, thanks to the brilliantly-conceived sensing gear on its bottom, had sensed its way easily down and down and down, through one of the very few ways in— down and down and down one of the very few ways out.

What Unk's soul hadn't suspected yet was the congenital stupidity of the pilot-navigator when it came to going up. It had never occurred to the designers that the ship might encounter problems in going up. All Martian ships, after all, were meant to take off from an unobstructed field on Mars, and to be abandoned after landing on Earth. Consequently, there was virtually no sensing equipment on the ship for hazards overhead.

"So long, old cave," said Boaz.

Casually, Unk pressed the *on* button.

The pilot-navigator hummed.

In ten Earthling seconds, the pilot-navigator was warm.

The ship left the cave floor with whispering ease, touched a wall, dragged its rim up the wall with a grinding, tearing scream, bashed its dome on an overhead projection, backed off, bashed its dome again, backed off, grazed the projection, climbed whisperingly again. Then came a grinding scream again—this time from all sides.

All upward motion had stopped.

The ship was wedged in solid rock.

The pilot-navigator whimpered.

It sent a wisp of mustard-coloured smoke up through the floorboards of the cabin.

The pilot-navigator stopped whimpering.

It had overheated, and overheating was a signal for the pilot-navigator to extricate the ship from a hopeless mess. This it proceeded to do—grindingly. Steel members groaned. Rivets snapped like rifle shots.

At last the ship was free.

The pilot-navigator knew when it was licked. It flew the ship back down to the cave floor, landing with a kiss.

The pilot-navigator shut itself off.

Unk pushed the *on* button again.

Again the ship blundered up into a blind passage, again retreated, again settled to the floor and shut itself off.

The cycle was repeated a dozen times, until it was plain that the ship would only bash itself to pieces. Already its frame was badly sprung.

When the ship settled to the cave floor for the twelfth time, Unk and Boaz went to pieces. They cried.

"We're dead, Unk—we're dead!" said Boaz.

"I've never been alive that I can remember," said Unk brokenly. "I thought I was finally going to get some living done."

Unk went to a porthole, looked out with streaming eyes.

He saw that the creatures nearest the porthole had outlined in aquamarine a perfect, pale yellow letter T.

The making of a T was well within the limits of probability for brainless creatures distributing themselves at random. But then Unk saw that the T was preceded by a perfect S. And the S was preceded by a perfect E.

Unk moved his head to one side, looked through the porthole obliquely. The movement gave him a perspective down a hundred yards of harmonium-infested wall.

Unk was flabbergasted to see that the harmoniums were forming a message in dazzling letters.

The message was this, in pale yellow, outlined in aquamarine:

IT'S AN INTELLIGENCE TEST!

CHAPTER NINE

A PUZZLE SOLVED

In the beginning, God became the Heaven and
the Earth. . . . And God said, 'Let Me be light,'
and He was light.
>   —*The Winston Niles Rumfoord*
>   *Authorized Revised Bible*

For a delicious tea snack, try young harmoniums rolled into tubes and filled with Venusian
cottage cheese.
>   —*The Beatrice Rumfoord*
>   *Galactic Cookbook*

In terms of their souls, the martyrs of Mars
died not when they attacked Earth but when they
were recruited for the Martian war machine.
>   —*The Winston Niles Rumfoord*
>   *Pocket History of Mars*

I found me a place where I can do good without
doing any harm.
>   —BOAZ IN SARAH HORNE CANBY'S
>   *Unk and Boaz in the Caves of Mercury*

THE BEST-SELLING book in recent times has been *The
Winston Niles Rumfoord Authorized Revised Bible*. Next
in popularity is that delightful forgery, *The Beatrice Rumfoord Galactic Cookbook*. The third most popular is *The
Winston Niles Rumfoord Pocket History of Mars*. The
fourth most popular is a children's book, *Unk and Boaz in
the Caves of Mercury*, by Sarah Horne Canby.

The publisher's bland analysis of Mrs. Canby's book's
success appears on the dust jacket: "What child wouldn't
like to be shipwrecked on a space ship with a cargo of
hamburgers, hot dogs, catsup, sporting goods, and soda
pop?"

Dr. Frank Minot, in his *Are Adults Harmoniums?*, sees
something more sinister in the love children have for the

book. "Dare we consider," he asks, "how close Unk and Boaz are to the everyday experience of children when Unk and Boaz deal solemnly and respectfully with creatures that are in fact obscenely unmotivated, insensitive, and dull?" Minot, in drawing a parallel between human parents and harmoniums, refers to the dealings of Unk and Boaz with harmoniums. The harmoniums spelled out for Unk and Boaz a new message of hope or veiled derision every fourteen Earthling days—for three years.

The messages were written, of course, by Winston Niles Rumfoord, who materialized briefly on Mercury at fourteen-day intervals. He peeled off harmoniums here, slapped others up there, making the block letters.

In Mrs. Canby's tale, the first intimation given that Rumfoord is around the caves from time to time is given in a scene very close to the end—a scene wherein Unk finds the tracks of a big dog in the dust.

At this point in the story it is mandatory, if an adult is reading the story aloud to a child, for the adult to ask the child with delicious hoarseness, "Who wuzza dog?"

Dog wuzza Kazak. Dog wuzza Winston Niles Rumfoord's great big mean chrono-synclastic infundibulated dog.

Unk and Boaz had been on Mercury for three Earthling years when Unk found Kazak's footprints in the dust on the floor of a cave corridor. Mercury had carried Unk and Boaz twelve and a half times around the Sun.

Unk found the prints on a floor six miles above the chamber in which the dented, scarred, and rock-bound space ship lay. Unk didn't live in the space ship any more, and neither did Boaz. The space ship served as a common supply base to which Unk and Boaz returned for provisions once every Earthling month or so.

Unk and Boaz rarely met. They moved in very different circles.

The circles in which Boaz moved were small. His abode was fixed and richly furnished. It was on the same level as the space ship, only a quarter of a mile away from it.

The circles in which Unk moved were vast and restless. He had no home. He travelled light and he travelled far, climbing ever higher until he was stopped by cold. Where the cold stopped Unk, the cold stopped the harmoniums, too. On the upper levels where Unk wandered, the harmoniums were stunted and few.

On the cozy lower level where Boaz lived, the harmoniums were plentiful and fast-growing.

Boaz and Unk had separated after one Earthling year together in the space ship. In that first year together, it had become clear to both of them that they weren't going to get out unless something or somebody came and got them out.

That had been clear, even though the creatures on the walls continued to spell out new messages emphasizing the *fairness* of the test to which Unk and Boaz were being subjected, the ease with which they might escape, if only they would think a little harder, if they would only think a little more intricately.

"THINK!" the creatures would say.

Unk and Boaz separated after Unk went temporarily insane. Unk had tried to murder Boaz. Boaz had come into the space ship with a harmonium, which was exactly like all the other harmoniums, and he'd said, "Ain't he a cute little feller, Unk?"

Unk had gone for Boaz's throat.

Unk was naked when he found the dog tracks. The lichen-green uniform and black fibre boots of the Martian Assault Infantry had been scoured to threads and dust by the touch of stone.

The dog tracks did not excite Unk. Unk's soul wasn't filled with the music of sociability or the light of hope when he saw a warm-blooded creature's tracks, saw the tracks of man's best friend. And he still had very little to say to himself when the tracks of a well-shod man joined those of the dog.

Unk was at war with his environment. He had come to regard his environment as being either malevolent or cruelly mismanaged. His response was to fight it with the only weapons at hand—passive resistance and open displays of contempt.

The footprints seemed to Unk to be the opening moves in one more fat-headed game his environment wanted to play. He would follow the tracks, but lazily, without excitement. He would follow them simply because he had nothing else scheduled for the time.

He would follow them.

He would see where they went.

His progress was knobby and ramshackle. Poor Unk had lost a lot of weight, and a lot of hair, too. He was aging fast. His eyes felt hot and his skeleton felt rickety.

Unk never shaved on Mercury. When his hair and beard got so long as to be a bother, he would hack away wads of thatch with a butcherknife.

Boaz shaved every day. Boaz gave himself a haircut twice an Earthling week with a barber kit from the space ship.

Boaz, twelve years younger than Unk, had never felt better in his life. He had gained weight in the caves of Mercury—and serenity, too.

Boaz's home vault was furnished with a cot, a table, two chairs, a punching bag, a mirror, dumbells, a tape recorder, and a library of recorded music on tape consisting of eleven hundred compositions.

Boaz's home vault had a door on it, a round boulder with which he could plug the vault's mouth. The door was necessary, since Boaz was God Almighty to the harmoniums. They could locate him by his heart beat.

Had he slept with his door open, he would have awakened to find himself pinned down by hundreds of thousands of his admirers. They would have let him up only when his heart stopped beating.

Boaz, like Unk, was naked. But he still had shoes. His genuine leather shoes had held up gorgeously. True—Unk had walked fifty miles to every mile walked by Boaz, but Boaz's shoes had not merely held up. They looked as good as new.

Boaz wiped, waxed, and shined them regularly.

He was shining them now.

The door of his vault was blocked by the boulder. Only four favored harmoniums were inside with him. Two were wrapped about his upper arms. One was stuck to his thigh. The fourth, an immature harmonium only three inches long, clung to the inside of his left wrist, feeding on Boaz's pulse.

When Boaz found a harmonium he loved more than all the rest, that was what he did—let the creature feed on his pulse.

"You like that?" he said in his thoughts to the lucky harmonium. "Ain't that nice?"

He had never felt better physically, had never felt better mentally, had never felt better spiritually. He was glad he and Unk had separated, because Unk liked to twist things around to where it seemed that anybody who was happy was dumb or crazy.

"What makes a man *be* like that?" Boaz asked the little harmonium in his thoughts. "What's he think he's gaining compared to what he's throwing away? No wonder he looks sick."

Boaz shook his head. "I kept trying to interest him in you fellers, and he just got madder. Never helps to get mad.

"I don't know what's going on," said Boaz in his thoughts, "and I'm probably not smart enough to understand if somebody was to explain it to me. All I know is we're being tested somehow, by somebody or something a whole lot smarter than us, and all I can do is be friendly and keep calm and try and have a nice time till it's over."

Boaz nodded. "That's my philosophy, friends," he said to the harmoniums stuck to him. "And if I'm not mistaken, that's yours, too. I reckon that's how come we hit it off so good."

The genuine leather toe of the shoe that Boaz was shining glowed like a ruby.

"Men—awww now, men, men, men," said Boaz to himself, staring into the ruby. When he shined his shoes, he imagined that he could see many things in the rubies of the toes.

Right now, Boaz was looking into a ruby and seeing Unk strangling poor old Stony Stevenson at the stone stake on the iron parade ground back on Mars. The horrible image wasn't a random recollection. It was dead centre in Boaz's relationship with Unk.

"Don't *truth* me," said Boaz in his thoughts, "and I won't *truth* you." It was a plea he had made several times to Unk.

Boaz had invented the plea, and its meaning was this: Unk was to stop telling Boaz truths about the harmoniums, because Boaz loved the harmoniums, and because Boaz was nice enough not to bring up truths that would make Unk unhappy.

Unk didn't know that he had strangled his friend Stony Stevenson. Unk thought Stony was still marvellously alive somewhere in the Universe. Unk was living on dreams of a reunion with Stony.

Boaz was nice enough to withhold the truth from Unk, no matter how great the provocation had been to club Unk between the eyes with it.

The horrible image in the ruby dissolved.

"Yes, Lord," said Boaz in his thoughts.

The adult harmonium on Boaz's upper left arm stirred.

"You are asking old Boaz for a concert?" Boaz asked the creature in his thoughts. "That what you trying to say? You trying to say, 'Ol' Boaz, I don't want to sound ungrateful, on account of I know it's a great honour to get to be right here close to your heart. Only I keep thinking about all my friends outside, and I keep wishing they could have something good, too.' That what you trying to say?" said Boaz in his thoughts. "You trying to say, 'Please, Papa Boaz—put on a concert for all the poor friends outside?' That what you trying to say?"

Boaz smiled. "You don't have to flatter me," he said to the harmonium.

The small harmonium on his wrist doubled up, extended itself again. "What *you* trying to tell me?" he asked it. "You trying to say 'Uncle Boaz—your pulse is just too rich for a little tad like me. Uncle Boaz—please just play some nice, sweet, easy music to eat?' That what you trying to say?"

Boaz turned his attention to the harmonium on his right arm. The creature had not moved. "Aren't *you* the quiet one, though?" Boaz asked the creature in his thoughts. "Don't say much, but thinking all the time. I guess you're thinking old Boaz is pretty mean not just letting the music play all the time, huh?"

The harmonium on his left arm stirred again. "What's that you say?" said Boaz in his thoughts. He cocked his head, pretended to listen, though no sounds could travel through the vacuum in which he lived. "You say, 'Please, King Boaz, play us the *1812 Overture*?'" Boaz looked shocked, then stern. "Just because something feels better than anything else," he said in his thoughts, "that don't mean it's good for you."

Scholars whose field is the Martian War often exclaim over the queer unevenness of Rumfoord's war preparations. In some areas, his plans were horribly flimsy. The shoes he issued his ordinary troops, for instance, were almost a satire on the temporariness of the Jerry-built society of Mars—on a society whose whole purpose was to destroy itself in uniting the peoples on Earth.

In the music libraries Rumfoord personally selected for the company mother ships, however, one sees a great cultural nest egg—a nest egg prepared as though for a monumental civilization that was going to endure for a thousand Earthling years. It is said that Rumfoord spent more time on the useless music libraries than he did on artillery and field sanitation combined.

As an anonymous wit has it: "The Army of Mars arrived with three hundred hours of continuous music, and didn't last long enough to hear *The Minute Waltz* to the end."

The explanation of the bizarre emphasis on the music carried by the Martian mother ships is simple: Rumfoord was crazy about good music—a craze, incidentally, that struck him only after he had been spread through time and space by the chrono-synclastic infundibulum.

The harmoniums in the caves of Mercury were crazy about good music, too. They had been feeding on one sustained note in the song of Mercury for centuries. When Boaz gave them their first taste of music, which happened to be *Le Sacré du Printemps*, some of the creatures actually died in ecstasy.

A dead harmonium is shrivelled and orange in the yellow light of the Mercurial caves. A dead harmonium looks like a dried apricot.

On that first occasion, which hadn't been planned as a concert for the harmoniums, the tape recorder had been on the floor of the space ship. The creatures who had actually died in ecstasy had been in direct contact with the metal hull of the ship.

Now, two and a half years later, Boaz demonstrated the proper way to stage a concert for the creatures so as not to kill them.

Boaz left his home vault, carrying the tape recorder and the musical selections for the concert with him. In the corridor outside were two aluminum ironing boards. These had fibre pads on their feet. The ironing boards were six feet apart, and spanning them was a stretcher made of aluminium poles and lichen-fibre canvas.

Boaz placed the tape recorder in the middle of the stretcher. The purpose of the engine resulting was to dilute and dilute and dilute the vibrations from the tape recorder. The vibrations, before they reached the stone floor, had to struggle through the dead canvas of the stretcher, down the stretcher handles, through the ironing boards, and finally through the fibre pads on the feet of the ironing boards.

The dilution was a safety measure. It guaranteed that no harmonium would get a lethal overdose of music.

Boaz now put the tape in the recorder and turned the recorder on. Throughout the concert, he would stand guard by the apparatus. His duty was to see that no creature crept too close to the apparatus. His duty, when a creature crept too close, was to peel the creature from the wall or floor, scold it, and paste it up again a hundred yards or more away.

"If you ain't got no more sense than that," he would say in his thoughts to the foolhardy harmonium, "you're going to wind up out here in left field ever' time. Think it over."

Actually, a creature placed a hundred yards from the tape recorder still got plenty of music to eat.

The walls of the caves were so extraordinarily conductive, in fact, that harmoniums on cave walls miles away got whiffs of Boaz's concerts through the stone.

Unk, who had been following the tracks deeper and deeper into the caves, could tell from the way the harmoniums were behaving that Boaz was staging a concert. He had reached a warm level where the harmoniums were thick. Their regular pattern of alternating yellow and aquamarine diamonds was breaking up—was degenerating into jagged clumps, pinwheels, and lightning bolts. The music was making them do it.

Unk laid his pack down, then laid himself down to rest.

Unk dreamed about colours other than yellow and aquamarine.

Then he dreamed that his good friend Stony Stevenson was waiting for him around the next bend. His mind became lively with the things he and Stony would say when they met. Unk's mind still had no face to go with the name of Stony Stevenson, but that didn't matter much.

"What a pair," Unk said to himself. By that he meant that he and Stony, working together, would be invincible.

"I tell you," Unk said to himself with satisfaction, "that is one pair they want to keep apart at all costs. If old Stony and old Unk ever get together again, they better watch out. When old Stony and old Unk get together, anything can happen, and it usually does."

Old Unk chuckled.

The people who were supposedly afraid of Unk's and Stony's getting together were the people in the big, beautiful buildings up above. Unk's imagination had done a lot in three years with the glimpses he'd had of the supposed buildings—of what were in fact solid, dead, dumb-cold crystals. Unk's imagination was now certain that the masters of all creation lived in those buildings. They were Unk's and Boaz's and maybe Stony's jailers. They were experimenting with Unk and Boaz in the caves. They wrote the messages in harmoniums. The harmoniums didn't have anything to do with the messages.

Unk knew all those things for sure.

Unk knew a lot of other things for sure. He even knew how the buildings up above were furnished. The furniture didn't have any legs on it. It just floated in air, suspended by magnetism.

And the people never worked at all, and they never worried about a thing.

Unk hated them.

He hated the harmoniums, too. He peeled a harmonium from the wall and tore it in two. It shriveled at once—turned orange.

Unk flipped the two-piece corpse at the ceiling. And, looking up at the ceiling, he saw a new message written there. The message was disintegrating, because of the music. But it was still legible.

The message told Unk in five words how to escape surely, easily, and swiftly from the caves. He was bound to admit, when given the solution to the puzzle that he had failed to solve in three years, that the puzzle was simple and fair.

Unk scuttled down through the caves until he came upon Boaz's concert for the harmoniums. Unk was wild and bug-eyed with big news. He could not speak in a vacuum, so he hauled Boaz to the space ship.

There, in the inert atmosphere of the cabin, Unk told Boaz of the message that meant escape from the caves.

It was now Boaz's turn to react numbly. Boaz had thrilled to the slightest illusion of intelligence on the part of the harmoniums—but now, having heard the news that he was about to be freed from his prison, Boaz was strangely reserved.

"That—that explains that other message," said Boaz softly.

"What other message?" asked Unk.

Boaz held up his hands to represent a message that had appeared on the wall outside his home four Earthling days before. "Said, 'BOAZ, DON'T GO!'" said Boaz. He looked down self-consciously. "'WE LOVE YOU, BOAZ.' That's what it said."

Boaz dropped his hands to his side, turned away as though turning away from unbearable beauty. "I saw that," he said, "and I had to smile. I looked at them sweet, gentle fellers on the wall there, and I says to myself, 'Boys—how's old Boaz ever going to go anywhere? Old Boaz, he going to be stuck here for quite some time yet!'"

"It's a trap!" said Unk.

"It's a what?" said Boaz.

"A trap!" said Unk. "A trick to keep us here!"

The comic book called *Tweety and Sylvester* was open on the table before Boaz. Boaz didn't answer Unk right away. He leafed through the ragged book instead. "I expect," he said at last.

Unk thought about the crazy appeal in the name of love. He did something he hadn't done for a long time. He laughed. He thought it was an hysterical ending for the nightmare—that the brainless membranes on the walls should speak of love.

Boaz suddenly grabbed Unk, rattled poor Unk's dry bones. "I'd appreciate it, Unk," said Boaz tautly, "if you'd just let me think whatever I'm going to think about that message about how they love me. I mean," he said, "you know," he said, "it don't necessarily have to make sense to you. I mean," he said, "you know," he said, "there ain't really any call for you to say anything about it, one way or the other. I mean," he said, "you know," he said, "these animals ain't necessarily your dish. You don't necessarily have to like 'em, or understand 'em, or say anything about 'em. I mean," said Boaz, "you know," said Boaz, "the message wasn't addressed to you. It's me they said they loved. That lets you out."

He let Unk go, turned attention to the comic book again. His broad, brown, slab-muscled back amazed Unk. Living apart from Boaz, Unk had flattered himself into thinking he was a physical match for Boaz. He saw now what a pathetic delusion this had been.

The muscles in Boaz's back slid over one another in slow patterns that were counterpoint to the quick movements of his page-turning fingers. "You know so much about traps and things," said Boaz. "How you know there ain't some worse trap waiting for us if we go flying out of here?"

Before Unk could answer him, Boaz remembered that he had left the tape recorder playing and unguarded.

"Ain't nobody watching out for 'em at all!" he cried. He left Unk, ran to rescue the harmoniums.

While Boaz was gone, Unk made plans for turning the space ship upside down. That was the solution to the puzzle of how to get out. That was what the harmoniums on the ceiling had said:

UNK, TURN SHIP UPSIDE DOWN.

The theory of turning the space ship over was sound, of course. The ship's sensing equipment was on its bottom. When turned over, the ship would be able to apply the same easy grace and intelligence to getting out of the caves that it had used in getting into them.

Thanks to a power winch and the feeble tug of gravity in the caves of Mercury, Unk had the ship turned over by the time Boaz got back. All that remained to be done for the trip out was to press the *on* button. The upside-down ship would then blunder against the cave floor, give up, retreat from the floor under the impression that the floor was a ceiling.

It would go up the system of chimneys under the impression that it was coming down. And it would inevitably find the way out, under the impression that it was seeking the deepest possible hole.

The hole it would eventually find itself in would be the bottomless, sideless pit of space eternal.

Boaz came into the upside-down ship, his arms loaded with dead harmoniums. He was carrying four quarts or more of the seeming dried apricots. Inevitably he dropped some. And, in stooping to pick them up reverently, he dropped more.

Tears were streaming down his face.

"You see?" said Boaz. He was raging heartbrokenly against himself. "You see, Unk?" he said. "See what happens when somebody just runs off and forgets?"

Boaz shook his head. "This ain't all of 'em," he said. "This ain't *near* all of 'em." He found an empty carton that had once contained candy bars. He put the harmonium corpses into that.

He straightened up, his hands on his hips. Just as Unk had been amazed by Boaz's physical condition, so was Unk now amazed by Boaz's dignity.

Boaz, when he straightened up, was a wise, decent, weeping, brown Hercules.

Unk, by comparison, felt scrawny, rootless, and soreheaded.

"You want to do the dividing, Unk?" said Boaz.

"Dividing?" said Unk.

"Goofballs, food, soda pop, candy," said Boaz.

"Divide it all?" said Unk. "My God—there's enough of everything for five hundred years." There had never been any talk of dividing things before. There had been no shortage, and no threat of a shortage of anything.

"Half for you to take with you, and half to leave here with me," said Boaz.

"*Leave* with you?" said Unk incredulously. "You're—you're coming with me, aren't you?"

Boaz held up his big right hand, and it was a tender gesture for silence, a gesture made by a thoroughly great human being. "Don't truth me, Unk," said Boaz, "and I won't truth you." He brushed away his tears with a fist.

Unk had never been able to brush aside the plea about truthing. It frightened him. Some part of his mind warned him that Boaz was not bluffing, that Boaz really knew a truth about Unk that could tear him to pieces.

Unk opened his mouth and closed it again.

"You come and tell me the big news," said Boaz. "'Boaz,' you say, 'we're going to be free!' And I get all

150

excited, and I drop everything I'm doin', and I get set to be free.

"And I keep saying it over to myself about how I'm going to be free," said Boaz, "and then I try to think what that's going to be like, and all I can see is people. They push me this way, then they push me that—and nothing pleases 'em, and they get madder and madder, on account of nothing makes 'em happy. And they holler at me on account of I ain't made 'em happy, and we all push and pull some more.

"And then, all of a sudden," said Boaz, "I remember all the crazy little animals I been making so happy so easy with music. And I go find thousands of 'em lying around dead, on account of Boaz forgot all about 'em, he was so excited about being free. And ever' one of them lost lives I could have saved, if I'd have just kept my mind on what I was doing.

"And then I say to myself," said Boaz, "'I ain't never been nothing good to people, and people never been nothing good to me. So what I want to be free in crowds of people for?'

"And then I knew what I was going to say to you, Unk, when I got back here," said Boaz.

Boaz now said it:

"I found me a place where I can do good without doing any harm, and I can see I'm doing good, and them I'm doing good for know I'm doing it, and they love me, Unk, as best they can. I found me a home.

"And when I die down here some day," said Boaz, "I'm going to be able to say to myself, 'Boaz—you made millions of lives worth living. Ain't nobody ever spread more joy. You ain't got an enemy in the Universe,'" Boaz became for himself the affectionate Mama and Papa he'd never had. "'You go to sleep now,'" he said to himself, imagining himself on a stone deathbed in the caves. "'You're a good boy, Boaz,'" he said. "'Good night.'"

CHAPTER TEN

AN AGE OF MIRACLES

"O Lord Most High, Creator of the Cosmos, Spinner of Galaxies, Soul of Electromagnetic Waves, Inhaler and Exhaler of Inconceivable Volumes of Vacuum, Spitter of Fire and Rock, Trifler with Millennia—what could we do for Thee that Thou couldst not do for Thyself one octillion times better? Nothing. What could we do or say that could possibly interest Thee? Nothing. Oh, Mankind, rejoice in the apathy of our Creator, for it makes us free and truthful and dignified at last. No longer can a fool like Malachi Constant point to a ridiculous accident of good luck and say, 'Somebody up there likes me.' And no longer can a tyrant say, 'God wants this or that to happen, and anybody who doesn't help this or that to happen is against God.' O Lord Most High, what a glorious weapon is Thy Apathy, for we have unsheathed it, have thrust and slashed mightily with it, and the claptrap that has so often enslaved us or driven us into the madhouse lies slain!"

————THE REVEREND C. HORNER REDWINE

It was a Tuesday afternoon. It was springtime in the northern hemisphere of Earth.

Earth was green and watery. The air of earth was good to breathe, as fattening as cream.

The purity of the rains that fell on Earth could be tasted. The taste of purity was daintily tart.

Earth was warm.

The surface of Earth heaved and seethed in fecund restlessness. Earth was most fertile where the most death was.

The daintily tart rain fell on a green place where there was a great deal of death. It fell on a New World country churchyard. The churchyard was in West Barnstaple, Cape

Cod, Massachusetts, U.S.A. The churchyard was full, the spaces between its naturally dead chinked tight by the bodies of the honoured war dead. Martians and Earthlings lay side by side.

There was not a country in the world that did not have graveyards with Earthlings and Martians buried side by side. There was not a country that had not fought a battle in the war of all Earth against the invaders from Mars.

All was forgiven.

All living things were brothers, and all dead things were even more so.

The church, which squatted among the headstones like a wet mother dodo, had been at various times Presbyterian, Congregationalist, Unitarian, and Universal Apocalyptic. It was now the Church of God the Utterly Indifferent.

A seeming wild man stood in the churchyard, wondering at the creamery air, at the green, at the wet. He was almost naked, and his blue-black beard and his hair were tangled and long and shot with gray. The only garment he wore was a clinking breechclout made of wrenches and copper wire.

The garment covered his shame.

The rain ran down his coarse cheeks. He tipped back his head to drink it. He rested his hand on a headstone, more for the feel than the support of it. He was used to the feel of stones—was deathly used to the feel of rough, dry stones. But stones that were wet, stones that were mossy, stones that were squared and written on by men—he hadn't felt stones like that for a long, long time.

Pro patria said the stone he touched.

The man was Unk.

He was home from Mars and Mercury. His space ship had landed itself in a wood next to the churchyard. He was filled with the heedless, tender violence of a man who has had his lifetime cruelly wasted.

Unk was forty-three years old.

He had every reason to wither and die.

All that kept him going was a wish that was more mechanical than emotional. *He wished to be reunited with Bee, his mate, with Chrono, his son, and with Stony Stevenson, his best and only friend.*

The Reverend C. Horner Redwine stood in the pulpit of his church that rainy Tuesday afternoon. There was no one else in the church. Redwine had climbed up to the pulpit in order simply to be as happy as possible. He was not being as happy as possible under adverse circumstances. He was being as happy as possible under extraordinarily happy circumstances—for he was a much loved minister of a religion that not only promised but delivered miracles.

His church, the Barnstable First Church of God the Utterly Indifferent, had a subtitle: *The Church of the Weary Space Wanderer*. The subtitle was justified by this prophecy: That a lone straggler from the Army of Mars would arrive at Redwine's church some day.

The church was ready for the miracle. There was a hand-forged iron spike driven into the rugged oak post behind the pulpit. The post carried the mighty beam that was the rooftree. And on the nail was hung a coathanger encrusted with semiprecious stones. And on the coathanger hung a suit of clothes in a transparent plastic bag.

The prophecy was that the weary Space Wanderer would be naked, that the suit of clothes would fit him like a glove. The suit was of such a design as to fit no one but the right man well. It was one piece, lemon-yellow, rubberized, closed by a zipper, and ideally skin-tight.

The garment was not in the mode of the day. It was a special creation to add glamour to the miracle.

Stitched into the back and front of the garment were orange question marks a foot high. These signified that the Space Wanderer would not know who he was.

No one would know who he was until Winston Niles Rumfoord, the head of all churches of God the Utterly Indifferent, gave the world the Space Wanderer's name.

The signal, should the Space Wanderer arrive, was for Redwine to ring the church bell madly.

When the bell was rung madly, the parishioners were to feel ecstasy, to drop whatever they were doing, to laugh, to weep, to come.

The West Barnstable Volunteer Fire Department was so dominated by members of Redwine's church that the fire engine itself was going to arrive as the only vehicle remotely glorious enough for the Space Wanderer.

The screams of the fire alarm on top of the firehouse

were to be added to the bedlam joy of the bell. One scream from the alarm meant a grass or woods fire. Two screams meant a house fire. Three screams meant a rescue. Ten screams would mean that the Space Wanderer had arrived.

Water seeped in around an ill-fitting window sash. Water crept under a loose shingle in the roof, dropped through a crack and hung in glittering beads from a rafter over Redwine's head. The good rain wet the old Paul Revere bell in the steeple, trickled down the bell rope, soaked the wooden doll tied to the end of the bell rope, dripped from the feet of the doll, made a puddle on the steeple's flagstone floor.

The doll had a religious significance. It represented a repellent way of life that was no more. It was called a *Malachi*. No home or place of business of a member of Redwine's faith was without a Malachi hanging somewhere.

There was only one proper way to hang a Malachi. That was by the neck. There was only one proper knot to use, and that was a hangman's knot.

And the rain dripped from the feet of Redwine's Malachi at the end of the bell rope.

The cold goblin spring of the crocuses was past.

The frail and chilly fairy spring of the daffodils was past.

The springtime for mankind had arrived, and the blooms of the lilac bowers outside Redwine's church hung fatly, heavy as Concord grapes.

Redwine listened to the rain, and imagined that it spoke Chaucerian English. He spoke aloud the words he imagined the rain to be speaking, spoke harmoniously, at just the noise level of the rain.

> *When that Aprille with his shoures sote*
> *The droughte of Marche hath perced to the rote*
> *And bathed every veyne in swich licour,*
> *Of which vertu engendered is the flour—*

A droplet fell twinkling from the rafter overhead, wet the left lens of Redwine's spectacles and his apple cheek.

Time had been kind to Redwine. Standing there in the pulpit, he looked like a ruddy, bespectacled country newsboy, though he was forty-nine. He raised his hand to brush away the wetness on his cheek, and rattled the blue canvas bag of lead shot that was strapped around his wrist.

There were similar bags of shot around his ankles and his other wrist, and two heavy slabs of iron hung on shoulder straps—one slab on his chest and one on his back.

These weights were his handicaps in the race of life.

He carried forty-eight pounds—carried them gladly. A stronger person would have carried more, a weaker person would have carried less. Every strong member of Redwine's faith accepted handicaps gladly, wore them proudly everywhere.

The weakest and meekest were bound to admit, at last, that the race of life was fair.

The liquid melodies of the rain made such lovely backgrounds for any sort of recitation in the empty church that Redwine recited some more. This time he recited something that Winston Niles Rumfoord, the Master of Newport, had written.

The thing that Redwine was about to recite with the rain chorus was a thing that the Master of Newport had written to define the position of himself with respect to his ministers, the position of his ministers with respect to their flocks, and the position of everybody with respect to God. Redwine read it to his flock on the first Sunday of every month.

"'I am not your father,'" said Redwine. "'Rather call me brother. But I am not your brother. Rather call me son. But I am not your son. Rather call me a dog. But I am not your dog. Rather call me a flea on your dog. But I am not a flea. Rather call me a germ on a flea on your dog. As a germ on a flea on your dog, I am eager to serve you in any way I can, just as you are willing to serve God Almighty, Creator of the Universe.'"

Redwine slapped his hands together, killing the imaginary germ-infested flea. On Sundays, the entire congregation slapped the flea in unison.

Another droplet fell shivering from the rafter, wet Redwine's cheek again. Redwine nodded his sweet thanks for the droplet, for the church, for peace, for the Master of Newport, for Earth, for a God Who didn't care, for everything.

He stepped down from the pulpit, making the lead balls in his handicap bags shift back and forth with a stately swish.

He went down the aisle and through the arch under the

steeple. He paused by the puddle under the bell rope, looked up to divine the course the water had taken down. It was a lovely way, he decided, for spring rain to come in. If ever he were in charge of remodelling the church, he would make sure that enterprising drops of rain could still come in that way.

Just beyond the arch under the steeple was another arch, a leafy arch of lilacs.

Redwine now stepped under that second arch, saw the space ship like a great blister in the woods, saw the naked, bearded Space Wanderer in his churchyard.

Redwine cried out for joy. He ran back into his church and jerked and swung on the bell rope like a drunken chimpanzee. In the clanging bedlam of the bells, Redwine heard the words that the Master of Newport said all bells spoke.

"NO HELL!" whang-clanged the bell—
"NO HELL,
"NO HELL,
"NO HELL!"

Unk was terrified by the bell. It sounded like an angry, frightened bell to Unk, and he ran back to his ship, gashing his shin badly as he scrambled over a stone wall. As he was closing the airlock, he heard a siren wailing answers to the bell.

Unk thought Earth was still at war with Mars, and that the siren and the bell were calling sudden death down on him. He pressed the *on* button.

The automatic navigator did not respond instantly, but engaged in a fuzzy, ineffectual argument with itself. The argument ended with the navigator's shutting itself off.

Unk pressed the *on* button again. This time he kept it down by jamming his heel against it.

Again the navigator argued stupidly with itself, tried to shut itself off. When it found it could not shut itself off, it made dirty yellow smoke.

The smoke became so dense and poisonous that Unk was obliged to swallow a goofball and practice Schliemann breathing again.

Then the pilot-navigator gave out a deep, throbbing organ note and died forever.

There was no taking off now. When the pilot-navigator died, the whole space ship died.

Unk went through the smoke to a porthole—looked out.

He saw a fire engine. The fire engine was breaking through the brush to the space ship. Men, women, and children were clinging to the engine—drenched by rain and expressing ecstasy.

Going in advance of the fire engine was the Reverend C. Horner Redwine. In one hand he carried a lemon-yellow suit in a transparent plastic bag. In the other hand he held a spray of fresh-cut lilacs.

The women threw kisses to Unk through the portholes, held their children up to see the adorable man inside. The men stayed with the fire engine, cheered Unk, cheered each other, cheered everything. The driver made the mighty motor backfire, blew the siren, rang the bell.

Everyone wore handicaps of some sort. Most handicaps were of an obvious sort—sashweights, bags of shot, old furnace grates—meant to hamper physical advantages. But there were, among Redwine's parishioners, several true believers who had chosen handicaps of a subtler and more telling kind.

There were women who had received by dint of dumb luck the terrific advantage of beauty. They had annihilated that unfair advantage with frumpish clothes, bad posture, chewing gum, and a ghoulish use of cosmetics.

One old man, whose only advantage was excellent eyesight, had spoiled that eyesight by wearing his wife's spectacles.

A dark young man, whose lithe, predaceous sex appeal could not be spoiled by bad clothes and bad manners, had handicapped himself with a wife who was nauseated by sex.

The dark young man's wife, who had reason to be vain about her Phi Beta Kappa key, had handicapped herself with a husband who read nothing but comic books.

Redwine's congregation was not unique. It wasn't especially fanatical. There were literally billions of happily self-handicapped people on Earth.

And what made them all so happy was that nobody took advantage of anybody any more.

Now the firemen thought of another way to express joy. There was a nozzle mounted amidships on the fire engine.

It could be swiveled around like a machine gun. They aimed it straight up and turned it on. A shivering, unsure fountain climbed into the sky, was torn to shreds by the winds when it could climb no more. The shreds fell all around, now falling on the space ship with splattering thumps; now soaking the firemen themselves; now soaking women and children, startling them, then making them more full of joy than ever.

That water should have played such an important part in the welcoming of Unk was an enchanting accident. No one had planned it. But it was perfect that everyone should forget himself in a festival of universal wetness.

The Reverend C. Horner Redwine, feeling as naked as a pagan wood sprite in the clinging wetness of his clothes, swished a spray of lilacs over the glass of a porthole, then pressed his adoring face against the glass.

The expression of the face that looked back at Redwine was strikingly like the expression on the face of an intelligent ape in a zoo. Unk's forehead was deeply wrinkled, and his eyes were liquid with a hopeless wish to understand.

Unk had decided not to be afraid.

Neither was he in any hurry to let Redwine in.

At last he went to the airlock, unlatched both the inner and outer doors. He stepped back, waiting for someone else to push the doors open.

"First let me go in and have him put on the suit!" said Redwine to his congregation. "Then you can have him!"

There in the space ship, the lemon-yellow suit fitted Unk like a coat of paint. The orange question marks on his chest and back clung without a wrinkle.

Unk did not yet know that no one else in the world was dressed like him. He assumed that many people had suits like this—question marks and all.

"This—this is Earth?" said Unk to Redwine.

"Yes," said Redwine. "Cape Cod, Massachusetts, United States of America, Brotherhood of Man."

"Thank God!" said Unk.

Redwine raised his eyebrows quizzically. "Why?" he said.

"Pardon me?" said Unk.

"Why thank God?" said Redwine. "He doesn't care what happens to you. He didn't go to any trouble to get you here safe and sound, any more than He would go to the trouble to kill you." He raised his arms, demonstrating the muscularity of his faith. The balls of shot in the handicap bags on his wrists shifted swishingly, drawing Unk's attention. From the handicap bags, Unk's attention made an easy jump to the heavy slab of iron on Redwine's chest. Redwine followed the trend of Unk's gaze, hefted the iron slab on his chest. "Heavy," he said.

"Um," said Unk.

"You should carry about fifty pounds, I would guess—after we build you up," said Redwine.

"Fifty pounds?" said Unk.

"You should be glad, not sorry, to carry such a handicap," said Redwine. "No one could then reproach you for taking advantage of the random ways of luck." There crept into his voice a beatifically threatening tone that he had not used much since the earliest days of the Church of God the Utterly Indifferent, since the thrilling mass conversions that had followed the war with Mars. In those days, Redwine and all the other young proselytizers had threatened unbelievers with the righteous displeasure of crowds—righteously displeased crowds that did not then exist.

The righteously displeased crowds existed now in every part of the world. The total membership of Churches of God the Utterly Indifferent was a good, round three billion. The young lions who had first taught the creed could now afford to be lambs, to contemplate such oriental mysteries as water trickling down a bell rope. The disciplinary arm of the Church was in crowds everywhere.

"I must warn you," Redwine said to Unk, "that when you go out among all those people you mustn't say anything that would indicate that God took a special interest in you, or that you could somehow be of help to God. The worst thing you could say, for instance, would be something like, 'Thank God for delivering me from all my troubles. For some reason He singled me out, and now my only wish is to serve Him.'

"The friendly crowd out there," continued Redwine, "could turn quite ugly quite fast, despite the high auspices under which you come."

Unk had been planning to say almost exactly what Redwine had warned him against saying. It had seemed the only proper speech to make. "What—what should I say?" said Unk.

"It has been prophesied what you will say," said Redwine, "word for word. I have thought long and hard about the words you are going to say, and I am convinced they cannot be improved upon."

"But I can't think of any words—except hello—thank you," said Unk. "What do you *want* me to say?"

"What you do say," said Redwine. "Those good people out there have been rehearsing this moment for a long time. They will ask you two questions, and you will answer them to the best of your ability."

He led Unk through the airlock to the outside. The fire engine's fountain had been turned off. The shouting and dancing had stopped.

Redwine's congregation now formed a semicircle around Unk and Redwine. The members of the congregation had their lips pressed tightly together and their lungs filled.

Redwine gave a saintly signal.

The congregation spoke as one. "Who are you?" they said.

"I—I don't know my real name," said Unk. "They called me Unk."

"What happened to you?" said the congregation.

Unk shook his head vaguely. He could think of no apt condensation of his adventures for the obviously ritual mood. Something great was plainly expected of him. He was not up to greatness. He exhaled noisily, letting the congregation know that he was sorry to fail them with his colourlessness. "I was a victim of a series of accidents," he said. He shrugged. "As are we all," he said.

The cheering and dancing began again.

Unk was hustled aboard the fire engine, and driven on it to the door of the church.

Redwine pointed amiably to an unfurled wooden scroll over the door. Incised in the scroll and gilded were these words:

I WAS A VICTIM OF A SERIES OF ACCIDENTS,
AS ARE WE ALL.

Unk was driven on the fire engine straight from the church to Newport, Rhode Island, where a materialization was due to take place.

According to a plan that had been set up years before, other fire apparatus on Cape Cod was shifted so as to protect West Barnstable, which would be without its pumper for a little while.

Word of the Space Wanderer's coming spread over the Earth like wildfire. In every village, town, and city through which the fire engine passed, Unk was pelted with flowers.

Unk sat high on the fire engine, on a two-by-six fir timber laid across the cockpit amidships. In the cockpit itself was the Reverend C. Horner Redwine.

Redwine had control of the fire engine's bell, which he rang assiduously. Attached to the clapper of the bell was a Malachi made of high-impact plastic. The doll was of a special sort that could be bought only in Newport. To display such a Malachi was to proclaim that one had made a pilgrimage to Newport.

The entire Volunteer Fire Department of West Barnstable, with the exception of two non-conformists, had made such a pilgrimage to Newport. The fire engine's Malachi had been bought with Fire Department funds.

In the parlance of the souvenir hawkers in Newport, the Fire Department's high-impact plastic Malachi was a "genuwine, authorized, official Malachi."

Unk was happy, because it was so good to be among people again, and to be breathing air again. And everybody seemed to adore him so.

There was so much good noise. There was so much good everything. Unk hoped the good everything would go on forever.

"What happened to you?" the people all yelled to him, and they laughed.

For the purposes of mass communications, Unk shortened the answer that had pleased the little crowd so much at the Church of the Space Wanderer. "Accidents!" he yelled.

He laughed.

Oh boy.

What the hell. He laughed.

In Newport, the Rumfoord estate had been packed to the walls for eight hours. Guards turned thousands away from the little door in the wall. The guards were hardly necessary, since the crowd inside was monolithic.

A greased eel couldn't have squeezed in.

The thousands of pilgrims outside the walls now jostled one another piously for positions close to the loudspeakers mounted at the corners of the walls.

From the speakers would come Rumfoord's voice.

The crowd was the largest yet and the most excited yet, for the day was the long-promised Great Day of the Space Wanderer.

Handicaps of the most imaginative and effective sort were displayed everywhere. The crowd was wonderfully drab and hampered.

Bee, who had been Unk's mate on Mars, was in Newport, too. So was Bee's and Unk's son, Chrono.

"Hey! —getcher genuwine, authorized, official Malachis here," said Bee hoarsely. "Hey! —getcher Malachis here. Gotta have a Malachi to wave at the Space Wanderer," said Bee. "Get a Malachi, so the Space Wanderer can bless it when he comes by."

She was in a booth facing the little iron door in the wall of the Rumfoord estate in Newport. Bee's booth was the first in the line of twenty booths that faced the door. The twenty booths were under one continuous shed roof, and were separated from one another by waist-high partitions.

The Malachis she was hawking were plastic dolls with movable joints and rhinestone eyes. Bee bought them from a religious supply house for twenty-seven cents apiece and sold them for three dollars. She was an excellent businesswoman.

And while Bee showed the world an efficient and flashy exterior, it was the grandeur within her that sold more merchandise than anything. The carnival flash of Bee caught the pilgrims' eyes. But what brought the pilgrims to her booth and made them buy was her aura. The aura said unmistakably that Bee was meant for a far nobler station in life, that she was being an awfully good sport about being stuck where she was.

"Hey! —getcher Malachi while there's still time," said Bee. "Can't get a Malachi while a materialization's going on!"

That was true. The rule was that the concessionaires had to close their shutters five minutes before Winston Niles

Rumfoord and his dog materialized. And they had to keep their shutters closed until ten minutes after the last trace of Rumfoord and Kazak had disappeared.

Bee turned to her son, Chrono, who was opening a fresh case of Malachis. "How long before the whistle?" she said. The whistle was a great steam whistle inside the estate. It was blown five minutes in advance of materializations.

Materializations themselves were announced by the firing of a three-inch cannon.

Dematerializations were announced by the release of a thousand toy balloons.

"Eight minutes," said Chrono, looking at his watch. He was eleven Earthling years old now. He was dark and smouldering. He was an expert short-changer, and was clever with cards. He was foul-mouthed, and carried a switch-knife with a six-inch blade. Chrono would not socialize well with other children, and his reputation for dealing with life courageously and directly was so bad that only a few very foolish and very pretty little girls were attracted to him.

Chrono was classified by the Newport Police Department and by the Rhode Island State Police as a juvenile delinquent. He knew at least fifty law-enforcement officers by their first names, and was a veteran of fourteen lie-detector tests.

All that prevented Chrono's being placed in an institution was the finest legal staff on Earth, the legal staff of the Church of God the Utterly Indifferent. Under the direction of Rumfoord, the staff defended Chrono against all charges.

The commonest charges brought against Chrono were larceny by sleight of hand, carrying concealed weapons, possessing unregistered pistols, discharging firearms within the city limits, selling obscene prints and articles, and being a wayward child.

The authorities complained bitterly that the boy's big trouble was his mother. His mother loved him just the way he was.

"Only eight more minutes to get your Malachi, folks," said Bee. "Hurry, hurry, hurry."

Bee's upper front teeth were gold, and her skin, like the skin of her son, was the colour of golden oak.

Bee had lost her upper front teeth when the space ship in which she and Chrono had ridden from Mars crash-landed in the Gumbo region of the Amazon Rain Forest. She and Chrono had been the only survivors of the crash, and had wandered through the jungles for a year.

The colour of Bee's and Chrono's skins was permanent, since it stemmed from a modification of their livers. Their livers had been modified by a three-month diet consisting of water and the roots of the salpa-salpa or Amazonian blue poplar. The diet had been a part of Bee's and Chrono's initiation into the Gumbo tribe.

During the initiation, mother and son had been staked at the ends of tethers in the middle of the village, with Chrono representing the Sun and Bee representing the Moon, as the Sun and the Moon were understood by the Gumbo people.

As a result of their experiences, Bee and Chrono were closer than most mothers and sons.

They had been rescued at last by a helicopter. Winston Niles Rumfoord had sent the helicopter to just the right place at just the right time.

Winston Niles Rumfoord had given Bee and Chrono the Lucrative Malachi concession outside the Alice-in-Wonderland door. He had also paid Bee's dental bill, and had suggested that her false front teeth be gold.

The man who had the booth next to Bee's was Harry Brackman. He had been Unk's platoon sergeant back on Mars. Brackman was portly and balding now. He had a cork leg and a stainless steel right hand. He had lost the leg and hand in the Battle of Boca Raton. He was the only survivor of the battle—and, if he hadn't been so horribly wounded, he would certainly have been lynched along with the other survivors of his platoon.

Brackman sold plastic models of the fountain inside the wall. The models were a foot high. The models had spring-driven pumps in their bases. The pumps pumped water from the big bowl at the bottom to the tiny bowls at the top. Then the tiny bowls spilled into the slightly larger bowls below and . . .

Brackman had three of them going at once on the counter before him. "Just like the one inside, folks," he said. "And you can take one of these home with you. Put it in the picture window, so all your neighbours'll know you've been to

165

Newport. Put it in the middle of the kitchen table for the kids' parties, and fill it with pink lemonade."

"How much?" said a rube.

"Seventeen dollars," said Brackman.

"Wow!" said the rube.

"It's a sacred shrine, cousin," said Brackman, looking at the rube levelly. "Isn't a toy." He reached under the counter, brought out a model of a Martian space ship. "You want a toy? Here's a toy. Forty-nine cents. I only make two cents on it."

The rube made a show of being a judicious shopper. He compared the toy with the real article it was supposed to represent. The real article was a Martian space ship on top of a column ninety-eight feet tall. The column and space ship were inside the walls of the Rumfoord estate—in the corner of the estate where the tennis courts had once been.

Rumfoord had yet to explain the purpose of the space ship, whose supporting column had been built with the pennies of school children from all over the world. The ship was kept in constant readiness. What was reputedly the longest free-standing ladder in history leaned against the column, led giddily to the door of the ship.

In the fuel cartridge of the space ship was the very last trace of the Martian war effort's supply of the Universal Will to Become.

"Uh huh," said the rube. He put the model back on the counter. "If you don't mind. I'll shop around a little more." So far, the only thing he had bought was a Robin Hood hat with a picture of Rumfoord on one side and a picture of a sailboat on the other, and with his own name stitched on the feather. His name, according to the feather, was *Delbert*. "Thanks just the same," said Delbert. "I'll probably be back."

"Sure you will, Delbert," said Brackman.

"How did you know my name was Delbert?" said Delbert, pleased and suspicious.

"You think Winston Niles Rumfoord is the only man around here with supernatural powers?" said Brackman.

A jet of steam went up inside the walls. An instant later, the voice of the great steam whistle rolled over the booths —mighty, mournful, and triumphant. It was the signal that Rumfoord and his dog would materialize in five minutes.

It was the signal for the concessionaires to stop their

irreverent bawling of brummagem wares, to close their shutters.

The shutters were banged shut at once.

The effect of the closing inside the booths was to turn the line of concessions into a twilit tunnel.

The isolation of the concessionaires in the tunnel had an extra dimension of spookiness, since the tunnel contained only survivors from Mars. Rumfoord had insisted on that—that Martians were to have first choice of the concessions at Newport. It was his way of saying, "Thanks."

There weren't many survivors—only fifty-eight in the United States, only three hundred and sixteen in the entire World.

Of the fifty-eight in the United States, twenty-one were concessionaires in Newport.

"Here we go again, kiddies," somebody said, far, far, far down the line. It was the voice of the blind man who sold the Robin Hood hats with a picture of Rumfoord on one side and a picture of a sailboat on the other.

Sergeant Brackman laid his folded arms on the half-partition between his booth and Bee's. He winked at young Chrono, who was lying on an unopened case of Malachis.

"Go to hell, eh, kid?" said Brackman to Chrono.

"Go to hell," Chrono agreed. He was cleaning his nails with the strangely bent, drilled and nicked piece of metal that had been his good-luck piece on Mars. It was still his good-luck piece on Earth.

The good-luck piece had probably saved Chrono's and Bee's lives in the jungle. The Gumbo tribesmen had recognized the piece of metal as an object of tremendous power. Their respect for it had led them to initiate rather than eat its owners.

Brackman laughed affectionately. "Yessir—there's a Martian for you," he said. "Won't even get off his case of Malachis for a look at the Space Wanderer."

Chrono was not alone in his apathy about the Space Wanderer. It was the proud and impudent custom of all the concessionaires to stay away from ceremonies—to stay in the twilit tunnel of their booths until Rumfoord and his dog had come and gone.

It wasn't that the concessionaires had real contempt for Rumfoord's religion. Actually, most of them thought the new religion was probably a pretty good thing. What they were dramatizing when they stayed in their shuttered booths was that they, as Martian veterans, had already done more than enough to put the Church of God the Utterly Indifferent on its feet.

They were dramatizing the fact of their having been all used up.

Rumfoord encouraged them in this pose—spoke of them fondly as his ". . . soldier saints outside the little door. Their apathy," Rumfoord once said, "is a great wound they suffered that we might be more lively, more sensitive, and more free."

The temptation of the Martian concessionaires to take a peek at the Space Wanderer was great. There were loud-speakers on the walls of the Rumfoord estate, and every word spoken by Rumfoord inside blatted in the ears of anyone within a quarter of a mile. The words had spoken again and again of the glorious moment of truth that would come when the Space Wanderer came.

It was a big moment true believers titillated themselves about—the big moment wherein true believers were going to find their beliefs amplified, clarified, and vivified by a factor of ten.

Now the moment had arrived.

The fire engine that had carried the Space Wanderer down from the Church of the Space Wanderer on Cape Cod was clanging and shrieking outside the booths.

The trolls in the twilight of the booths refused to peek.

The cannon roared within the walls.

Rumfoord and his dog, then, had materialized—and the Space Wanderer was passing in through the Alice-in-Wonderland door.

"Probably some broken-down actor he hired from New York," said Brackman.

This got no response from anyone, not even from Chrono, who fancied himself the chief cynic of the booths. Brackman didn't take his own suggestion seriously—that the Space Wanderer was a fraud. The concessionaires knew all too well about Rumfoord's penchant for realism. When Rumfoord staged a passion play, he used nothing but real people in real hells.

Let it be emphasized here that, passionately fond as Rumfoord was of great spectacles, he never gave in to the temptation to declare himself God or something a whole lot like God.

His worst enemies admit that. Dr. Maurice Rosenau, in his *Pan-Galactic Humbug or Three Billion Dupes* says:

Winston Niles Rumfoord, the interstellar Pharisee, Tartufe, and Cagliostro, has taken pains to declare that he is not God Almighty, that he is not a close relative of God Almighty, and that he has received no plain instructions from God Almighty. To these words of the Master of Newport we can say Amen! And may we add that Rumfoord is so far from being a relative or agent of God Almighty as to make all communication with God Almighty Himself impossible so long as Rumfoord is around!

Ordinarily, talk by the Martian veterans in the shuttered booths was sprightly—bristling with entertaining irreverence and tips on selling trashy religious articles to boobs.

Now, with Rumfoord and the Space Wanderer about to meet, the concessionaires found it very hard not to be interested.

Sergeant Brackman's good hand went up to the crown of his head. It was the characteristic gesture of a Martian veteran. He was touching the area over his antenna, over the antenna that had once done all his important thinking for him. He missed the signals.

"Bring the Space Wanderer here!" blatted Rumfoord's voice from the Gabriel horns on the walls.

"Maybe—maybe we should go," said Brackman to Bee.

"What?" murmured Bee. She was standing with her back to the closed shutters. Her eyes were shut. Her head was down. She looked cold.

She always shivered when a materialization was taking place.

Chrono was rubbing his good-luck piece slowly with the ball of his thumb, watching a halo of mist on the cold metal, a halo around the thumb.

"The hell with 'em—eh, Chrono?" said Brackman.

The man who sold twittering mechanical birds swung his wares overhead listlessly. A farm wife had stabbed him with a pitchfork in the Battle of Toddington, England, had left him for dead.

The International Committee for the Identification and Rehabilitation of Martians had, with the help of finger-prints, identified the bird man as Bernard K. Winslow, an itinerant chicken sexer, who had disappeared from the alcoholic ward of a London hospital.

"Thanks very much for the information," Winslow had told the committee. "Now I don't have that lost feeling any more."

Sergeant Brackman had been identified by the commit-tee as Private Francis J. Thompson, who had disappeared in the dead of night while walking a lonely guard post around a motor pool in Fort Bragg, North Carolina, U.S.A.

The committee had been baffled by Bee. She had no fingerprints on record. The committee believed her to be either Florence White, a plain and friendless girl who had disappeared from a steam laundry in Cohoes, New York, or Darlene Simpkins, a plain and friendless girl who had last been seen accepting a ride with a swarthy stranger in Brownsville, Texas.

And down the line of booths from Brackman and Chrono and Bee were Martian husks who had been identified as Myron S. Watson, an alcoholic, who had disappeared from his post as a wash room attendant at Newark Airport . . . as Charlene Heller, assistant dietician of the cafeteria of Stivers High School in Dayton, Ohio . . . as Krishna Garu, a typesetter still wanted, technically, on charges of bigamy, pandering, and nonsupport in Calcutta, India . . . as Kurt Schneider, also an alcoholic, manager of a failing travel agency in Bremen, Germany.

"The mighty Rumfoord—" said Bee.

"Pardon me?" said Brackman.

"He snatched us out of our lives," said Bee. "He put us to sleep. He cleaned out our minds the way you clean the seeds out of a jack-o'-lantern. He wired us like robots, trained us, aimed us—burned us out in a good cause." She shrugged.

"Could we have done any better if he'd left us in charge of our own lives?" said Bee. "Would we have become any more—or less? I guess I'm glad he used me. I guess he had a lot better ideas about what to do with me than Florence White or Darlene Simpkins or whoever I was.

"But I hate him all the same," said Bee.

"That's your privilege," said Brackman. "He said that was the privilege of every Martian."

"There's one consolation," said Bee. "We're all used up. We'll never be of any use to him again."

"Welcome, Space Wanderer," blatted Rumfoord's oleomargarine tenor from the Gabriel horns on the wall. "How meet it is that you should come to us on the bright red pumper of a volunteer fire department. I can think of no more stirring symbol of man's humanity to man than a fire engine. Tell me, Space Wanderer, do you see anything here—anything that makes you think you may have been here before?"

The Space Wanderer murmured something unintelligible.

"Louder, please," said Rumfoord.

"The fountain—I remember that fountain," said the Space Wanderer gropingly. "Only—only—"

"Only?" said Rumfoord.

"It was dry then—whenever that was. It's so wet now," said the Space Wanderer.

A microphone near the fountain was now tuned into the public address system, so that the actual babble, spatter and potch of the fountain could underline the Space Wanderer's words.

"Anything else familiar, O Space Wanderer?" said Rumfoord.

"Yes," said the Space Wanderer shyly. "You."

"I am familiar?" said Rumfoord archly. "You mean there's a possibility that I played some small part in your life before?"

"I remember you on Mars," said the Space Wanderer. "You were the man with the dog—just before we took off."

"What happened after you took off?" said Rumfoord.

"Something went wrong," said the Space Wanderer. He sounded apologetic, as though the series of misfortunes were somehow his own fault. "A lot of things went wrong."

"Have you ever considered the possibility," said Rumfoord, "that everything went absolutely right?"

"No," said the Space Wanderer simply. The idea did not startle him, could not startle him—since the idea proposed was so far beyond the range of his jerry-built philosophy.

"Would you recognize your mate and child?" said Rumfoord.

"I—I don't know," said the Space Wanderer.

"Bring me the woman and the boy who sell Malachis outside the little iron door," said Rumfoord. "Bring Bee and Chrono."

The Space Wanderer and Winston Niles Rumfoord and Kazak were on a scaffold before the mansion. The scaffold was at eye-level for the standing crowd. The scaffold before the mansion was a portion of a continuous system of catwalks, ramps, ladders, pulpits, steps, and stages that reached into every corner of the estate.

The system made possible the free and showy circulation of Rumfoord around the grounds, unimpeded by crowds. It meant, too, that Rumfoord could offer a glimpse of himself to every person on the grounds.

The system was not suspended magnetically, though it looked like a miracle of levitation. The seeming miracle was achieved by means of a cunning use of paint. The underpinnings were painted a flat black, while the superstructures were painted flashing gold.

Television cameras and microphones on booms could follow the system anywhere.

For night materializations, the superstructures of the system were outlined in flesh-coloured electric lamps.

The Space Wanderer was only the thirty-first person to be invited to join Rumfoord on the elevated system.

An assistant had now been dispatched to the Malachi booth outside to bring in the thirty-second and thirty-third persons to share the eminence.

Rumfoord did not look well. His colour was bad. And, although he smiled as always, his teeth seemed to be gnashing behind the smile. His complacent glee had become a caricature, betraying the fact that all was not well by any means.

But on and on the famous smile went. The magnificently snobbish crowd-pleaser held his big dog Kazak by a choke chain. The chain was twisted so as to nip warningly into the dog's throat. The warning was necessary, since the dog plainly did not like the Space Wanderer.

The smile faltered for an instant, reminding the crowd

of what a load Rumfoord carried for them—warning the crowd that he might not be able to carry it forever.

Rumfoord carried in his palm a microphone and transmitter the size of a penny. When he did not want his voice carried to the crowd, he simply smothered the penny in his fist.

The penny was smothered in his fist now—and he was addressing bits of irony to the Space Wanderer that would have bewildered the crowd, had the crowd been able to hear them.

"This is certainly your day, isn't it?" said Rumfoord. "A perfect love feast from the instant you arrived. The crowd simply adores you. Do you adore crowds?"

The joyful shocks of the day had reduced the Space Wanderer to a childish condition—a condition wherein irony and even sarcasm were lost to him. He had been the captive of many things in his troubled times. He was now a captive of a crowd that thought he was a marvel. "They've certainly been wonderful," he said, in reply to Rumfoord's last question. "They've been grand."

"Oh—they're a grand bunch," said Rumfoord. "No mistake about that. I've been racking my brains for the right word to describe them, and you've brought it to me from outer space. *Grand* is what they are." Rumfoord's mind was plainly elsewhere. He wasn't much interested in the Space Wanderer as a person—hardly looked at him. Neither did he seem very excited about the approach of the Space Wanderer's wife and child.

"Where are they, where are they?" said Rumfoord to an assistant below. "Let's get on with it. Let's get it over with."

The Space Wanderer was finding his adventures so satisfying and stimulating, so splendidly staged, that he was shy about asking questions—was afraid that asking questions might make him seem ungrateful.

He realized that he had a terrific ceremonial responsibility and that the best thing to do was to keep his mouth shut, to speak only when spoken to, and to make his answer to all questions short and artless.

The Space Wanderer's mind did not teem with questions. The fundamental structure of his ceremonial situation was obvious—was as clean and functional as a three-legged milking stool. He had suffered mightily, and now he was being rewarded mightily.

The sudden change in fortunes made a bang-up show. He smiled, understanding the crowd's delight—pretending to be in the crowd himself, sharing the crowd's delight.

Rumfoord read the Space Wanderer's mind. "They'd like it just as much the other way around, you know," he said.

"The other way around?" said the Space Wanderer.

"If the big reward came first, and then the great suffering," said Rumfoord. "It's the *contrast* they like. The order of events doesn't make any difference to them. It's the thrill of the *fast reverse*—"

Rumfoord opened his fist, exposed the microphone. With his other hand he beckoned pontifically. He was beckoning to Bee and Chrono, who had been hoisted onto a tributary of the gilded system of catwalks, ramps, ladders, pulpits, steps, and stages. "This way, please. We haven't got all day, you know," said Rumfoord schoolmarmishly.

During the lull, the Space Wanderer felt the first real tickle of plans for a good future on Earth. With everyone so kind and enthusiastic and peaceful, not only a good life but a perfect life could be lived on Earth.

The Space Wanderer had already been given a fine new suit and a glamorous station in life, and his mate and son were to be restored to him in a matter of minutes.

All that was lacking was a good friend, and the Space Wanderer began to tremble. He trembled, for he knew in his heart that his best friend, Stony Stevenson, was hidden somewhere on the grounds, awaiting a cue to appear.

The Space Wanderer smiled, for he was imagining Stony's entrance. Stony would come running down a ramp, laughing and a little drunk. "Unk, you bloody bastard," Stony would roar right into the public address system, "by God, I've looked in every flaming pub on bloody Earth for you—and here you've been hung up on Mercury the whole bloody time!"

As Bee and Chrono reached Rumfoord and the Space Wanderer, Rumfoord walked away. Had he separated himself from Bee, Chrono, and the Space Wanderer by a mere arm's length, his separateness might have been understood. But the gilded system enabled him to put a really respectable distance between himself and the three, and not only a distance, but a distance made tortuous by rococo and variously symbolic hazards.

It was undeniably great theatre, notwithstanding Dr. Maurice Rosenau's carping comment (*op. cit.*): "The people who watch reverently as Winston Niles Rumfoord goes dancing over his golden jungle gym in Newport are the same idiots one finds in toy stores, gaping reverently at toy trains as the trains go *chuffa-chuffa-chuffa* in and out of papier-mâché tunnels, over toothpick trestles, through cardboard cities, and into papier-mâché tunnels again. Will the little trains or will Winston Niles Rumfoord *chuffa-chuffa-chuffa* into view again? Oh, *mirabile dictu!* . . . they will!"

From the scaffold in front of the mansion Rumfoord went to a stile that arched over the crest of a boxwood hedge. On the other side of the stile was a catwalk that ran for ten feet to the trunk of a copper beech. The trunk was four feet through. Gilded rungs were fixed to the trunk by lag screws.

Rumfoord tied Kazak to the bottom rung, then climbed out of sight like Jack on the beanstalk.

From somewhere up in the tree he spoke.

His voice came not from the tree but from the Gabriel horns on the walls.

The crowd weaned its eyes from the leafy treetops, turned its eyes to the nearest loudspeakers.

Only Bee, Chrono, and the Space Wanderer continued to look up, to look up at where Rumfoord really was. This wasn't so much a result of realism as it was a result of embarrassment. By looking up, the members of the little family avoided looking at each other.

None of the three had any reason to be pleased with the reunion.

Bee was not drawn to the scrawny, bearded, happy boob in lemon-yellow long underwear. She had dreamed of a big, angry, arrogant free-thinker.

Young Chrono hated the bearded intruder on his sublime relationship with his mother. Chrono kissed his good-luck piece and wished that his father, if this really was his father, would drop dead.

And the Space Wanderer himself, sincerely as he tried, could see nothing he would have chosen of his own free will in the dark, malevolent mother and son—

175

By accident, the Space Wanderer's eyes met the one good eye of Bee. Something had to be said.

"How do you do?" said the Space Wanderer.

"How do *you* do?" said Bee.

They both looked up into the tree again.

"Oh, my happy, handicapped brethren," said Rumfoord's voice, "let us thank God—God, who appreciates our thanks as much as the mighty Mississippi appreciates a raindrop—that we are not like Malachi Constant."

The back of the Space Wanderer's neck ached some. He lowered his gaze. His eyes were caught by a long, straight golden runway in the middle distance. His eyes followed it.

The runway ended at Earth's longest free-standing ladder. The ladder was painted gold, too.

The Space Wanderer's gaze climbed the ladder to the tiny door of the space ship on top of the column. He wondered who would have nerve enough or reason enough to climb such a frightening ladder to such a tiny door.

The Space Wanderer looked at the crowd again. Maybe Stony Stevenson was in the crowd somewhere. Maybe he would wait for the whole show to end before he presented himself to his best and only friend from Mars.

CHAPTER ELEVEN

WE HATE MALACHI CONSTANT BECAUSE...

"Tell me one good thing you ever did in your life."
—WINSTON NILES RUMFOORD

AND THIS is how the sermon went:

"We are *disgusted* by Malachi Constant," said Winston Niles Rumfoord up in his treetop, "because he used the fantastic fruits of his fantastic good luck to finance an unending demonstration that man is a pig. He wallowed in sycophants. He wallowed in worthless women. He wallowed in lascivious entertainments and alcohol and drugs. He wallowed in every known form of voluptuous turpitude.

"At the height of his good luck, Malachi Constant was worth more than the states of Utah and North Dakota combined. Yet, I daresay, his moral worth was not that of the most corrupt little fieldmouse in either state.

"We are *angered* by Malachi Constant," said Rumfoord up in his treetop, "because he did nothing to deserve his billions, and because he did nothing unselfish or imaginative with his billions. He was as benevolent as Marie Antoinette, as creative as a professor of cosmetology in an embalming college.

"We *hate* Malachi Constant," said Rumfoord up in his treetop, "because he accepted the fantastic fruits of his fantastic good luck without a qualm, as though luck were the hand of God. To us of the Church of God the Utterly Indifferent, there is nothing more cruel, more dangerous, more blasphemous that a man can do than to believe that —that luck, good or bad, is the hand of God!

"Luck, good or bad," said Rumfoord up in his treetop, "is *not* the hand of God.

"Luck," said Rumfoord up in his treetop, "is the way the wind swirls and the dust settles eons after God has passed by.

"Space Wanderer!" called Rumfoord from up in his treetop.

The Space Wanderer was not paying strict attention. His powers of concentration were feeble—possibly because he had been in the caves too long, or on goofballs too long, or in the Army of Mars too long.

He was watching clouds. They were lovely things, and the sky they drifted in was, to the colour-starved Space Wanderer, a thrilling blue.

"Space Wanderer!" called Rumfoord again.

"You in the yellow suit," said Bee. She nudged him. "Wake up."

"Pardon me?" said the Space Wanderer.

"Space Wanderer!" called Rumfoord.

The Space Wanderer snapped to attention. "Yes, sir?" he called up into the leafy bower. The greeting was ingenuous, cheerful, and winsome. A microphone on the end of a boom was swung to dangle before him.

"Space Wanderer!" called Rumfoord, and he was peeved now, for the ceremonial flow was being impeded.

"Right here, sir!" cried the Space Wanderer. His reply boomed earsplittingly from the loudspeaker.

"Who are you?" said Rumfoord. "What is your real name?"

"I don't know my real name," said the Space Wanderer. "They called me Unk."

"What happened to you before you arrived back on Earth, Unk?" said Rumfoord.

The Space Wanderer beamed. He had been led to a repetition of the simple statement that had caused so much laughing and dancing and singing on Cape Cod. "I was a victim of a series of accidents, as are we all," he said.

There was no laughing and dancing and singing this time, but the crowd was definitely in favour of what the Space Wanderer had said. Chins were raised, and eyes were widened, and nostrils were flared. There was no outcry, for the crowd wanted to hear absolutely everything that Rumfoord and the Space Wanderer might have to say.

"A victim of a series of accidents, were you?" said Rumfoord up in his treetop. "Of all the accidents," he said, "which would you consider the most significant?"

The Space Wanderer cocked his head. "I'd have to think," he said.

"I'll spare you the trouble," said Rumfoord. "The most significant accident that happened to you was your being born. Would you like me to tell you what you were named when you were born?"

The Space Wanderer hesitated only a moment, and all that made him hesitate was a fear that he was going to spoil a very gratifying ceremonial career by saying the wrong thing. "Please do," he said.

"They called you Malachi Constant," said Rumfoord up in his treetop.

To the extent that crowds can be good things, the crowds that Winston Niles Rumfoord attracted to Newport were good crowds. They were not crowd-minded. The members remained in possession of their own consciences, and Rumfoord never invited them to participate as one in any action —least of all in applause or catcalls.

When the fact had sunk in that the Space Wanderer was the disgusting, irking, and hateful Malachi Constant, the members of the crowd reacted in quiet, sighing, personal ways—ways that were by and large compassionate. It was on their generally decent consciences, after all, that they had hanged Constant in effigy in their homes and places of work. And, while they had been cheerful enough about hanging the effigies, very few felt that Constant, in the flesh, actually deserved hanging. Hanging Malachi Constant in effigy was an act of violence of the order of trimming a Christmas tree or hiding Easter eggs.

And Rumfoord up in his treetop said nothing to discourage their compassion. "You have had the singular accident, Mr. Constant," he said sympathetically, "of becoming a central symbol of wrong-headedness for a perfectly enormous religious sect.

"You would not be attractive to us as a symbol, Mr. Constant," he said, "if our hearts did not go out to you to a certain extent. Our hearts *have* to go out to you, since all your flamboyant errors are errors that human beings have made since the beginning of time.

"In a few minutes, Mr. Constant," said Rumfoord up in his treetop, "you are going to walk down the catwalks and ramps to that long golden ladder, and you are going to climb that ladder, and you are going to get into that space ship, and you are going to fly away to Titan, a warm and fecund moon of Saturn. You will live there in safety and comfort, but in exile from your native Earth.

"You are going to do this voluntarily, Mr. Constant, so that the Church of God the Utterly Indifferent can have a drama of dignified self-sacrifice to remember and ponder through all time.

"We will imagine, to our spiritual satisfaction," said Rumfoord up in his treetop, "that you are taking all mistaken ideas about the meaning of luck, all misused wealth and power, and all disgusting pastimes with you."

The man who had been Malachi Constant, who had been Unk, who had been the Space Wanderer, the man who was Malachi Constant again—that man felt very little upon being declared Malachi Constant again. He might, possibly, have felt some interesting things, had Rumfoord's timing been different. But Rumfoord told him what his ordeal was to be only seconds after telling him he was Malachi Constant—and the ordeal was sufficiently ghastly to command Constant's full attention.

The ordeal had been promised not in years or months or days—but in minutes. And, like any condemned criminal, Malachi Constant became a student, to the exclusion of all else, of the apparatus on which he was about to perform.

Curiously, his first worry was that he would stumble, that he would think too hard about the simple matter of walking, and that his feet would cease to work naturally, and that he would stumble on those wooden feet.

"You won't stumble, Mr. Constant," said Rumfoord up in his treetop, reading Constant's mind. "There is nowhere else for you to go, nothing else for you to do. By putting one foot in front of the other, while we watch in silence, you will make of yourself the most memorable, magnificent, and meaningful human being of modern times."

Constant turned to look at his dusky mate and child. Their gazes were direct. Constant learned from their gazes that Rumfoord had spoken the truth, that no course save the course to the space ship was open to him. Beatrice and young Chrono were supremely cynical about the festivities —but not about courageous behaviour in the midst of them.

They dared Malachi Constant to behave well.

Constant rubbed his left thumb and index finger together in a careful rotary motion. He watched this pointless enterprise for perhaps ten seconds.

And then he dropped his hands to his sides, raised his eyes, and stepped off firmly toward the space ship.

As his left foot struck the ramp, his head was filled with a sound he had not heard for three Earthling years. The sound was coming from the antenna under the crown of his skull. Rumfoord, up in his treetop, was sending signals to Constant's antenna by means of a small box in his pocket.

He was making Constant's long and lonely walk more bearable by filling Constant's head with the sound of a snare drum.

The snare drum had this to say to him:

Rented a tent, a tent, a tent;
Rented a tent, a tent.
Rented a tent!
Rented a tent!
Rented a, rented a tent!

The snare drum fell silent as Malachi Constant's hand closed for the first time on a gilded rung of the world's tallest free-standing ladder. He looked up, and perspective made the ladder's summit seem as tiny as a needle. Constant rested his brow for a moment against the rung to which his hand clung.

"You have something you would like to say, Mr. Constant, before you go up the ladder?" said Rumfoord up in his treetop.

A microphone on the end of a boom was again dangled before Constant. Constant licked his lips.

"You're about to say something, Mr. Constant?" said Rumfoord.

"If you're going to talk," the technician in charge of the microphone said to Constant, "speak in a perfectly normal tone, and keep your lips about six inches away from the microphone."

"You're going to speak to us, Mr. Constant?" said Rumfoord.

"It's—it's probably not worth saying," said Constant quietly, "but I'd still like to say that I haven't understood a single thing that's happened to me since I reached Earth."

"You haven't got that feeling of participation?" said Rumfoord up in his treetop. "Is that it?"

"It doesn't matter," said Constant. "I'm still going up the ladder."

"Well," said Rumfoord up in his treetop, "if you feel we are doing you some sort of injustice here, suppose you tell us something really good you've done at some point in your life, and let us decide whether that piece of goodness might excuse you from this thing we have planned for you."

"Goodness?" said Constant.

"Yes," said Rumfoord expansively. "Tell me one good thing you ever did in your life—what you can remember of it."

Constant thought hard. His principal memories were of scuttling through endless corridors in the caves. There had been a few opportunities for what might pass for goodness with Boaz and the harmoniums. But Constant could not say honestly that he had availed himself of these opportunities to be good.

So he thought about Mars, about all the things that had been contained in his letter to himself. Surely, among all those items, there was something about his own goodness.

And then he remembered Stony Stevenson—his friend. He had had a friend, which was certainly a good thing. "I had a friend," said Malachi Constant into the microphone.

"What was his name?" said Rumfoord.

"Stony Stevenson," said Constant.

"Just one friend?" said Rumfoord up in his treetop.

"Just one," said Constant. His poor soul was flooded with pleasure as he realized that one friend was all that a man needed in order to be well-supplied with friendship.

"So your claim of goodness would stand or fall, really," said Rumfoord up in his treetop, "depending on how good a friend you really were of this Stony Stevenson."

"Yes," said Constant.

"Do you recall an execution on Mars, Mr. Constant," said Rumfoord up in his treetop, "wherein you were the executioner? You strangled a man at the stake before three regiments of the Army of Mars."

This was one memory that Constant had done his best to eradicate. He had been successful to a large extent—and the rummaging he did through his mind now was sincere. He couldn't be sure that the execution had taken place. "I—I think I remember," said Constant.

"Well—that man you strangled was your great and good friend Stony Stevenson," said Winston Niles Rumfoord.

Malachi Constant wept as he climbed the gilded ladder. He paused halfway up, and Rumfoord called to him again through the loudspeakers.

"Feel more like a vitally-interested participant now, Mr. Constant?" called Rumfoord.

Mr. Constant did. He had a thorough understanding now of his own worthlessness, and a bitter sympathy for anyone who might find it good to handle him roughly.

And when he got to the top, he was told by Rumfoord not to close the airlock yet, because his mate and child would be up shortly.

Constant sat on the threshold of his space ship at the top of the ladder, and listened to Rumfoord's brief sermon about Constant's dark mate, about the one-eyed, gold-toothed woman called Bee. Constant did not listen closely to the sermon. His eyes saw a larger, more comforting sermon in the panorama of town, bay, and islands so far below.

The sermon of the panorama was that even a man without a friend in the Universe could still find his home planet mysteriously, heartbreakingly beautiful.

"I shall tell you now," said Winston Niles Rumfoord in his treetop so far below Malachi Constant, "about Bee, the woman who sells Malachis outside the gate, the dark woman who, with her son, now glowers at us all.

"While she was on route to Mars so many years ago, Malachi Constant forced his attention on her, and she bore him this son. Before then, she was my wife and mistress of this estate. Her true name is Beatrice Rumfoord."

A groan went up from the crowd. Was it any wonder that the dusty puppets of other religions had been put away for want of audiences, that all eyes were turned to Newport? Not only was the head of the Church of God the Utterly Indifferent capable of telling the future and fighting the cruellest inequalities of all, inequalities in luck—but his supply of dumfounding new sensations was inexhaustible.

He was so well supplied with great material that he could actually let his voice trail off as he announced that the one-eyed, gold-toothed woman was his wife, and that he had been cuckolded by Malachi Constant.

"I now invite you to despise the example of her life as you have so long despised the example of the life of Malachi Constant," he said up in his treetop mildly. "Hang her alongside Malachi Constant from your window blinds and light fixtures, if you will.

"The excesses of Beatrice were excesses of reluctance," said Rumfoord. "As a younger woman, she felt so exquisitely bred as to do nothing and to allow nothing to be done to her, for fear of contamination. Life, for Beatrice as a younger woman, was too full of germs and vulgarity to be anything but intolerable.

"We of the Church of God the Utterly Indifferent damn her as roundly for refusing to risk her imagined purity in living as we damn Malachi Constant for wallowing in filth.

"It was implicit in Beatrice's every attitude that she was intellectually, morally, and physically what God intended human beings to be when perfected, and that the rest of humanity needed another ten thousand years in which to catch up. Again we have a case of an ordinary and uncreative person's tickling God Almighty pink. The proposition that God Almighty admired Beatrice for her touch-me-not breeding is at least as questionable as the proposition that God Almighty wanted Malachi Constant to be rich.

"Mrs. Rumfoord," said Winston Niles Rumfoord up in his treetop, "I now invite you and your son to follow Malachi Constant into the space ship bound for Titan. Is there something you would like to say before you leave?"

There was a long silence in which mother and son drew closer together and looked, shoulder to shoulder, at a world much changed by the news of the day.

"Are you planning to address us, Mrs. Rumfoord?" said Rumfoord up in his treetop.

"Yes," said Beatrice. "But it won't take me long. I believe everything you say about me is true, since you so seldom lie. But when my son and I walk together to that ladder and climb it, we will not be doing it for you, or for your silly crowd. We will be doing it for ourselves—and we will be proving to ourselves and to anybody who wants to watch that we aren't afraid of anything. Our hearts won't be breaking when we leave this planet. It disgusts us at least as much as we, under your guidance, disgust it.

"I do not recall the old days," said Beatrice, "when I was mistress of this estate, when I could not stand to do anything or to have anything done to me. But I loved myself the instant you told me I'd been that way. The human race is a scummy thing, and so is Earth, and so are you."

Beatrice and Chrono walked quickly over the catwalks and ramps to the ladder, climbed the ladder. They brushed past Malachi Constant in the doorway of the space ship without any sort of greeting. They disappeared inside.

Constant followed them into the space ship, and joined them as they considered the accommodations.

The condition of the accommodations was a surprise— and would have been a surprise to the custodians of the estate in particular. The space ship, seemingly inviolable at the top of a shaft in sacred precincts patrolled by watch-men, had plainly been the scene of one or perhaps several wild parties.

The bunks were all unmade. The bedding was rumpled, twisted, and wadded. The sheets were stained with lipstick and shoe polish.

Fried clams crunched greasily underfoot.

Two quart bottles of Mountain Moonlight, one pint of Southern Comfort, and a dozen cans of Narragansett Lager Beer, all empty, were scattered through the ship.

Two names were written in lipstick on the white wall by the door: *Bud and Sylvia*. And from a flange on the central shaft in the cabin hung a black brassière.

Beatrice gathered up the bottles and beer cans. She dropped them out the door. She took the brassière down, and fluttered it out the doorway, awaiting a favourable wind.

Malachi Constant, sighing and shaking his head and mourning Stony Stevenson, used his feet for push-brooms. He scuffed the fried clams toward the door.

Young Chrono sat on a bunk, rubbing his good-luck piece. "Let's go, Mom," he said tautly. "For crying out loud, let's go."

Beatrice let go of the brassière. A gust caught it, carried it over the crowd, hung it in a tree next to the tree in which Rumfoord sat.

"Good-bye, all you clean and wise and lovely people," said Beatrice.

CHAPTER TWELVE

THE GENTLEMAN FROM TRALFAMADORE

"In a punctual way of speaking, good-bye."
WINSTON NILES RUMFOORD

SATURN HAS nine moons, the greatest of which is Titan.

Titan is only slightly smaller than Mars.

Titan is the only moon in the Solar System that has an atmosphere. There is plenty of oxygen to breathe.

The atmosphere of Titan is like the atmosphere outside the back door of an Earthling bakery on a spring morning.

Titan has a natural chemical furnace at its core that maintains a uniform air temperature of sixty-seven degrees Fahrenheit.

There are three seas on Titan, each the size of Earthling Lake Michigan. The waters of all three are fresh and emerald clear. The names of the three are the Winston Sea, the Niles Sea, and the Rumfoord Sea.

There is a cluster of ninety-three ponds and lakes, incipiently a fourth sea. The cluster is known as the Kazak Pools.

Connecting the Winston Sea, the Niles Sea, the Rumfoord Sea and the Kazak Pools are three great rivers. These rivers, with their tributaries, are moody—variously roaring, listless, and torn. Their moods are determined by the wildly fluctuating tugs of eight fellow moons, and by the prodigious influence of Saturn, which has ninety-five times the mass of Earth. The three rivers are known as the Winston River, the Niles River, and the Rumfoord River.

There are woods and meadows and mountains.

The tallest mountain is Mount Rumfoord, which is nine thousand, five hundred and seventy-one feet high.

Titan affords an incomparable view of the most appallingly beautiful things in the Solar System, the rings of Saturn. These dazzling bands are forty thousand miles across and scarcely thicker than a razor blade.

On Titan the rings are called Rumfoord's Rainbow.

Saturn describes a circle around the Sun.

It does it once every twenty-nine and a half Earthling years.

Titan describes a circle around Saturn.

Titan describes, as a consequence, a spiral around the Sun.

Winston Niles Rumfoord and his dog Kazak were wave phenomena—pulsing in distorted spirals, with their origins in the Sun and their terminals in Betelgeuse. Whenever a heavenly body intercepted their spirals, Rumfoord and his dog materialized on that body.

For reasons as yet mysterious, the spirals of Rumfoord, Kazak, and Titan coincided exactly.

So Rumfoord and his dog were permanently materialized on Titan.

Rumfoord and Kazak lived there on an island one mile from shore in the Winston Sea. Their home was a flawless reproduction of the Taj Mahal in Earthling India.

It was built by Martian labour.

It was Rumfoord's wry fancy to call his Titan home *Dun Roamin.*

Before the arrival of Malachi Constant, Beatrice Rumfoord, and Chrono, there was only one other person on Titan. That other person was named *Salo*. He was old. Salo was eleven million Earthling years old.

Salo was from another galaxy, from the Small Magellanic Cloud. He was four and a half feet tall.

Salo had a skin with the texture and colour of the skin of an Earthling tangerine.

Salo had three light deer-like legs. His feet were of an extraordinarily interesting design, each being an inflatable sphere. By inflating these spheres to the size of German batballs, Salo could walk on water. By reducing them to the size of golf balls, Salo could bound over hard surfaces at high speeds. When he deflated the spheres entirely, his feet became suction cups. Salo could walk up walls.

Salo had no arms. Salo had three eyes, and his eyes could perceive not only the so-called visible spectrum, but infrared and unltraviolet and X-rays as well. Salo was punctual—that is, he lived one moment at a time—and he liked to tell Rumfoord that he would rather see the wonderful colour at the far ends of the spectrum than either the past or the future.

This was something of a weasel, since Salo had seen, living a moment at a time, far more of the past and far more of the Universe than Rumfoord had. He remembered more of what he had seen, too.

Salo's head was round and hung on gimbals.

His voice was an electric noise-maker that sounded like a bicycle horn. He spoke five thousand languages, fifty of them Earthling languages, thirty-one of them *dead* Earthling languages.

Salo didn't live in a palace, though Rumfoord had offered to have one built for him. Salo lived in the open, near the space ship that had brought him to Titan two hundred thousand years before. His space ship was a flying saucer, the prototype for the Martian invasion fleet.

Salo had an interesting history.

In the Earthling year 483,441 B.C., he was chosen by popular telepathic enthusiasm as the most handsome, healthy, clean-minded specimen of his people. The occasion was the hundred-millionth anniversary of the government of his home planet in the Small Magellanic Cloud. The name of his home planet was Tralfamadore, which old Salo once translated for Rumfoord as meaning both *all of us* and the *number 541*

The length of a year on his home planet, according to his own calculations, was 3.6162 times the length of an Earthling year—so the celebration in which he participated was actually in honour of a government 361,620,000 Earthling years old. Salo once described this durable form of government to Rumfoord as hypnotic anarchy, but he declined to explain its workings. "Either you understand at once what it is," he told Rumfoord, "or there is no sense in trying to explain it to you, Skip."

His duty when he was elected to represent Tralfamadore, was to carry a sealed message from "One Rim of the Universe to the Other." The planners of the ceremonies were not so deluded as to believe that Salo's projected route spanned the Universe. The image was poetic, as was Salo's expedition. Salo would simply take the message and go as fast and as far as the technology of Tralfamadore could send him.

The message itself was unknown to Salo. It had been

prepared by what Salo described to Rumfoord as, "A kind of university—only nobody goes to it. There aren't any buildings, isn't any faculty. Everybody's in it and nobody's in it. It's like a cloud that everybody has given a little puff of mist to, and then the cloud does all the heavy thinking for everybody. I don't mean there's *really* a cloud. I just mean it's something *like* that. If you don't understand what I'm talking about, Skip, there's no sense in trying to explain it to you. All I can say is, there aren't any meetings."

The message was contained in a sealed lead wafer that was two inches square and three-eights of an inch thick. The wafer itself was contained in a gold mesh reticule which was hung on a stainless steel band clamped to the shaft that might be called Salo's neck.

Salo had orders not to open the reticule and wafer until he arrived at his destination. His destination was not Titan. His destination was in a galaxy that began eighteen million light-years beyond Titan. The planners of the ceremonies in which Salo had participated did not know what Salo was going to find in the galaxy. His instructions were to find creatures in it somewhere, to master their language, to open the message, and to translate it for them.

Salo did not question the good sense of his errand, since he was, like all Tralfamadorians, a machine. As a machine, he had to do what he was supposed to do.

Of all the orders Salo received before taking off from Tralfamadore, the one that was given the most importance was that *he was not, under any circumstances, to open the message along the way.*

This order was so emphasized that it became the very core of the little Tralfamadorian messenger's being.

In the Earthling year 203,117 B.C., Salo was forced down in the Solar System by mechanical difficulties. He was forced down by a complete disintegration of a small part in his ship's power plant, a part about the size of an Earthling beer-can opener. Salo was not mechanically inclined, and so had only a hazy idea as to what the missing part looked like or was supposed to do. Since Salo's ship was powered by UWTB, the Universal Will to Become, it's power plant was nothing for a mechanical dilettante to tinker with.

Salo's ship wasn't entirely out of commission. It would still run—but limpingly, at only about sixty-eight thousand miles an hour. It was adequate for short hops around the Solar System, even in its crippled condition, and copies of the crippled ship did yeoman service for the Martian war effort. But the crippled ship was impossibly slow for the purposes of Salo's intergalactic errand.

So old Salo holed up on Titan and he sent home to Tralfamadore word of his plight. He sent the message home with the speed of light, which meant that it would take one hundred and fifty thousand Earthling years to get to Tralfamadore.

He developed several hobbies that helped him to pass the time. Chief among these were sculpture, the breeding of Titanic daisies, and watching the various activities on Earth. He could watch the activities on Earth by means of a viewer on the dash panel of his ship. The viewer was sufficiently powerful to let Salo follow the activities of Earthling ants, if he so wished.

It was through this viewer that he got his first reply from Tralfamadore. The reply was written on Earth in huge stones on a plain in what is now England. The ruins of the reply still stand, and are known as Stonehenge. The meaning of Stonehenge in Tralfamadorian, when viewed from above is: *"Replacement part being rushed with all possible speed."*

Stonehenge wasn't the only message old Salo had received.

There had been four others, all of them written on Earth.

The Great Wall of China means in Tralfamadorian, when viewed from above: *"Be patient. We haven't forgotten about you."*

The Golden House of the Roman Emperor Nero meant: *"We are doing the best we can."*

The meaning of the Moscow Kremlin when it was first walled was: *"You will be on your way before you know it."*

The meaning of the Palace of the League of Nations in Geneva, Switzerland, is: *"Pack up your things and be ready to leave on short notice."*

Simple arithmetic will reveal that these messages all arrived with speeds considerably in excess of the speed of light. Salo had sent his message of distress home with the speed of light, and it had taken one hundred and fifty thousand years to reach Tralfamadore. He had received a reply from Tralfamadore in less than fifty thousand years.

It is grotesque for anyone as primitive as an Earthling to explain how these swift communications were effected. Suffice it to say, in such primitive company, that the Tralfamadorians were able to make certain impulses from the Universal Will to Become echo through the vaulted architecture of the Universe with about three times the speed of light. And they were able to focus and modulate these impulses so as to influence creatures far, far away, and inspire them to serve Tralfamadorian ends.

It was a marvellous way to get things done in places far, far away from Tralfamadore. It was easily the fastest way.

But it wasn't cheap.

Old Salo was not equipped himself to communicate and get things done in this way, even over short distances. The apparatus and the quantities of Universal Will to Become used in the process was colossal, and they demanded the services of thousands of technicians.

And even the heavily-powered, heavily-manned, heavily-built apparatus of Tralfamadore was not particularly accurate. Old Salo had watched many communications failures on Earth. Civilizations would start to bloom on Earth, and the participants would start to build tremendous structures that were obviously to be messages in Tralfamadorian— and then the civilizations would poop out without having finished the messages.

Old Salo had seen this happen hundreds of times.

Old Salo had told his friend Rumfoord a lot of interesting things about the civilization of Tralfamadore, but he had never told Rumfoord about the messages and the techniques of their delivery.

All that he had told Rumfoord was that he had sent home a distress message, and that he expected a replacement part to come any day now. Old Salo's mind was so different from Rumfoord's that Rumfoord couldn't read Salo's mind.

Salo was grateful for that barrier between their thoughts, because he was mortally afraid of what Rumfoord might say if he found out that Salo's people had so much to do with gumming up the history of Earth. Even though Rumfoord was chrono-synclastic infundibulated, and might be expected to take a larger view of things, Salo had found Rumfoord to be, still, a surprisingly parochial Earthling at heart.

Old Salo didn't want Rumfoord to find out what the Tralfamadorians were doing to Earth, because he was sure that Rumfoord would be offended—that Rumfoord would turn against Salo and all Tralfamadorians. Salo didn't think he could stand that because he loved Winston Niles Rumfoord.

There was nothing offensive in this love. That is to say, it wasn't homosexual. It couldn't be, since Salo had no sex.

He was a machine, like all Tralfamadorians.

He was held together by cotter pins, hose clamps, nuts, bolts, and magnets. Salo's tangerine-coloured skin, which was so expressive when he was emotionally disturbed, could be put on or taken off like an Earthling windbreaker. A magnetic zipper held it shut.

The Tralfamadorians, according to Salo, manufactured each other. No one knew for certain how the first machine had come into being.

The legend was this:

Once upon a time on Tralfamadore there were creatures who weren't anything like machines. They weren't dependable. They weren't efficient. They weren't predictable. They weren't durable. And these poor creatures were obsessed by the idea that everything that existed had to have a purpose, and that some purposes were higher than others.

These creatures spent most of their time trying to find out what their purpose was. And every time they found out what seemed to be a purpose of themselves, the purpose seemed so low that the creatures were filled with disgust and shame.

And, rather than serve such a low purpose, the creatures would make a machine to serve it. This left the creatures free to serve higher purposes. But whenever they found a higher purpose, the purpose still wasn't high enough.

So machines were made to serve higher purposes, too.

And the machines did everything so expertly that they were finally given the job of finding out what the highest purpose of the creatures could be.

The machines reported in all honesty that the creatures couldn't really be said to have any purpose at all.

The creatures thereupon began slaying each other, because they hated purposeless things above all else.

And they discovered that they weren't even very good at slaying. So they turned that job over to the machines, too. And the machines finished up the job in less time than it takes to say "Tralfamadore".

Using the viewer on the dash panel of his space ship, Old Salo now watched the approach to Titan of the space ship carrying Malachi Constant, Beatrice Rumfoord, and their son Chrono. Their ship was set to land automatically on the shore of the Winston Sea.

It was set to land amid two million life-sized statues of human beings. Salo had made the statues at the rate of about ten an Earthling year.

The statues were concentrated in the region of the Winston Sea because the statues were made of Titanic peat. Titanic peat abounds by the Winston Sea, only two feet under the surface soil.

Titanic peat is a curious substance—and, for the facile and sincere sculptor, an attractive one.

When first dug, Titanic peat has the consistency of Earthling putty.

After one hour's exposure to Titan's light and air, the peat has the strength and hardness of plaster of Paris.

After two hours' exposure, it is as durable as granite, and must be worked with a cold chisel.

After three hours' exposure, nothing but a diamond will scratch Titanic peat.

Salo was inspired to make so many statues by the showy ways in which Earthlings behaved. It wasn't so much what the Earthlings did as the way they did it that inspired Salo.

The Earthlings behaved at all times as though there were a big eye in the sky—as though that big eye were ravenous for entertainment.

The big eye was a glutton for great theatre. The big eye was indifferent as to whether the Earthling shows were comedy, tragedy, farce, satire, athletics, or vaudeville. Its demand, which Earthlings apparently found as irresistible as gravity, was that the shows be great.

The demand was so powerful that Earthlings did almost nothing but perform for it, night and day—and even in their dreams.

The big eye was the only audience that Earthlings really cared about. The fanciest performances that Salo had seen had been put on by Earthlings who were terribly alone. The imagined big eye was their only audience.

Salo, with his diamond-hard statues, had tried to preserve some of the mental states of those Earthlings who had put on the most interesting shows for the imagined big eye.

Hardly less surprising than the statues were the Titanic daisies that abounded by the Winston Sea. When Salo arrived on Titan in 203,117 B.C., the blooms of Titanic daisies were tiny, star-like, yellow flowers barely a quarter of an inch across.

Then Salo began to breed them selectively.

When Malachi Constant, Beatrice Rumfoord, and their son Chrono arrived on Titan, the typical Titanic daisy had a stalk four feet in diameter, and a lavender bloom shot wih pink and having a mass in excess of a ton.

Salo, having watched the approaching space ship of Malachi Constant, Beatrice Rumfoord, and their son Chrono, inflated his feet to the size of German batballs. He stepped onto the emerald clear waters of the Winston Sea, crossed the waters to Winston Niles Rumfoord's Taj Mahal.

He entered the walled yard of the palace, let the air out of his feet. The air hissed. The hiss echoed from the walls.

Winston Niles Rumfoord's lavender contour chair by the pool was empty.

"Skip?" called Salo. He used this most intimate of all possible names for Rumfoord. Rumfoord's childhood name, in spite of Rumfoord's resentment of his use of it. He didn't use the name in order to tease Rumfoord. He used it in order to assert the friendship he felt for Rumfoord—to test the friendship a little, and to watch it endure the test handsomely.

There was a reason for Salo's putting friendship to such a sophomoric test. He had never seen, never even heard of friendship before he hit the Solar System. It was a fascinating novelty to him. He had to play with it.

"Skip?" Salo called again.

There was an unusual tang in the air. Salo identified it tentatively as ozone. He was unable to account for it.

A cigarette still burned in the ash tray by Rumfoord's contour chair, so Rumfoord hadn't been out of his chair long.

"Skip? Kazak?" called Salo. It was unusual for Rumfoord not to be snoozing in his chair, for Kazak not to be snoozing beside it. Man and dog spent most of their time by the pool, monitoring signals from their other selves through space and time. Rumfoord was usually motionless in his chair, the fingers of one languid, dangling hand buried in Kazak's coat. Kazak was usually whimpering and twitching dreamingly.

Salo looked down into the water of the rectangular pool. In the bottom of the pool, in eight feet of water, were the three sirens of Titan, the three beautiful human females who had been offered to the lecherous Malachi Constant so long ago.

They were statues made by Salo of Titanic peat. Of the millions of statues made by Salo, only these three were painted with lifelike colours. It had been necessary to paint them in order to give them importance in the sumptuous, oriental scheme of things in Rumfoord's palace.

"Skip?" Salo called again.

Kazak, the hound of space, answered the call. Kazak came from the domed and minareted building that was reflected in the pool. Kazak came stiffly from the lacy shadows of the great octagonal chamber within.

Kazak looked poisoned.

Kazak shivered, and stared fixedly at a point to one side of Salo. There was nothing there.

Kazak stopped, and seemed to be preparing himself for a terrible pain that another step would cost him.

And then Kazak blazed and crackled with Saint Elmo's fire.

Saint Elmo's fire is a luminous electrical discharge, and any creature afflicted by it is subject to discomfort no worse than the discomfort of being tickled by a feather. All the same, the creature appears to be on fire, and can be forgiven for being dismayed.

The luminous discharge from Kazak was horrifying to watch. And it renewed the stench of ozone.

Kazak did not move. His capacity for surprise at the amazing display had long since been exhausted. He tolerated the blaze with tired rue.

The blaze died.

Rumfoord appeared in the archway. He, too, looked frowzy and palsied. A band of dematerialization, a band of nothingness about a foot wide, passed over Rumfoord from foot to head. This was followed by two narrow bands an inch apart.

Rumfoord held his hands high, and his fingers were spread. Streaks of pink, violet, and pale green Saint Elmo's fire streamed from his fingertips. Short streaks of pale gold fizzed in his hair, conspiring to give him a tinsel halo.

"Peace," said Rumfoord wanly.

Rumfoord's Saint Elmo's fire died.

Salo was aghast. "Skip," he said. "What's—what's the matter, Skip?"

"Sunspots," said Rumfoord. He shuffled to his lavender contour chair, lay his great frame on it, covered his eyes with a hand as limp and white as a damp handkerchief.

Kazak lay down beside him. Kazak was shivering.

"I—I've never seen you like this before," said Salo.

"There's never been a storm on the Sun like this before," said Rumfoord.

Salo was not surprised to learn that sunspots affected his chrono-synclastic infundibulated friends. He had seen Rumfoord and Kazak sick with sunspots many times before —but the most severe symptom had been fleeting nausea. The sparks and the bands of dematerialization were new.

As Salo watched Rumfoord and Kazak now, they became momentarily two-dimensional, like figures painted on rippling banners.

They steadied, became rounded again.

"Is there anything I can do, Skip?" said Salo.

Rumfoord groaned. "Will people never stop asking that dreadful question?" he said.

"Sorry," said Salo. His feet were so completely deflated now that they were concave, were suction cups. His feet made sucking sounds on the polished pavement.

"Do you *have* to make those noises?" said Rumfoord peevishly.

Old Salo wanted to die. It was the first time his friend Winston Niles Rumfoord had spoken a harsh word to him. Salo couldn't stand it.

Old Salo closed two of his three eyes. The third scanned the sky. The eye was caught by two streaking blue dots in the sky. The dots were soaring Titanic bluebirds.

The pair had found an updraft.

Neither great bird flapped a wing.

No movement of so much as a pinfeather was inharmonious. Life was but a soaring dream.

"*Graw*," said one Titanic bluebird sociably.

"*Graw*," the other agreed.

The birds closed their wings simultaneously, fell from the heights like stones.

They seemed to plummet to certain death outside Rumfoord's walls. But up they soared again, to begin another long and easy climb.

This time they climbed a sky that was streaked by the vapour trail of the space ship carrying Malachi Constant, Beatrice Rumfoord, and their son Chrono. The ship was about to land.

"Skip—?" said Salo.

"Do you *have* to call me that?" said Rumfoord.

"No," said Salo.

"Then don't," said Rumfoord. "I'm not fond of the name—unless somebody I've grown up with happens to use it."

"I thought—as a friend of yours," said Salo, "I might be entitled—"

"Shall we just drop this guise of friendship?" said Rumfoord curtly.

Salo closed his third eye. The skin of his torso tightened. "Guise?" he said.

"Your feet are making that noise again!" said Rumfoord.

"Skip!" cried Salo. He corrected this insufferable familiarity. "*Winston*—it's like a nightmare, your talking to me this way. I thought we were friends."

"Let's say we've managed to be of some *use* to each other, and let it go at that," said Rumfoord.

Salo's head rocked gently in its gimbals. "I thought there'd been a little more to it than that," he said at last.

"Let's say," said Rumfoord acidly, "that we discovered in each other a means to our separate ends."

"I—I was glad to help you—and I hope I really *was* a help to you," said Salo. He opened his eyes. He had to see Rumfoord's reaction. Surely Rumfoord would become friendly again, for Salo had helped him unselfishly.

"Didn't I give you half my UWTB?" said Salo. "Didn't I let you copy my ship for Mars? Didn't I fly the first few recruiting missions? Didn't I help you figure out how to control the Martians, so they wouldn't make trouble? Didn't I spend day after day helping you to design the new religion?"

"Yes," said Rumfoord. "But what have you done for me lately?"

"What?" said Salo.

"Never mind," said Rumfoord curtly. "It's the tag-line on an old Earthling joke, and not a very funny one, under the circumstances."

"Oh," said Salo. He knew a lot of Earthling jokes, but he didn't know that one.

"Your feet!" cried Rumfoord.

"I'm sorry!" cried Salo. "If I could weep like an Earthling, I would!" His grieving feet were out of his control. They went on making the sounds Rumfoord suddenly hated so. "I'm sorry for everything! All I know is, I've tried every way I know how to be a true friend, and I never asked for *anything* in return."

"You didn't have to!" said Rumfoord. "You didn't have to ask for a thing. All you had to do was sit back and wait for it to be dropped in your lap."

"What was it I wanted dropped in my lap?" said Salo incredulously.

"The replacement part for your space ship," said Rumfoord. "It's almost here. It's arriving, sire. Constant's boy has it—calls it his good-luck piece—as though you didn't know."

Rumfoord sat up, turned green, motioned for silence. "Excuse me," he said. "I'm going to be sick again."

Winston Niles Rumfoord and his dog Kazak *were* sick again—more violently sick than before. It seemed to poor old Salo that this time they would surely sizzle to nothing or explode.

Kazak howled in a ball of Saint Elmo's fire.

Rumfoord stood bolt upright, his eyes popping, a fiery column.

This attack passed, too.

"Excuse me," said Rumfoord with scathing decency. "You were saying—?"

"What?" said Salo bleakly.

"You were saying something—or about to say something," said Rumfoord. Only the sweat at his temples betrayed the fact that he had just been through something harrowing. He put a cigarette in a long, bone cigarette holder, lighted it. He thrust out his jaw. The cigarette holder pointed straight up. "We won't be interrupted again for three minutes," he said. "You were saying?"

Salo recalled the subject of conversation only with effort. When he did recall it, it upset him more than ever. The worst possible thing had happened. Not only had Rumfoord found out, seemingly, about the influence of Tralfamadore on Earthling affairs, which would have offended him quite enough—but Rumfoord also regarded himself, seemingly, as one of the principal victims of that influence.

Salo had had an uneasy suspicion from time to time that Rumfoord was under the influence of Tralfamadore, but he'd pushed the thought out of his mind, since there was nothing he could do about it. He hadn't even discussed it, because to discuss it with Rumfoord would surely have ruined their beautiful friendship at once. Very lamely, Salo explored the possibility that Rumfoord did not know as much as he seemed to know. "Skip—" he said.

"Please!" said Rumfoord.

"Mr. Rumfoord," said Salo, "you think I somehow used you?"

"Not you," said Rumfoord. "Your fellow machines back on your precious Tralfamadore."

"Um," said Salo. "You—you think you—you've been used, Skip?"

"Tralfamadore," said Rumfoord bitterly, "reached into the Solar System, picked me up, and used me like a handy-dandy potato peeler!"

"If you could see this in the future," said Salo miserably, "why didn't you mention it before?"

"Nobody likes to think he's being used," said Rumfoord. "He'll put off admitting it to himself until the last possible instant." He smiled crookedly. "It may surprise you to learn that I take a certain pride, no matter how foolishly mistaken that pride may be, in making my own decisions for my own reasons."

"I'm not surprised," said Salo.

"Oh?" said Rumfoord unpleasantly. "I should have thought it was too subtle an attitude for a *machine* to grasp."

This, surely, was the low point in their relationship. Salo *was* a machine, since he had been designed and manufactured. He didn't conceal the fact. But Rumfoord had never used the fact as an insult before. He had definitely used the fact as an insult now. Through a thin veil of noblesse oblige, Rumfoord let Salo know that to be a machine was to be insensitive, was to be unimaginative, was to be vulgar, was to be purposeful without a shred of conscience.

Salo was pathetically vulnerable to this accusation. It was a tribute to the spiritual intimacy he and Rumfoord had once shared that Rumfoord knew so well how to hurt him.

Salo closed two of his three eyes again, watched the soaring Titanic bluebirds again. The birds were as big as Earthling eagles.

Salo wished he were a Titanic bluebird.

The space ship carrying Malachi Constant, Beatrice Rumfoord, and their son Chrono sailed low over the palace, landed on the shore of the Winston Sea.

"I give you my word of honour," said Salo, "I didn't know you were being used, and I haven't the slightest idea what you—"

"Machine," said Rumfoord nastily.

"Tell me what you've been used for—please?" said Salo. "My word of honour—I don't have the foggiest—"

"Machine!" said Rumfoord.

"If you think so badly of me, Skip—Winston—Mr. Rumfoord," said Salo, "after all I've done and tried to do in the name of friendship alone, there's certainly nothing I can say or do now to change your mind."

"Precisely what a machine *would* say," said Rumfoord.

"It's what a machine did say," said Salo humbly. He inflated his feet to the size of German batballs, preparing to walk out of Rumfoord's palace and onto the waters of the Winston Sea—never to return. Only when his feet were fully inflated did he catch the challenge in what Rumfoord had said. There was a clear implication that there was something Old Salo could still do to make things right again.

Even if he was a machine, Salo was sensitive enough to know that to ask what that something was would be to grovel. He steeled himself. In the name of friendship, he was going to grovel.

"Skip," he said, "tell me what to do. Anything—anything at all."

"In a very short time," said Rumfoord, "an explosion is going to blow the terminal of my spiral clear off the Sun, clear out of the Solar System."

"No!" cried Salo. "Skip! Skip!"

"No, no—not pity, *please*," said Rumfoord, stepping back, afraid of being touched. "It's a very good thing, really, I'll be seeing a lot of new things, a lot of new creatures." He tried to smile. "One gets tired, you know, being caught up in the monotonous clockwork of the Solar System." He laughed harshly. "After all," he said, "it isn't as though I were dying or something. Everything that ever was always will be, and everything that ever will be always was." He shook his head quickly, and cast away a tear he hadn't known was on his eyelid.

"Comforting as that chrono-synclastic infundibulated thought is," he said, "I should still like to know just what the main point of this Solar System episode has been."

"You—you've summed it up far better than anyone else could—in your *Pocket History of Mars*," said Salo.

"*The Pocket History of Mars*," said Rumfoord, "makes no mention of the fact that I have been powerfully influenced by forces emanating from the planet Tralfamadore." He gritted his teeth.

"Before my dog and I go crackling off through space like buggywhips in the hands of a lunatic," said Rumfoord, "I should very much like to know what the message you are carrying is."

"I—I don't know," said Salo. "It's sealed. I have orders—"

"Against all orders from Tralfamadore," said Winston Niles Rumfoord, "against all your instincts as a machine, but in the name of our friendship, Salo, I want you to open the message and read it to me now."

Malachi Constant, Beatrice Rumfoord, and young Chrono, their savage son, picnicked sulkily in the shade of a Titanic daisy by the Winston Sea. Each member of the family had a statue against which to lean.

Bearded Malachi Constant, playboy of the Solar System, still wore his bright yellow suit with the orange question marks. It was the only suit he had.

Constant leaned against a statue of St. Francis of Assisi. St. Francis was trying to befriend two hostile and terrifying huge birds, apparently bald eagles. Constant was unable to identify the birds properly as Titanic bluebirds, since he hadn't seen a Titanic bluebird yet. He had arrived on Titan only an hour before.

Beatrice, looking like a gypsy queen, smouldered at the foot of a statue of a young physical student. At first glance, the laboratory-gowned scientist seemed to be a perfect servant of nothing but truth. At first glance, one was convinced that nothing but truth could please him as he beamed at his test tube. At first glance, one thought that he was as much above the beastly concerns of mankind as the harmoniums in the caves of Mercury. There, at first glance, was a young man without vanity, without lust—and one accepted at its face value the title Salo had engraved on the statue, *Discovery of Atomic Power*.

And then one perceived that the young truth-seeker had a shocking erection.

Beatrice hadn't perceived this yet.

Young Chrono, dark and dangerous like his mother, was already committing his first act of vandalism—or was trying to. Chrono was trying to inscribe a dirty Earthling word on the base of the statue against which he had been leaning. He was attempting the job with a sharp corner of his good-luck piece.

The seasoned Titanic peat, almost as hard as diamonds, did the cutting instead, rounding off the corner's point.

The statue on which Chrono was working was of a family group—a Neanderthal man, his mate, and their baby. It was a deeply-moving piece. The squat, shaggy, hopeful creatures were so ugly they were beautiful.

Their importance and universality was not spoiled by the satiric title Salo had given the piece. He gave frightful titles to all his statues, as though to proclaim desperately that he did not take himself seriously as an artist, not for an instant. The title he gave to the Neanderthal family derived from the fact that the baby was being shown a human foot roasting on a crude spit.

The title was *This Little Piggy*.

"No matter what happens, no matter what beautiful or sad or happy or frightening thing happens," Malachi Constant told his family there on Titan, "I'm damned if I'll respond. The minute it looks like something or somebody wants me to act in some special way, I will freeze." He glanced up at the rings of Saturn, curled his lip. "Isn't that just too beautiful for words?" He spat on the ground.

"If anybody ever expects to use me again in some tremendous scheme of his," said Constant, "he is in for one big disappointment. He will be a lot better off trying to get a rise out of one of these statues."

He spat again.

"As far as I'm concerned," said Constant, "the Universe is a junk yard, with everything in it overpriced. I am through poking around in the junk heaps, looking for bargains. Every so-called bargain," said Constant, "has been connected by fine wires to a dynamite bouquet." He spat again.

"I resign," said Constant.

"I withdraw," said Constant.

"I quit," said Constant.

Constant's little family agreed without enthusiasm. Constant's brave speech was stale stuff. He had delivered it many times during the seventeen-month voyage from Earth to Titan—and it was, after all, a routine philosophy for all Martian veterans.

Constant wasn't really speaking to his family anyway. He was speaking loudly, so his voice would carry some distance into the forest of statuary and over the Winston Sea. He was making a policy statement for the benefit of Rumfoord or anybody else who might be lurking near by.

"We have taken part for the last time," said Constant loudly, "in experiments and fights and festivals we don't like or understand!"

"'Understand—'" came an echo from the wall of a palace on an island two hundred yards offshore. The place was, of course, Dun Roamin, Rumfoord's Taj Mahal. Constant wasn't surprised to see the palace out there. He had seen it when he disembarked from his space ship, had seen it shining out there like St. Augustine's City of God.

"What happens next?" Constant asked the echo. "All the statues come to life?"

"'Life!'" said the echo.

"It's an echo," said Beatrice.

"I know it's an echo," said Constant.

203

"I didn't know if you knew it was an echo or not," said Beatrice. She was distant and polite. She had been extremely decent to Constant, blaming him for nothing, expecting nothing from him. A less aristocratic woman might have put him through hell, blaming him for everything and demanding miracles.

There had been no love-making during the voyage. Neither Constant nor Beatrice had been interested. Martian veterans never were.

Inevitably, the long voyage had drawn Constant closer to his mate and child—closer than they had been on the gilded system of catwalks, ramps, ladders, pulpits, steps, and stages in Newport. But the only love in the family unit was still the love between young Chrono and Beatrice. Other than the love between mother and son there was only politeness, glum compassion, and suppressed indignation at having been forced to be a family at all.

"Oh, my," said Constant, "life is funny when you stop to think of it."

Young Chrono did not smile when his father said life was funny.

Young Chrono was the member of the family least in a position to think life was funny. Beatrice and Constant, after all, could laugh bitterly at the wild incidents they had survived. But young Chrono couldn't laugh with them, because he himself was a wild incident.

Small wonder that young Chrono's chief treasures were a good-luck piece and a switchblade knife.

Young Chrono now drew his switchblade knife, flicked open the blade nonchalantly. His eyes narrowed. He was preparing to kill, if killing should become necessary. He was looking in the direction of a gilded rowboat that had put out from the palace on the island.

It was being rowed by a tangerine-coloured creature. The oarsman was, of course, Salo. He was bringing the boat in order to transport the family back to the palace. Salo was a bad oarsman, never having rowed before. He grasped the oars with his suction-cup feet.

He had one advantage over human oarsmen, in that he had an eye in the back of his head.

Young Chrono flashed light into Old Salo's eye, flashed it with his bright knife blade.

Salo's back eye blinked.

Flashing the light into the eye was not a piece of sky-larking on Chrono's part. It was a piece of jungle cunning, a piece of cunning calculated to make almost any sort of sighted creature uneasy. It was one of a thousand pieces of jungle cunning that young Chrono and his mother had learned in their year together in the Amazon Rain Forest.

Beatrice's brown hand closed on a rock. "Worry him again," she said softly to Chrono.

Young Chrono again flashed the light in Old Salo's eye.

"His body looks like the only soft part," said Beatrice, without moving her lips. "If you can't get his body, try for an eye."

Chrono nodded.

Constant was chilled, seeing what an efficient unit of self-defence his mate and son made together. Constant was not included in their plans. They had no need of him.

"What should I do?" whispered Constant.

"Sh!" said Beatrice sharply.

Salo beached his gilded craft. He made it fast with a clumsy landlubber's knot to the wrist of a statue by the water. The statue was of a nude woman playing a slide trombone. It was entitled, enigmatically, *Evelyn and her Magic Violin*.

Salo was too jangled by sorrow to care for his own safety—to understand, even, that he might be frightening to someone. He stood for a moment on a block of seasoned Titanic peat near his landing. His grieving feet sucked at the damp stone. He prised loose his feet with a tremendous effort.

On he came, the flashes from Chrono's knife dazzling him.

"Please," he said.

A rock flew out of the knife's dazzle.

Salo ducked.

A hand siezed his bony throat, threw him down.

Young Chrono now stood astride Old Salo, his knife point pricking Salo's chest. Beatrice knelt by Salo's head, a rock poised to smash his head to bits.

"Go on—kill me," said Salo raspingly. "You'd be doing me a favour. I wish I were dead. I wish to God I'd never been assembled and started up in the first place. Kill me, put me out of my misery, and then go see him. He's asking for you."

"Who is?" said Beatrice.

"Your poor husband—my former friend, Winston Niles Rumfoord," said Salo.

"Where is he?" said Beatrice.

"In that palace on the island," said Salo. "He's dying —all alone, except for his faithful dog. He's asking for you," said Salo, "asking for all of you. And he says he never wants to lay his eyes on me again."

Malachi Constant watched the lead-coloured lips kiss thin air soundlessly. The tongue behind the lips clicked infinitesimally. The lips suddenly drew back, baring the perfect teeth of Winston Niles Rumfoord.

Constant was himself showing his teeth, preparing to gnash them appropriately at the sight of this man who had done him so much harm. He did not gnash them. For one thing, no one was looking—no one would see him do it and understand. For another thing, Constant found himself destitute of hate.

His preparations for gnashing his teeth decayed into a yokel gape—the gape of a yokel in the presence of a spectacularly mortal disease.

Winston Niles Rumfoord was lying, fully materialized, on his back on his lavender contour chair by the pool. His eyes were directed at the sky, unblinkingly and seemingly sightless. One fine hand dangled over the side of the chair, its limp fingers laced in the choke chain of Kazak, the hound of space.

The chain was empty.

An explosion on the Sun had separated man and dog. A Universe schemed in mercy would have kept man and dog together.

The Universe inhabited by Winston Niles Rumfoord and his dog was not schemed in mercy. Kazak had been sent ahead of his master on the great mission to nowhere and nothing.

Kazak had left howling in a puff of ozone and sick light, in a hum like swarming bees.

Rumfoord let the empty choke chain slip from his fingers. The chain expressed deadness, made formless sound and a formless heap, was a soulless slave of gravity, born with a broken spine.

Rumfoord's lead-coloured lips moved. "Hello, Beatrice—wife," he said sepulchrally.

"Hello, Space Wanderer," he said. He made his voice affectionate this time. "Gallant of you to come, Space Wanderer—to take one more chance with me.

"Hello, illustrious young bearer of the illustrious name of Chrono," said Rumfoord. "Hail, oh German batball star —hail, him of the good-luck piece."

The three to whom he spoke stood just inside the wall. The pool was between them and Rumfoord.

Old Salo, who had not been granted his wish to die, grieved in the stern of the gilded rowboat that was beached outside the wall.

"I am not dying," said Rumfoord. "I am merely taking my leave of the Solar System. And I am not even doing that. In the grand, in the timeless, in the chrono-synclastic infundibulated way of looking at things, I shall always be here. I shall always be wherever I've been.

"I'm honeymooning with you still, Beatrice," he said. "I'm talking to you still in a little room under the stairway in Newport, Mr. Constant. Yes—and playing peek-a-boo in the caves of Mercury with you and Boaz. And Chrono," he said, "I'm watching you still as you play German batball so well on the iron playground of Mars."

He groaned. It was a tiny groan—and so sad.

The sweet, mild air of Titan carried the tiny groan away.

"Whatever we've said, friends, we're saying still—such as it was, such as it is, such as it will be," said Rumfoord.

The tiny groan came again.

Rumfoord watched it leave as though it were a smoke ring.

"There is something you should know about life in the Solar System," he said. "Being chrono-synclastic infundibulated, I've known about it all along. It is, none the less, such a sickening thing that I've thought about it as little as possible.

"The sickening thing is this:

"*Everything that every Earthling has ever done has been warped by creatures on a planet one-hundred-and-fifty thousand light years away*. The name of the planet is Tralfamadore.

"How the Tralfamadorians controlled us, I don't know.

But I know to what end they controlled us. *They controlled us in such a way as to make us deliver a replacement part to a Tralfamadorian messenger who was grounded right here on Titan.*"

Rumfoord pointed a finger at young Chrono. "You young man," he said. "You have it in your pocket. In your pocket is the culmination of all Earthling history. In your pocket is the mysterious something that every Earthling was trying so desperately, so earnestly, so gropingly, so exhaustingly to produce and deliver."

A fizzing twig of electricity grew from the tip of Rumfoord's accusing finger.

"The thing you call your good-luck piece," said Rumfoord, "is the replacement part for which the Tralfamadorian messenger has been waiting so long!

"The messenger," said Rumfoord, "is the tangerine-coloured creature who now cowers outside the walls. His name is Salo. I had hoped that the messenger would give mankind a glimpse of the message he was carrying, since mankind was giving him such a nice boost on his way. Unfortunately, he is under orders to show the message to no one. He is a machine, and, as a machine, he has no choice but to regard orders as orders.

"I asked him politely to show me the message," said Rumfoord. "He desperately refused."

The fizzing twig of electricity on Rumfoord's finger grew, forming a spiral around Rumfoord. Rumfoord considered the spiral with sad contempt. "I think perhaps this is it," he said of the spiral.

It was indeed. The spiral telescoped slightly, making a curtsey. And then it began to revolve around Rumfoord, spinning a continuous cocoon of green light.

It barely whispered as it spun.

"All I can say," said Rumfoord from the cocoon, "is that I have tried my best to do good for my native Earth while serving the irresistible wishes of Tralfamadore.

"Perhaps, now that the part has been delivered to the Tralfamadorian messenger, Tralfamadore will leave the Solar System alone. Perhaps Earthlings will now be free to develop and follow their own inclinations, as they have not been free to do for thousands of years." He sneezed. "The wonder is that Earthlings have been able to make as much sense as they have," he said.

The green cocoon left the ground, hovered over the dome. "Remember me as a gentleman of Newport, Earth, and the Solar System," said Rumfoord. He sounded serene again, at peace with himself, and at least equal to any creature that he might encounter anywhere.

"In a punctual way of speaking," came Rumfoord's glottal tenor from the cocoon, "good-bye."

The cocoon and Rumfoord disappeared with a *pft*.

Rumfoord and his dog were never seen again.

Old Salo came bounding into the courtyard just as Rumfoord and his cocoon disappeared.

The little Tralfamadorian was wild. He had torn the message from its band around his throat with a suction-cup foot. One foot was still a suction cup, and in it was the message.

He looked up at the place where the cocoon had hovered. "Skip!" he cried into the sky. "Skip! The message! I'll tell you the message! *The message! Skiiiiiiiiiiiiiiiiiiip!*"

His head did a somersault in its gimbals. "Gone," he said emptily. He whispered, "Gone.

"Machine?" said Salo. He was speaking haltingly, as much to himself as to Constant, Beatrice, and Chrono. "A machine I am, and so are my people," he said. "I was designed and manufactured, and no expense, no skill, was spared in making me dependable, efficient, predictable, and durable. I was the best machine my people could make.

"How good a machine have I proved to be?" asked Salo.

"*Dependable?*" he said. "I was depended upon to keep my message sealed until I reached my destination, and now I've torn it open.

"*Efficient?*" he said. "Having lost my best friend in the Universe, it now costs me more energy to step over a dead leaf than it once cost me to bound over Mount Rumfoord.

"*Predictable?*" he said. "After watching human beings for two hundred thousand Earthling years, I have become as skittish and sentimental as the silliest Earthling schoolgirl.

"*Durable?*" he said darkly. "We shall see what we shall see."

He laid the message he had been carrying so long on Rumfoord's empty, lavender contour chair.

"There it is—friend," he said to his memory of Rumfoord, "and much consolation may it give you, Skip. Much pain it cost your old friend Salo. In order to give it to you —even too late—your old friend Salo had to make war against the core of his being, against the very nature of being a machine.

"You asked the impossible of a machine," said Salo. "and the machine complied.

"The machine is no longer a machine," said Salo. "The machine's contacts are corroded, his bearings fouled, his circuits shorted, and his gears stripped. His mind buzzes and pops like the mind of an Earthling—fizzes and overheats with thoughts of love, honour, dignity, rights, accomplishment, integrity, independence—"

Old Salo picked up the message again from Rumfoord's contour chair. It was written on a thin square of aluminum. The message was a single dot.

"Would you like to know how I have been used, how my life has been wasted?" he said. "Would you like to know what the message is that I have been carrying for almost half a million Earthling years—the message I am supposed to carry for eighteen million more years?"

He held out the square of aluminium in a cupped foot.

"A dot," he said.

"A single dot," he said.

"The meaning of a dot in Tralfamadorian," said Old Salo, "is—

"Greetings."

The little machine from Tralfamadore, having delivered this message to himself, to Constant, to Beatrice, and to Chrono over a distance of one hundred and fifty thousand light years, bounded abruptly out of the courtyard and onto the beach outside.

He killed himself out there. He took himself apart and threw his parts in all directions.

Chrono went out on the beach alone, wandered thoughtfully among Salo's parts. Chrono had always known that his good-luck piece had extraordinary powers and extraordinary meanings.

And he had always suspected that some superior creature would eventually come to claim the good-luck piece as his own. It was in the nature of truly effective good-luck pieces that human beings never really owned them.

They simply took care of them, had the benefit of them, until the real owners, the superior owners, came along.

Chrono did not have a sense of futility and disorder.

Everything seemed in apple-pie order to him.

And the boy himself participated fitly in that perfect order.

He took his good-luck piece from his pocket, dropped it without regret to the sand, dropped it among Salo's scattered parts.

Sooner or later, Chrono believed, the magical forces of the Universe would put everything back together again.

They always did.

REUNION WITH STONY

"You are tired, so very tired, Space Wanderer, Malachi, Unk. Stare at the faintest star, Earthling, and think how heavy your limbs are growing."
SALO

THERE ISN'T much more to tell.

Malachi Constant grew to be an old man on Titan.

Beatrice Rumfoord grew to be an old woman on Titan.

They died peacefully, died within twenty-four hours of each other. They died in their seventy-fourth years.

Only the Titanic bluebirds know for sure what happened, finally, to Chrono, their son.

When Malachi Constant turned seventy-four years old, he was crusty, sweet, and bandy-legged. He was totally bald, and went naked most of the time, wearing nothing but a neatly-trimmed, white vandyke beard.

He lived in Salo's grounded space ship, had been living there for thirty years.

Constant had not tried to fly the space ship. He hadn't dared to touch a single control. The controls of Salo's ship were far more complex than those of a Martian ship. Salo's dash panel offered Constant two hundred and seventy-three knobs, switches, and buttons, each with a Tralfamadorian inscription or calibration. The controls were anything but a hunch-player's delight in a Universe composed of one trillionth part matter to one decillion parts black velvet futility.

Constant had tinkered with the ship only to the extent of finding out gingerly if, as Rumfoord had said, Chrono's good-luck piece really would serve as a part of the power plant.

Superficially, at any rate, the good-luck piece would. There was an access door to the ship's power plant that had plainly leaked smoke at one time. Constant opened it, found a sooty compartment within. And under the soot were smudged bearings and cams that related to nothing.

Constant was able to slip the holes in Chrono's good-luck piece onto those bearings and between the cams. The good-luck piece conformed to close tolerances and surrounding clearances in a way that would have pleased a Swiss machinist.

Constant had many hobbies that helped him to pass the balmy time in the salubrious clime of Titan.

His most interesting hobby was puttering around with Salo, the dismantled Tralfamadorian messenger. Constant spent thousands of hours trying to get Salo back together and going again.

So far, he had had no luck.

When Constant first undertook the reconstruction of the little Tralfamadorian, it had been with the express hope that Salo would then agree to fly young Chrono back to Earth.

Constant wasn't eager to fly back to Earth, and neither was his mate Beatrice. But Constant and Beatrice had agreed that their son, with most of his life ahead of him, should live that life with busy and jolly contemporaries on Earth.

By the time Constant was seventy-four, however, getting young Chrono back to Earth was no longer a pressing problem. Young Chrono was no longer particularly young. He was forty-two. And he had made such a thorough and specialized adjustment on Titan that it would have been cruel in the extreme to send him anywhere else.

At the age of seventeen, young Chrono had run away from his palatial home to join the Titanic bluebirds, the most admirable creatures on Titan. Chrono now lived among their nests by the Kazak pools. He wore their feathers and sat on their eggs and shared their food and spoke their language.

Constant never saw Chrono. Sometimes, late at night, he would hear Chrono's cries. Constant did not answer the cries. The cries were for nothing and nobody on Titan.

They were for Phoebe, a passing moon.

Sometimes, when Constant was out gathering Titanic strawberries or the speckled, two-pound eggs of the Titanic plover, he would come upon a little shrine made of sticks and stones in a clearing. Chrono made hundreds of these shrines.

The elements in the shrines were always the same. One large stone was at the center, representing Saturn. A Wooden hoop made of a green twig was placed around it— to represent Saturn's rings. And beyond the rings were small stones to represent the nine moons. The largest of these satellite stones was Titan. And there was always the feather of a Titanic bluebird under it.

The marks on the ground made it clear that young Chrono, no longer so young, spent hours moving the elements of the system about.

When old Malachi Constant found one of his strange son's shrines in a state of neglect, he would tidy it up as best he could. Constant would weed it and rake it, and make a new twig ring for the stone that was Saturn. He would put a fresh bluebird feather under the stone that was Titan.

Tidying up the shrines was as close, spiritually, as Constant could get to his son.

He respected what his son was trying to do with religion.

And sometimes, when Constant gazed at a refurbished shrine, he moved the elements of his own life about experimentally—but he did it in his head. At such times he was likely to reflect in melancholy on two things in particular— his murder of Stony Stevenson, his best and only friend, and his winning, so late in life, the love of Beatrice Rumfoord.

Constant never found out whether Chrono knew who tidied up the shrines. Chrono may have thought his god or gods were doing it.

It was all so sad. But it was all so beautiful, too.

Beatrice Rumfoord lived alone in Rumfoord's Taj Mahal. Her contacts with Chrono were far more harrowing than Constant's. At unpredictable intervals, Chrono would swim out to the palace, dress himself from Rumfoord's wardrobe, announce that it was his mother's birthday, and spend the day in indolent, sullen, reasonably civilized discourse.

At the end of such a day, Chrono would rage at the clothes and his mother and civilization. He would tear off the clothes, scream like a bluebird, and dive into the Winston Sea.

When Beatrice had suffered through one of these birthday parties, she would thrust an oar into the sand of the beach that faced the nearest shore, and she would fly a white sheet from it.

It was a signal for Malachi Constant, begging him please to come at once, to help her calm down.

And when Constant arrived in response to the signal of distress, Beatrice always comforted herself with the same words.

"At least," she would say, "he isn't a mama's boy. And at least he had the greatness of soul to join the noblest, most beautiful creatures in sight."

The white sheet, the signal of distress, was flying now.

Malachi Constant put out from shore in a dugout canoe. The gilded rowboat that had come with the palace had long since been sunk by dry rot.

Constant was wearing an old blue wool bathrobe that had once belonged to Rumfoord. He had found it in the palace, had taken it when his Space Wanderer's suit wore out. It was his only garment, and he wore it only when he went calling on Beatrice.

Constant had in the dugout canoe with him six plovers' eggs, two quarts of wild Titanic strawberries, a three-gallon peat crock of fermented daisy milk, a bushel of daisy seeds, eight books he had borrowed from the forty-thousand-volume library in the palace, and a home-made broom and a home-made shovel.

Constant was self-sufficient. He raised or gathered or made everything he needed. This satisfied him enormously.

Beatrice was not dependent on Constant. Rumfoord had stocked the Taj Mahal lavishly with Earthling food and Earthling liquor. Beatrice had plenty to eat and drink, and always would have.

Constant was bringing native foods to Beatrice because he was so proud of his skills as a woodsman and husbandman. He liked to show off his skills as a provider.

It was a compulsion.

Constant had his broom and shovel along in the dugout canoe because Beatrice's palace was always a broom-and-shovel mess. Beatrice did no cleaning, so Constant got rid of the worst of the refuse whenever he paid her a visit.

Beatrice Rumfoord was a springy, one-eyed, gold-toothed, brown old lady—as lean and tough as a chair slat. But the class of the damaged and roughly-used old lady showed through.

To anyone with a sense of poetry, mortality, and wonder, Malachi Constant's proud, high-cheekboned mate was as handsome as a human being could be.

She was probably a little crazy. On a moon with only two other people on it, she was writing a book called *The True Purpose of Life in the Solar System*. It was a refutation of Rumfoord's notion that the purpose of human life in the Solar System was to get a grounded messenger from Tralfamadore on his way again.

Beatrice began the book after her son left her to join the bluebirds. The manuscript so far, written in longhand, occupied thirty-eight cubic feet inside the Taj Mahal.

Every time Constant visited her, she read aloud her latest additions to the manuscript.

She was reading out loud now, sitting in Rumfoord's old contour chair while Constant puttered about the court-yard. She was wearing a pink and white chenille bedspread that had come with the palace. Worked into the tufts of the bedspread was the message, *God does not care*.

It had been Rumfoord's own personal bedspread.

On and on Beatrice read, spinning arguments against the importance of the forces of Tralfamadore.

Constant did not listen attentively. He simply enjoyed Beatrice's voice, which was strong and triumphant. He was down in a manhole by the pool, turning a valve that would drain the water out. The water of the pool had been turned into something like cream of pea soup by Titanic algae. Every time Constant visited Beatrice he fought a losing battle against the prolific green murk.

"'I would be the last to deny,'" said Beatrice, reading her own work out loud, "'that the forces of Tralfamadore have had something to do with the affairs of Earth. However, those persons who have served the interests of Tralfamadore have served them in such highly personalized ways that Tralfamadore can be said to have had practically nothing to do with the case.'"

Constant, down in the manhole, put his ear to the valve he had opened. From the sound of it, the water was draining slowly.

Constant swore. One of the vital pieces of information that had disappeared with Rumfoord and died with Salo was how they had managed, in their time, to keep the pool so crystal clean. Ever since Constant had taken over maintenance of the pool, the algae had been building up. The pool's bottoms and sides were lined with a blanket of viscid slime, and the three statues in the middle, the three Sirens of Titan, were under a mucilaginous hump.

Constant knew of the significance of the three sirens in his life. He had read about it—both in the *Pocket History of Mars* and *The Winston Niles Rumfoord Authorized Revised Bible*. The three great beauties didn't mean so much to him now, really, except to remind him that sex had once bothered him.

Constant climbed out of the manhole. "Drains slower every time," he said to Beatrice. "I don't guess I can put off digging up the pipes much longer."

"That so?" said Beatrice, looking up from her writing.

"That's so," said Constant.

"Well—you do whatever needs to be done," said Beatrice.

"That's the story of my life," said Constant.

"I just had an idea that ought to go in the book," said Beatrice, "if I can just keep it from getting away."

"I'll hit it with a shovel, if it comes this way," said Constant.

"Don't say anything for a minute," said Beatrice. "Just let me get it straight in my head." She stood, and went into the entry of the palace to escape the distractions of Constant and the rings of Saturn.

She looked long at a large oil painting hanging on the entry wall. It was the only painting in the palace. Constant had had it brought all the way from Newport.

It was a painting of an immaculate little girl in white, holding the reins of a white pony all her own.

Beatrice knew who the little girl was. The painting was labelled with a brass plate that said, *Beatrice Rumfoord as a Young Girl*.

It was quite a contrast—between the little girl in white and the old lady looking at her.

Beatrice suddenly turned her back on the painting, walked out into the courtyard again. The idea she wanted to add to her book was straight in her mind now.

"The worst thing that could possibly happen to anybody," she said, "would be to not be used for anything by anybody."

The thought relaxed her. She lay down on Rumfoord's old contour chair, looked up at the appallingly beautiful rings of Saturn—at Rumfoord's Rainbow.

"Thank you for using me," she said to Constant, "even though I didn't want to be used by anybody."

"You're welcome," said Constant.

He began to sweep the courtyard. The litter he was sweeping was a mixture of sand, which had blown in from the outside, daisy-seed hulls, Earthling peanut hulls, empty cans of boned chicken, and discarded wads of manuscript paper. Beatrice subsisted mostly on daisy seeds, peanuts, and boned chicken because she didn't have to cook them, because she didn't even have to interrupt her writing in order to eat them.

She could eat with one hand and write with the other—and, more than anything else in life, she wanted to get everything written down.

With his sweeping half done, Constant paused to see how the pool was draining.

It was draining slowly. The slimy green hump that covered the three Sirens of Titan was just breaking the descending surface.

Constant leaned over the open manhole, listened to the water sounds.

He heard the music of the pipes. And he heard something else, too.

He heard the absence of a familiar and a beloved sound.

His mate Beatrice wasn't breathing any more.

Malachi Constant buried his mate in Titanic peat on the shore of the Winston Sea. She was buried where there were no statues.

Malachi Constant said good-bye to her when the sky was filled with Titanic bluebirds. There must have been ten thousand, at least, of the great and noble birds.

They made night of day, made the air quake with their beating wings.

Not one bird cried out.

And in that night in the midst of day, Chrono, the son of Beatrice and Malachi, appeared on a knoll overlooking the new grave. He wore a feather cape which he flapped like wings.

He was gorgeous and strong.

"Thank you, Mother and Father," he shouted, "for the gift of life. Good-bye."

He was gone, and the birds went with him.

Old Malachi Constant went back to the palace with a heart as heavy as a cannonball. What drew him back to that sad place was a wish to leave it in good order.

Sooner or later, someone else would come.

The palace should be neat and clean and ready for them. The palace should speak well of the former tenant.

Around Rumfoord's worn contour chair were the plovers' eggs and wild Titanic strawberries, and the crock of fermented daisy milk and the basket of daisy seeds that Constant had given to Beatrice. They were perishables. They would not last until the next tenant came.

These Constant put back in his dugout canoe.

He didn't need them. Nobody needed them.

As he straightened up his old back from the canoe, he saw Salo, the little messenger from Tralfamadore, walking across the water toward him.

"How do you do," said Constant.

"How do you do," said Salo. "Thank you for putting me back together again."

"I didn't think I did it right," said Constant. "I couldn't get a peep out of you."

"You did it right," said Salo. "I just couldn't make up my mind whether or not I wanted to peep." He let the air out of his feet with a hiss. "I guess I'll be moseying along," he said.

"You're going to deliver your message after all?" said Constant.

"Anybody who has travelled this far on a fool's errand," said Salo, "has no choice but to uphold the honour of fools by completing the errand."

"My mate died today," said Constant.

"Sorry," said Salo. "I would say, 'Is there anything I can do?'—but Skip once told me that that was the most hateful and stupid expression in the English language."

Constant rubbed his hands together. The only company

he had left on Titan was whatever company his right hand could be for his left. "I miss her," he said.

"You finally fell in love, I see," said Salo.

"Only an Earthling year ago," said Constant. "It took us that long to realize that a purpose of human life, no matter who is controlling it, is to love whoever is around to be loved."

"If you or your son would like a ride back to Earth," said Salo, "it wouldn't be much out of my way."

"My boy joined the bluebirds," said Constant.

"Good for him!" said Salo. "I'd join them, if they'd have me."

"Earth," said Constant wonderingly.

"We could be there in a matter of hours," said Salo, "now that the ship's running right again."

"It's lonely here," said Constant, "now that—" He shook his head.

On the trip back to Earth, Salo suspected that he had made a tragic mistake in suggesting to Constant that he return to Earth. He had begun to suspect this when Constant insisted on being taken to Indianapolis, Indiana, U.S.A.

This insistence of Constant's was a dismaying development, since Indianapolis was far from an ideal place for a homeless old man.

Salo wanted to let him off by a shuffleboard court in St. Petersburg, Florida, U.S.A., but Constant, after the fashion of old men, could not be shaken from his first decision. He wanted to go to Indianapolis, and that was that.

Salo assumed that Constant had relatives or possibly old business connections in Indianapolis, but this turned out not to be the case.

"I don't know anybody in Indianapolis, and I don't know anything about Indianapolis except for one thing," said Constant, "a thing I read in a book."

"What did you read in a book?" said Salo uneasily.

"Indianapolis, Indiana," said Constant, "is the first place in the United States of America where a white man was hanged for the murder of an Indian. The kind of people who'll hang a white man for murdering an Indian," said Constant, "that's the kind of people for me."

Salo's head did a somersault in its gimbals. His feet made grieved sucking sounds on the iron floor. His passenger, obviously, knew almost nothing about the planet toward which he was being carried with a speed approaching that of light.

At least Constant had money.

There was hope in that. He had close to three thousand dollars in various Earthling currencies, taken from the pockets of Rumfoord's suits in the Taj Mahal.

And at least he had clothes.

He had on a terribly baggy but good tweed suit of Rumfoord's, complete with a Phi Beta Kappa key that hung from the watch chain that spanned the front of the vest.

Salo had made Constant take the key along with the suit.

Constant had a good overcoat, a hat, and overshoes, too.

With Earth only an hour away, Salo wondered what else he could do to make the remainder of Constant's life supportable, even in Indianapolis.

And he decided to hypnotize Constant, in order that the last few seconds of Constant's life, at least, would please the old man tremendously. Constant's life would end well.

Constant was already in a nearly hypnotic state, staring out at the Cosmos through a porthole.

Salo came up behind him and spoke to him soothingly.

"You are tired, so very tired, Space Wanderer, Malachi, Unk," said Salo. "Stare at the faintest star, Earthling, and think how heavy your limbs are growing."

"Heavy," said Constant.

"You are going to die some day, Unk," said Salo. "Sorry, but it's true."

"True," said Constant. "Don't be sorry."

"When you know you are dying, Space Wanderer," said Salo hypnotically, "a wonderful thing will happen to you." He then described to Constant the happy things that Constant would imagine before his life flickered out.

It would be a post-hypnotic illusion.

"Awake!" said Salo.

Constant shuddered, turned away from the porthole. "Where am I?" he said.

"On a Tralfamadorian space ship out of Titan, bound for Earth," said Salo.

"Oh," said Constant, "Of course," he said a moment later. "I must have been asleep."

"Take a nap," said Salo.

"Yes—I—I think I will," said Constant. He lay down on a bunk. He dropped off to sleep.

Salo strapped the sleeping Space Wanderer to his bunk. Then he strapped himself to his seat at the controls. He set three dials, double-checked the reading on each. He pressed a bright red button.

He sat back. There was nothing more to do now. From now on everything was automatic. In thirty-six minutes, the ship would land itself near the end of a bus line on the outskirts of Indianapolis, Indiana, U.S.A., Earth, Solar System, Milky Way.

It would be three in the morning there.

It would also be winter.

The space ship landed in four inches of fresh snow in a vacant lot on the south side of Indianapolis. No one was awake to see it land.

Malachi Constant got out of the space ship.

"That's your bus stop over there, old soldier," whispered Salo. It was necesary to whisper, for a two-story frame house with an open bedroom window was only thirty feet away. Salo pointed to a snowy bench by the street. "You'll have to wait about ten minutes," he whispered. "The bus will take you right into the centre of town. Ask the driver to let you off near a good hotel."

Constant nodded. "I'll be all right," he whispered.

"How do you feel?" whispered Salo.

"Warm as toast," whispered Constant.

The complaint of a vaguely disturbed sleeper came from the open bedroom window near by. "Aw, somebody," the sleeper complained, "*afo wa, de-yah, ummmmmmmmmmm.*"

"You really all right?" whispered Salo.

"Yes. Fine," whispered Constant. "Warm as toast."

"Good luck," whispered Salo.

"We don't say that down here," whispered Constant.

Salo winked. "I'm not *from* down here," he whispered. He looked around at the perfectly white world, felt the wet kisses of the snowflakes, pondered hidden meanings in the pale yellow streetlights that shone in a world so whitely asleep. "Beautiful," he whispered.

"Isn't it?" whispered Constant.

"*Sim-faw!*" cried the sleeper menacingly, to anyone who

might menace his sleep. *"Soo! A-s! What's a mabba? Nf."*

"You better go," whispered Constant.

"Yes," whispered Salo.

"Good-bye," whispered Constant, "and thanks."

"You're entirely welcome," whispered Salo. He backed into the ship, closed the airlock. The ship arose with the sound of man blowing over the mouth of a bottle. It disappeared into the swirling snow and was gone.

"Toodle-oo," it said.

Malachi Constant's feet squeaked in the snow as he walked to the bench. He brushed aside the snow on the bench and sat down.

"Fraugh!" cried the sleeper, as though he suddenly understood all.

"Braugh!" he cried, not liking at all what he suddenly understood.

"Sup-foe!" he said, saying in no uncertain terms what he was going to do about it.

"Floof!" he cried.

The conspirators presumably fled.

More snow fell.

The bus Malachi Constant was waiting for ran two hours late that morning—on account of the snow. When the bus did come it was too late. Malachi Constant was dead.

Salo had hypnotized him so that he would imagine, as he died, that he saw his best and only friend, Stony Stevenson.

As the snow drifted over Constant, he imagined that the clouds opened up, letting through a sunbeam, a sunbeam all for him.

A golden space ship encrusted with diamonds came skimming down the sunbeam, landed in the untouched snow of the street.

Out stepped a stocky, red-headed man with a big cigar. He was young. He wore the uniform of the Martian Assault Infantry, Unk's old outfit.

"Hello, Unk," he said. "Get in."

"Get in?" said Constant. "Who are you?"

"Stony Stevenson, Unk. You don't recognize me?"

"Stony?" said Constant. "That's you, Stony?"

"Who else could stand the bloody pace?" said Stony. He laughed. "Get in," he said.

"And go where?" said Constant.

"Paradise," said Stony.

"What's Paradise like?" said Constant.

"Everybody's happy there forever," said Stony, "or as long as the bloody Universe holds together. Get in, Unk. Beatrice is already there, waiting for you."

"Beatrice?" said Unk, getting into the space ship.

Stony closed the airlocks, pressed the *on* button.

"We're—we're going to Paradise now?" said Constant. "I—I'm going to get into Paradise?"

"Don't ask me why, old sport," said Stony, "but somebody up there likes you."